COLD DAY
DAY
in the
SUN

COLD DAY in the SUN

SARA BIREN

AMULET BOOKS

NEW YORK

Cataloging-in-Publication Data has been applied for and may be obtained from the Library of Congress.

ISBN 978-1-4197-3367-3

Text copyright © 2019 Sara Biren
Book design by Siobhán Gallagher

Printed and bound in U.S.A.
10 9 8 7 6 5 4 3 2 1

Amulet Books are available at special discounts when purchased in quantity for premiums and promotions as well as fundraising or educational use. Special editions can also be created to specification. For details, contact specialsales@abramsbooks.com or the address below.

Amulet Books® is a registered trademark of Harry N. Abrams, Inc.

ABRAMS The Art of Books
195 Broadway, New York, NY 10007
abramsbooks.com

To Troy,
my favorite metalhead, my favorite everything

Chapter One

I'M LATE. THE FIRST SONG ON THE WARM-UP PLAYLIST IS ALMOST over.

The music from the arena's sound system is loud, heavy, fast. It drills through me as I step onto the ice and skate toward the bench, my gloves tucked under my arm. I shake out the stiff, weighted feeling of exhaustion that comes from a day of early-morning practice followed by seven hours of riveting public education. I both dread and welcome the hour of intense drills, the stretch and burn in my muscles, the pure instinct of movement and play.

I also dread the beatdown I'm going to get for being late, even though I have a good reason.

I grab a water bottle and squirt some into my mouth before snapping the strap of my helmet closed and dropping the cage.

"Hey, Princess." My linemate Justin "Slacks" Swenson skates up next to me. "You're late. I'd watch out if I were you, because Captain Hot Shit is in a *mood* today." Justin has a different name for our co-captain, Wes "Hot Sauce" Millard, every other day.

I try to laugh away some of the tension. "Tell me something I don't know," I say as Justin skates away.

"Dutch." The word is sharp. Here we go.

I spin around and pinch my lips together as I stare down our co-captain. Even through the wire cage on the front of his helmet, I can see that Hot Shit—er, Hot *Sauce*—Millard's eyes flash with irritation.

"You're late," he growls. "Unacceptable."

I roll my eyes. "I had to stay after class to talk to one of my teachers, OK? I mean, last I checked, academics come first, right?"

I hate that every sentence ends with a question mark, like I'm asking for his approval. Which, I guess, I sort of am.

He sighs. "Which teacher?" he asks, his words laced with frustration.

He thinks I'm lying. Ass.

"Rieland. Journalism. She rejected my story idea. Happy now?"

I don't tell him that it was the *third* story idea for the *Jack Pine* print edition that she's rejected this week. I need to come up with something good—and fast.

He holds my gaze for another second, then looks away. "Just get out there, Dutch," he mutters. Can't argue with grades, although I'm somewhat surprised that he doesn't at least try.

"And don't call me Dutch," I snap as I join my teammates, Hot Sauce on my heels.

In all my years of playing hockey—eleven total between the Halcyon Lake Area Youth Hockey Association and on the high school team, thirteen if you count falling on my ass as a toddler, chasing after my brothers—I've never had a nickname.

Most of the guys have them, usually something to do with how they play or some twisted version of their last name. One of our coaches started calling my older brother Carter "Six-Four" back in our Squirt days because he was already so tall, and sure as shit, he's six-four. Most people shorten it to Six. Wes, apparently, has been called Hot Sauce for years because he puts Cholula on *everything*. Holls and Holly are the closest things I've had to a nickname, until Hot Sauce moved to town, along with his giant ego and state championship medal. He snagged a co-captain spot alongside Carter a year later.

A spot that rightfully should have gone to someone with team history, in my opinion. But obviously my opinion wasn't shared by the majority of my teammates who voted him in.

"What's your secret?" Justin asks me as I skate up behind him. "I expected him to bitch you out."

I shrug. "My irresistible charm, Slacks. What the fuck else?"

He snorts. "Nice mouth, Princess."

I'm a lot of things, but a princess is not one of them.

"Hot Flash thinks his shit doesn't stink because he scored that goddamn game-winning overtime goal," Justin goes on. "Then he moves here and kisses Coach's ass and the next thing we know, he's captain." He's on a roll now, although it's a quiet one. He skates off, catching a pass.

Justin and I go way back, linemates since Peewees, and I trust him almost as much as I do my brothers. And he's found me to be an easy confidant for years. Two months ago, I was the first person he told about his crush on Joseph Lincoln, senior class treasurer and track star. "Slacks-n-Tracks," I like to call them—well, now that they're together and out, that is.

I follow the action on the ice, leaning in and waiting for Justin to swing back around to pass me the puck.

"Dutch! You're up!" Hot Sauce yells from behind me. Thank you, Captain Obvious.

I connect with the puck and drive it toward the net, flick it neatly past the goalie's right shoulder.

Yessss.

"Nice shot," Carter says from his perch near the net.

When I return to the back of the line, though, Hot Sauce doesn't say a word.

Five minutes before practice is scheduled to end, Coach Giles blows his whistle and motions for us to join him at the bench. His typically stoic face crinkles into something like a smile. "Great news," he says. "Just got a text from the activities office. Halcyon Lake has been selected as one of this year's HockeyFest cities."

Carter whoops and Justin lifts me off my skates and spins me around as the guys talk over one another in their excitement.

"Holy crap," Showbiz Schroeder says. "Ho. Ly. Crap."

This is the closest Showbiz comes to swearing (admirable, considering the potty mouths on our team), further evidence that this announcement is a big deal.

Minnesota is known as the State of Hockey, and the annual HockeyFest weekend is one of the most anticipated of the year. Five cities are chosen to represent different regions of the state. The event brings scouts from colleges across the country and sometimes even from the NHL. Some people view HockeyFest as a popularity contest, and technically there's not a stated, official requirement that you have a decent record, but everyone knows you need one to be considered.

The team quiets and Coach continues. "One host city will be selected to have their game televised statewide. Last year, a national station picked up the game. This could be a huge opportunity for us. And I'm sure you all know the selection process."

A few of the guys nod, and I bite my bottom lip. Jason Fink, a wacky sports anchor from one of the Twin Cities news stations, travels around the state and interviews players from each town's teams about what makes the place special, and viewers then vote for their favorite. Last year, the high school game that was televised nationwide? Mondale-Petersburg in northwest Minnesota, known for seven Olympic gold medalists, five state championships, and an arena shaped like a giant hockey puck.

Halcyon Lake? We've got a recently renovated outdoor rink originally built in 1930 called Hole in the Moon. It has stone walls and a stone warming house, and it's on the National Register of Historic Places.

And we've got me.

The girl.

I cringe as Coach turns his gaze toward me. "Fink will interview players from a few teams—the girls' team, a couple of Peewees—and Holland."

All the guys turn to stare at me like something choreographed straight out of *High School Musical.* I look down at my skates.

"Holland," Carter says. I look over as he nods. "Deep breath," he mouths.

I inhale for four beats, hold it, and blow it out through my mouth for six, this new thing that Coach taught us at the beginning of the season that I thought was total bullshit until I realized it actually works. I take another breath.

"Holland hates to be the center of attention," Luke Abbott, the center on my line, says, not unsympathetically.

He isn't wrong. I didn't have to worry about being *the girl* until I made the JV team freshman year and, suddenly, a girl playing on the boys' team was newsworthy. I've done everything I can to stay out of the spotlight. I *write* the articles. I don't star in them.

Hmm. Maybe I could write an article about HockeyFest. I doubt Ms. Rieland would reject *that* idea.

"Well," Hot Sauce says, skating over and patting me on the shoulder. "I guess Dutch will have to take one for the team, then."

I shrug his hand off and glance up at him, annoyed. Something flashes across his face that can only be described as intense frustration.

The feeling's mutual, buddy. At the moment, I can't even tell him not to call me Dutch, because I'm afraid that other, more vicious words will spill out. Or that I'll start to cry, which would be much, much worse.

"She's got a great story," Coach says. "And you all know it. I don't have many details yet, but I can tell you that Holland's interview is scheduled for a week from Saturday. And they'll send a crew up sometime that week to get footage from practice. I'll know more tomorrow. That's all I got."

That's plenty. I turn and skate away, the first off the ice.

Chapter Two

BEING THE ONLY GIRL ON THE BOYS' HOCKEY TEAM OFFERS EXACTLY one perk: my own personal locker room. It's not actually *mine*, of course. It's the designated girls' locker room at the arena, and when our team practices, there aren't any other girls around. Well, except for Darla, who runs concessions, and sometimes her daughter, Molly, who's a year younger than me and helps out on game nights.

It's quiet in the locker room, especially after the loud reception of Coach's news. I relish the peacefulness but don't waste any time stripping off my stinking, sweaty gear and pulling on jeans and a clean T-shirt. Today it's a long-sleeved Foo Fighters tee. Soft, washed-out charcoal gray with the double-*F* logo surrounded by the band name and WASTING LIGHT in a circular border. My favorite band, my favorite album, and my number one go-to when the stress and pressure settle in. I even named my blog after the album. Pretty sure there's some *Wasting Light* in my very near future.

I sling my gear bag over my shoulder and head out to the lobby to wait for Carter. The Bantam game must be starting soon, because parent volunteers have set up a card table in front of the main entrance to collect the three-dollar entry fee and pass out rosters. I hang out next to a pillar near the concession stand to avoid the traffic.

Two guys in their fifties or sixties hand over their crisp singles at the card table and step into the short line at the concession stand.

"It's embarrassing, is what it is," I hear one of the old-timers saying. I recognize him as George, from Third Street Rental, the DVD and video-game rental place. Not that I spend a lot of time renting movies, but I have gone in a time or two for their other draw—homemade popcorn of every flavor imaginable. George isn't exactly the friendliest guy in town, at least not to me.

His buddy, the owner of Pete's Hardware on Main Street, nods in agreement. "Embarrassing," he repeats.

"I don't care if they think they'll have a better chance of getting that broadcast. That girl playing with the boys is an embarrassment to the sanctity of the sport."

My stomach drops, crash-lands.

An embarrassment to the sanctity of the sport.

I've heard that one a time or two hundred.

"Not to mention a real liability. Hockey's too rough for girls," Pete says. "My granddaughter wanted to play, and her father said, 'Absolutely not.' She's figure skating instead. What is Marcus Delviss thinking, letting his only daughter play with the boys?"

I roll my eyes. What is Marcus thinking? How fucking awesome his daughter is, for one.

"And she's taking a spot that rightfully belongs to someone else. It's a *boys'* hockey team."

"At the very least, they never should have moved her up from junior varsity. There's a boy out there who'll never have a shot at varsity because she took his spot."

I *earned* that spot.

No matter how many times I hear it, this stuff still hurts. I close my eyes, lean my head against the pillar, and pinch my lips together to stop from saying anything. That would only add fuel to the fire.

Pete buys them two small cups of coffee and stuffs the change into the tip jar. Tonight's tips support the upcoming Bantam boys' tournament in St. Paul. I'd bet all the money in that jar that Pete and George wouldn't turn over their hard-earned cash for a girls' team.

The high school has a girls' team, too, and it's not that I don't want to play with them or that I think I'm too good for them. I've grown up playing with my brothers, with boys. I like the extra challenge. I like to push myself. My dad and my brothers have pushed me, too. They've never treated me any differently because I'm a girl. I've worked hard to get where I am. I belong here. End of story.

I scowl as George and Pete walk through the double doors to the rink. Screw them.

My scowl deepens when I see Hot Sauce leaning against a pillar on the other side of the lobby, scrolling on his phone. *Shit.* I cling to the small hope that he didn't overhear the two old-timers. For all I know, he could agree with them.

I'll just pretend he's not standing there and get some coffee for the ride home.

"Hey, Darla," I say as I drop the heavy bag at my feet and lean up against the concessions counter. "Fresh pot?"

"Just gave Pete and George the last of it, but I should have a fresh one in a minute," Darla says.

I experience a disproportionate amount of satisfaction that Pete and George got the dregs of the last pot.

I chitchat with Darla (and continue to ignore Hot Sauce—why is he still here, anyway?) until the light on the coffee maker clicks off. She calls to Molly for a large. "Two sugars and a cream. Don't forget a straw for our girl."

Molly pours the coffee, taps in two packets of sugar and one little tub of cream, and gives it a stir with a wooden stick. She carefully places the lid on top, grabs a straw, and walks up to the counter. She points the straw at me. I reach for it, but she pulls back.

"Do you know that Americans use five hundred million plastic straws every day? Where do you think those straws end up?"

Here we go. Molly's headed up the school's Earth Day efforts for as long as I can remember. She went vegetarian at the age of twelve. At fourteen, she partnered with the electric co-op to provide every single Halcyon Lake household with two reusable shopping bags, and she convinced the local grocery store to stop using plastic bags. She's a force.

"A landfill?" I guess.

"If we're lucky!" she says. "More likely, up a poor sea turtle's nose! Plastic pollution kills *millions* of seabirds every year. That includes straws."

"Good thing we're so far from the ocean, then," Darla mutters.

"What about *our* lakes, Mom?" Molly asks. "*Our* birds? *Our* fish?"

Darla rolls her eyes.

"No, it's OK," I say. "I want to know." At this, Molly tentatively holds out the straw, and I grab it before she can change her mind, tearing the thin paper wrapper open with my teeth and sliding the straw into the hole in the lid. "I'd love to write an article about you for the *Jack Pine*. For Earth Day, maybe?"

She nods excitedly.

I reach back and rub my tense neck muscles. I started drinking everything with a straw a couple of years ago after a nasty hit that resulted in a trip headfirst into the boards and a mild concussion. Tipping my head back to drink gave me the spins. I recovered from the concussion but haven't kicked the straw habit.

Let's be honest. At the moment, I've got bigger things to worry about than a straw stuck up a sea turtle's nose.

She's moved on to her spiel about plastic shopping bags when the doors between the lobby and the rink bang open and the boys fill up the space with their big personalities, noise, and stench.

"Hey, Holland."

I turn to find Jack "Lumberjack" Lewis leaning against the counter. Jack is a year younger than me, a buddy of my younger brother, Jesse. He's the starting center on the JV squad, leads the team in goals, and dresses once in a while for varsity. Cocky. Obnoxious. Especially when he flips his long hair away from his face. He skated practice with us this afternoon.

"Oh, hey, Jack," I say and turn my attention back to Molly. "Thanks for the tip."

She sighs. "Holland. I've been telling you this for months. I just got the grocery store and the drugstore to carry metal straws, so pick some up, OK?"

"Oh, OK, sure," I say and then turn back to Lumberjack, who for some reason is tugging at my sleeve. "What?"

"Pretty exciting about HockeyFest, huh?" he says.

"Yep." The *p* pops.

"And so cool that you get to be interviewed."

I blink. Lumberjack's lived in town about three years, and I don't know him as well as some of the other guys. I'm not sure where he's going with this. "And?"

"And," he says, winking. "And I thought we could go out after the pasta feed Friday night."

And *that's* where he's going with this. "What?"

"Go out? To the movies, maybe, or—"

I move my lips into something resembling a tight smile. "Wow, thanks, Jack, but I can't."

I make a point of *not* saying I can't go out with him *on Friday night*, because that would leave the door open for another night. And this door is definitely *not* open.

"That's OK," he says. "How about Saturday after the game?"

My smile fades. "No, thank you."

Jack's brow furrows. "Next weekend?"

SARA BIREN

Even if I would consider dating a teammate, which I would not, my tolerance level for Lumberjack's cockiness is basically zero. "I appreciate the offer. But the answer is no."

He takes a step toward me and I take one backward. "Why not?"

He's persistent, I'll give him that. I try not to sigh. "I don't really go out with hockey players."

He grins. "I heard that about you. Maybe you just haven't met the *right* hockey player."

Arrogant ass. "You're a great teammate, Jack, but anything more could create a really weird dynamic for the team, you know? Fishing off the company dock and all that?"

"Oh, come on, babe."

Babe? *Babe?*

Behind me, Molly sucks in a breath.

"Uh-oh," Darla mutters.

"'Babe,' Lumberjack? Really? I am *not* your *babe.* Do you have any idea how derogatory and demeaning that is?"

Lumberjack puts his hands up in front of his chest and steps back. "Chill already," he says. "You always seemed so cool, Holland."

He turns, hauls his bag over his shoulder, and is out the door before I can think of a response other than *fuck you.* I gape after him, my hand tight and burning around the hot cup of coffee.

Someone takes the cup from me and sets it on the counter. Hot Sauce. Of course. Exactly what I need right now. I'd actually forgotten about him.

"You're going to crush that cup if you're not careful, Dutch," he says. His eyes land on my T-shirt for a few seconds, then snap back up to my face. "What's the matter? You don't like being compared to a big blue ox?"

"What are you talking about?"

"Babe? The big blue ox? Lumberjack? Paul Bunyan? Surely this is ringing a bell. You've lived up north your whole life."

"Yeah, yeah, I get it."

Carter blows into the lobby and jangles his keys in my direction. "Holls, let's move," he calls, and I'm more than happy to leave Hot Sauce Millard and his stupid Paul Bunyan references behind.

Except he follows me through the lobby, out the door, into the frosty January night, and across the parking lot.

Right up to Carter's Suburban.

I whirl around. "What are you doing?" I spit. "Why are you following me?"

"I call shotgun." He laughs and grabs my duffel to throw it into the back. "Truck's in the shop. I'm catching a ride."

And I cannot catch a break.

Chapter Three

I GRUMBLE UNDER MY BREATH AS I YANK OPEN THE BACK DOOR AND slide across the ass-biting cold seat. It's about as cold in the truck as it is outdoors. Carter and Hot Sauce carry on a conversation up front as though I'm not even here.

"HockeyFest. Shit," Carter says. "Can you believe it?"

He flips the radio to his favorite station—the Power Loon, *the Brainerd Lakes Home for the BEST in Classic Rock*— and the song playing is "Babe" by Styx. You've got to be kidding me.

"Right?" Hot Sauce says. He must not notice the song, or he would surely give me more shit about the blue ox.

"It's so awesome," Carter says. "Senior year, maybe a shot at state, and now statewide coverage with HockeyFest."

"Statewide if Holland can nail that interview and we get enough votes," Hot Sauce adds.

Oh, I'll nail that interview. I am going to *rock* that interview and get us the broadcast.

"Hello," I say. "I'm *right here.*"

The guys ignore me. The song on the radio ends and another begins: Poison, "Every Rose Has Its Thorn." Ah, one of my all-time favorite songs of any style or decade. I lean forward.

"Can you turn this up?" I ask.

Carter groans. "You and your glam bands," he says. He's always been more of a late-'70s/early-'80s classic rock guy. Journey, Boston, Supertramp, the Eagles. Oh Lord, how he loves the Eagles.

Hot Sauce turns to look at me, disbelief on his face. "You like Poison?"

Carter barks out a laugh. "She loves Poison. She's single-handedly trying to revive the hair metal movement."

"You cannot revive what never died," I snap. "Yes, I like Poison. Is there something wrong with that?"

Hot Sauce laughs. "Oh, no, Dutch, everything about that is right."

He turns back around and I'm about to request, for the nine hundredth time, that he not call me Dutch when he starts to sing.

Sing.

Hot Sauce Millard, singing along to "Every Rose Has Its Thorn."

His voice is gravelly and smooth at the same time and, not going to lie here, a little bit sexy, and that annoys the hell out of me.

He is *ruining* this song for me forever with his beautiful voice–slash–arrogant, intolerable personality. A personality that, quite frankly, we didn't need on our team.

I've played with the same guys my whole life—my brothers, Showbiz, Luke, T.J. MacMillan, Slacks and his brothers. So, when you throw a new guy into the mix—one from a state champion team, no less—things go a little off-kilter. Especially when he's elected co-captain after only one year on the team. No one was surprised when Carter got it, but we all figured the other one would be T.J. or Showbiz. Not the new guy.

I met Hot Sauce the week before school started my sophomore year, right after he'd moved to Halcyon Lake. I'd ridden my bike into town to meet Morgan and our other best friend, Cora, at Little Dipper's, the ice cream shop where Morgan works. Hot Sauce was there, too, with T.J.

"Hey, ladies," T.J. had said in his smarmy way. He's tall, with blond surfer hair and blue eyes so dark they're almost black. He reeks of Ralph Lauren Polo Blue and insincerity. "Meet the new sniper."

New sniper? I'd tilted my head and scrutinized the boy in the booth. Taller than T.J., with deep brown hair that stuck up in every direction, he looked familiar, but I couldn't place him. I figured I'd probably played against him at some point over the years.

"Meet the ladies," T.J. continued. "Cora Delmar and Holland Delviss."

"Delviss?" Hot Sauce had said. "This is *the girl*?"

Cora put her hands on her hips and opened her mouth, but he spoke again before she could unload. "I heard you're not bad. Maybe you think you're good enough for varsity, but don't think anyone is going to give you a free pass because you're a *girl*. You have to *earn* it."

T.J. snorted.

My mouth dropped open. "Who the hell are *you*?"

"*He*," T.J. said as he tried to contain his laughter, "is Wes Millard. He scored the game-winning overtime goal in the semifinals to take the Great River Thunder to the state championship tourney as a *sophomore*—which they *won*—and *now* he plays for *us*. So, show some respect, Holland."

"I'll show some respect when *he* does," I'd said, jabbing my thumb in his direction. "Don't think anyone is going to give you a free pass because you're a . . . a . . . *Thunder*. Scratch that. *Former* Thunder. Now you're a *Hawk*. You have to *earn* my respect."

"Yeah, girl!" Cora said, giving me a high five.

Hot Sauce went on to set a school record for goals scored in one season, earned co-captain, and has had it out for me ever since.

Thank God he lives so close to the arena. The song ends as we pull into the driveway of a blue rambler on Third Street up the hill from downtown. The house is kind of plain, but there's a fence with a cool mural of the four seasons of Halcyon Lake, including a group of kids playing pond hockey.

"Thanks for the ride, Six," he says to Carter as he opens the passenger side door. "Hey, Dutch."

I snap my head up. "Don't call me—"

He waves a hand and cuts me off. "Whatever. I heard what those guys said about you tonight."

"What guys?"

"Pete and George. Don't let that shit bother you."

He heard. At least I don't have to wonder anymore. "I don't—"

He cuts me off again. "Look, George is a friend of mine. I'll talk to him. He shouldn't be shooting off his mouth like that."

"George is a friend of yours? He's, like, sixty."

"Don't let them get to you," he says again. "You're good. You skate hard. You hold your own against a bunch of guys who are bigger and stronger. So don't let a couple of old guys stop you from getting out there and playing your heart out."

Well, this is unusual. Is he being *nice* to me?

"I *always* play my heart out," I say in a low, steady voice.

He shrugs. "Yeah, well, I'm not just talking about games. I'm talking about practice, too. And that starts with being on time. No more bullshit about staying late to talk to a teacher."

Nope. Not being nice.

"That wasn't bullshit," I hiss.

He raises an eyebrow. The one with the little scar cutting through it, a still-pink half-moon indentation from when he took a high stick from T.J. during a pickup game with a few of the guys over winter break. A game I wasn't invited to.

"'Night, Dutch," he says and waits a beat for me to return the sentiment. I don't.

And then, finally, he looks away. He gets out of the truck without another word.

Chapter Four

Mom is beside herself at the HockeyFest news and can talk of nothing else. She even video calls Dad while we eat dinner. He's a landscape architect for a nursery and landscaping company and is at a big industry expo in Minneapolis. He beams with pride like we're going to the state tournament or something. Jesse and Carter talk over themselves in their excitement.

"The chair of the HockeyFest committee called me today to see if I could cater a sponsor dinner," Mom says.

"Catering?" Dad asks from Mom's phone. "Is that even in the plan?"

Mom is a well-known food blogger with a special angle—how to feed growing, hungry hockey players. She's been writing her blog—*Top Shelf Pantry*, a nod to when you shoot high on the net—for about ten years. She needed to figure out ways to keep four growing hockey players fed, healthy, and satisfied—for cheap—while at the same time driving us to practices and games. She started a blog to keep track of her attempts. She was a huge hit with the online hockey mom community, and it all began with a recipe for cheesy shredded chicken and broccoli with rice. The slow cooker and pressure cooker companies love her, sending her new products to feature, and she brings in a ton of money from advertisers.

That cheesy chicken is still one of my favorites.

"Might be fun to try it," Mom says. "This would be for about fifty people, the night before the game. I was thinking about doing a Hotdish Feed. I'd need volunteers to help serve." She points at the three of us.

They chat for another minute or two before Dad says good night.

"You're awfully quiet, Holland," Mom says as she scoops more au gratin potatoes onto my plate. At least today's news hasn't affected my appetite. "Aren't you excited for HockeyFest?"

"Yeah, I'm excited," I say and shovel a forkful of potatoes into my mouth. Mom has a strict rule about not talking with food in our mouths, so I hope that answer will be good enough for her.

"She's nervous," Carter says helpfully. "About the interview."

Gee, thanks, Carter.

"Plus, Pete and George were shooting off their mouths at the arena tonight and she heard them," he continues.

"Carter!" I swallow the mouthful of potatoes.

"Why do you care what those guys think, anyway?" he asks.

"How do you even know about that? You were still in the locker room!"

He shrugs. "I heard Wes say something about it to you in the truck, so I called him when we got home."

I stare at him, wide-eyed, and shake my head. Nosy bastard.

Carter scrapes his fork across his plate and shoves the last of his dinner into his mouth. "Your turn for dishes, Holls." He scoots his chair back from the table and stands up. "Me and Jess got a little playoff football to attend to downstairs."

Jesse shoves his plate back. "You're going down, Six."

"Homework!" Mom calls as they pound down the stairs. Jesse grunts in response. "Those two would play video games twenty-four seven if I let them." She sighs.

I stand up to clear the table. "I think it's good stress relief for them." Too bad I'm not into video games.

"I'm sorry you're stressed about the interview," Mom says. "Even when you were a little girl, you never were much for the spotlight."

"That's part of it," I say slowly. I keep a lot to myself, but Mom has this way of drawing things out of me.

"What's the other part of it?"

I stack plates and utensils and take them to the sink. "So many people are counting on me. Like, the whole town."

"Hmm," she says as she brings over the leftover potatoes. "Now that we know we're one of the HockeyFest towns, it's a matter of pulling everything together. The broadcast is one piece of the puzzle. But remember, just like when you're on the ice, this is a team effort. You're not the only person they'll interview."

"Yeah, but I'm kinda the reason, right? That we got picked in the first place?"

"Maybe. Grandpa Delviss might have something to say about that."

My grandfather is a founding member and past president of the Rotary Club. The organization donated money to renovate the rink and the stone warming house at Hole in the Moon. Yes, the renovation has historical significance, and no, I'm not the only girl in the State of Hockey to play on a boys' team, but let's be honest: I'm the reason.

"Still. Why can't I just be a hockey player, instead of *the girl*?"

"I know, sweetheart," Mom says. "Just be yourself and you can't go wrong."

Sounds super easy.

Once I've loaded and started the dishwasher, I grab a few of Mom's famous organic chewy coconut oatmeal cookies. (Seriously, they are famous. She made them on the *Katy Bakes Live!* show in October and that post has about two million hits. Not an exaggeration.) I pound up the stairs to my room and pull my textbooks and notebooks out of my backpack. I set them in a neat stack on my desk, but I don't open any. Instead, I stare at the items on the corkboard on the wall next to my window. Memories and milestones. The roster from my first varsity game. A laminated, autographed Zach Parise rookie card that my brother Hunter had found at a garage sale for an unbelievable ten bucks. A photo of me and my brothers and my dad, all in hockey gear, posing in front of the goal on the frozen lake behind our house. A picture of me and Morgan and Cora at Little Dipper's.

And a newspaper clipping, curling at the one corner that's not tacked down.

It's a letter to the editor, a letter I've committed to memory, written by a Halcyon Lake resident named Don O'Rourke. Big Donnie, I call him. An old-timer whose granddaughter played for the girls' team and graduated last year. Don had plenty of things to say after I played my first varsity game. A lot of bullshit concerns about my safety and well-being, for one. The same old song and dance that allowing a girl to play on the boys' team is a travesty, a disservice to me and to whoever's spot I took on the team. An embarrassment to the sanctity of the sport, blah blah blah. And then this:

Allowing Ms. Delviss to play with the boys at this advanced age introduces a concern that coaches hadn't worried about when the players were younger, that a female on the ice and in the locker room with teenage boys will cause a significant distraction, at the very least affecting the quality of their play. As much as I'd like to state otherwise, boys will be boys, and I, for one, will feel no sympathy for Ms. Delviss should something unfortunate occur because of her presence on the team.

More than anything else in the letter, those words—his unfounded assumptions—pierced me.

I've collected Don O'Rourke's phrases like stones. I carry them with me every day. I take them out and turn them over, reminders of what I'm up against. Reminders of what I can do.

A travesty and a disservice.

An embarrassment to the sanctity of the sport.

Significant distraction.

Boys will be boys.

I reach out and touch the words, remember the anger that curled into me when I first read them, anger that fuels me most days, motivates me to prove him wrong. Him and Pete and George and anyone else who believes those things.

Tonight, the weight of the stones exhausts me.

Wasting Light: A Blog About Music, Hockey, and Life

January 11 12:04 a.m.

By HardRock_Hockey

The Power of the Power Ballad

Now Spinning: Poison, *Open Up and Say . . . Ahh!*

Hello, Hard Rockers.

I'm not a sappy love song kind of girl. I'm not swoony or romantic. I don't cry at happy endings, or sad ones, for that matter. I don't even *need* a happy ending. Give me a five-gallon bucket of battered pucks for sniper practice over roses and a box of chocolates any day of the week.

But there's one thing I cannot resist, and that's a romantic power ballad. Power ballads have been around a long time, but the '80s, kids . . . That's my favorite power ballad era—hair bands and glam metal.

Not every power ballad is a love song, although it could be ("Love Song" by Tesla). It might tell the story of the end of a relationship ("Time for Change" by Mötley Crüe); it might be an anti-war anthem ("When the Children Cry" by White Lion).

Sometimes there's hope in the lyrics, sometimes simmering fury. Either way, the power ballad gives you something, well, *something to believe in* (yeah, I went there: "Something to Believe In" by Poison).

Which brings me, naturally, to Poison. Tonight, my brother told someone that I'm single-handedly trying to revive the hair metal movement of the late '80s. I crisply informed him that you can't revive what hasn't died. Case in point, the power ballad to rule over all power ballads: "Every Rose Has Its Thorn" by, of course, Poison. A song that a heartbroken Bret Michaels wrote in a laundromat in the middle of the night after discovering that his girlfriend was cheating on him! A song that the label didn't even want to release as a single! A timeless classic!

Power ballads soothe. They take away the sting, whether you're *headed for a heartache* or you *don't know what you've got (till it's gone)*. Power ballads offer an outlet for your emotions and, at the same time, a place to tuck them away, unseen.

Here's the deal. I'm a girl in a guys' world, a world where showing any emotion besides rage (or elation after a sweet save or a killer goal) is a sign of weakness. I've never—not once—cried on the ice (alone in the locker room after the game? Yeah, a couple of times). For as long as I can remember, I've worked through my feelings with music. Yeah, the lyrics speak to me, but sometimes it's a riff or the drumbeat that hits me hard and stays with me.

Or that breath at the beginning of "Every Rose Has Its Thorn." You know what I'm talking about. If you don't, turn on the Power Loon. They're probably playing it right this minute.

I'm lucky. I haven't experienced true heartbreak in my young life. Sure, I've had my share of crushes (Zach Parise counts, right?). But I'm not naive. I know it could happen someday. Part of life, right?

Here's the real reason I'm writing tonight and listening

to Poison on repeat: power ballads—and music in general—also have the power to take your mind off the shit that's really bothering you. The worries, the pressure, the stress, you know? Some people might listen to classical or new age or whatever when they're stressed. I gravitate toward something harder, grittier. Sometimes that means a power ballad.

And maybe I haven't experienced the kind of heartbreak that Bret Michaels felt writing that song in the laundromat, but I know disappointment. I know pressure. I know stress. Tonight, I'm going to de-stress with Poison and the Power Loon and also this awesome, chill playlist I just put together.

HARDROCK_HOCKEY TOP 10: DE-STRESS

10. "Planet Caravan"—Pantera (Black Sabbath cover)

9. "Black Book of Fear"—Mad Season

8. "Vulgar Before Me"—Candlebox

7. "The Rain Song"—Led Zeppelin

6. "Big Empty"—Stone Temple Pilots

5. "I am the Highway"—Audioslave

4. "Fall to Pieces"—Velvet Revolver

3. "Drive"—Incubus

2. "Black Hole Sun"—Soundgarden

1. "One Ocean"—Chevelle

BONUS TRACKS:

"Chloe Dancer/Crown of Thorns"—Mother Love Bone

"Change (In the House of Flies)"—Deftones

"The Kill"—30 Seconds to Mars

Tell me, what's your favorite power ballad?

\m/

19

Comments

12:12 a.m.

You've never experienced heartbreak? I guess you've never experienced love, then. Don't just live through the music. LIVE. Get your heart broken. Get kicked to the curb or slammed into the boards or whatever analogy you want to use. But you're right about the healing power. My girlfriend dumped me at a Mötley Crüe concert, and even though hearing "Without You" kills me every time, it helped me get through a bad breakup, you know?

    Cooper1970

    Reply from HardRock_Hockey

    5:07 a.m.

    Sorry about your girlfriend. AT the concert? That's cold.

12:30 a.m.

Good tunes. I'm glad I found your blog. I play hockey, just a local bar league, basically, we're called Zero Pucks Given, funny, right? I'm going to school for HVAC repair. My favorite band is Foo Fighters, that's how I found you. If you're ever in SoCal, look me up. We'll talk metal. Also, my favorite power ballad is probably "Wait" by White Lion.

MetalManiac (Jim)
Reply from HardRock_Hockey
5:08 a.m.
California sounds pretty good right now. It's like twenty below here. I love White Lion.

3:03 a.m.
You put this playlist on Spotify yet? Let me know when you do. Also: C told me about the interview. You know you're going to rock that thing, right?
Hunter_Not_The_Hunted
Reply from HardRock_Hockey
5:10 a.m.
Please come home for it.

About Me
Hockey player. Number 19. Lover of hard rock, grunge, some heavy metal, '80s glam bands. Yeah, I'm a girl. Living the good life on the lake in the heart of Minnesota.

Chapter Five

BREATHE IN.

Breathe out.

Breathe. In.

Out.

My breaths come fast and heavy, puffs of white in the frigid air. The temperature is negative eleven, and the sun's not up yet to add any warmth, but at least there's no windchill. The only light comes from the two spotlights on the barn, weak by the time it reaches the lake.

This is my favorite time of day, early morning. I was up long before anyone else, out on the frozen lake. It's just me and my skates, my stick, the puck, the net. The only sounds: my breathing and the sharp edge of blades on ice.

I gave up on sleep at five. I responded to comments on my most recent blog post. My blog that somehow has several hundred followers, only one of whom knows me in real life: my brother Hunter. I don't go out of my way to tell people about the blog—it's mostly like an online diary for me to record my thoughts about music and engage with other like-minded (or not) music lovers. And, I suppose, it's a way for me to gain experience for my dream career as the founder and managing editor of a music magazine.

Then I tried to study for today's English quiz on the transcendentalists, but the pull of the ice was greater than anything I might feel for Emerson or Thoreau. Besides, wouldn't they want me out here instead, *living*, experiencing the outdoors, getting in tune with the natural world?

I'm in tune with this world. The crisp winter air, the ice beneath my blades, the dance of my stick with the puck.

I love it. I love this game. But in the back of my mind, there's always the reminder to bust my ass so I don't get benched or dropped to JV. Wouldn't Pete and George and good old Donnie love that.

I set up four orange pylons and work an iron cross drill, *side step-stop, side step-stop-forward, side step-stop, side step-stop-backward*, over and over. We have an amazing practice space in the basement of the farmhouse with state-of-the-art synthetic ice tiles and drill equipment, but there's nothing like the real thing, a frozen lake beneath your skates, striving for balance, finding your power.

My legs ache with cold and effort, my lungs tighten with exertion. The best feelings. Even when I was a little girl, I wanted to skate outside on the lake or at Hole in the Moon. There's something pure about it, authentic. I'm well aware that even a couple of decades ago, I might not have had the opportunity to play this game.

This is my junior year, my second year on varsity. I get more ice time than when I was a sophomore, true, but things can change quickly in this game.

I can't give anyone a reason to say that I'm not good

enough because I'm a girl. That I don't deserve to play on this team.

Refuse to lose. Whatever it takes.

The team battle cry means a little more for a girl who has to prove herself day in and day out. I take nothing for granted, and I work twice as hard as my brothers. It pisses me off that Hot Sauce thinks he needs to remind me every other minute.

Like it pisses me off that Pete and George and who knows who else are still saying that my spot rightfully belongs to a boy.

I've got to nail that interview.

By the time I complete the drill, I'm breathing heavily again. I pause with my hands on my thighs, and when I look up, the kitchen light is on. As much as I'd like to spend the day out on the ice, real life calls.

I stash the pylons back in the barn, kill the lights, and walk up the hill to the house. I'm surprised that the boys are in the kitchen, too. It must be later than I thought. Carter's hockey hair—long, flowing locks frequently called "salad," "flow," "lettuce," or "chop" by aficionados of the sport—is slicked back from a shower, but Jesse's in sweatpants and an old Minnesota Wild sweatshirt with holes at the cuffs.

"You reek," Carter says as he butters a slice of toast. "Go take a shower."

"How long have you been out there?" Jesse asks. "That's messed up."

Mom hands me a cup of coffee and smiles. "That's called dedication, Jess."

Or desperation.

"He wouldn't know dedication if it bit him in the rear end," I murmur. I take a sip of the hot coffee and cringe. I reach across the table for the sugar dish and spoon some in. "You didn't put any sugar in this? Two sugars and a cream, Mom. Even Darla at the arena knows how I like my coffee."

"You mean, 'Thanks, Mom.'"

"That shit's going to stunt your growth," Carter says.

"Carter, language," Mom says, and I snort. That's tame for him.

Or me, but I try to keep it clean around Mom.

"Good." Jesse shovels a spoonful of sugary cereal into his mouth. "Drink more coffee, Holly. I need you to stay runty."

"I am *not* runty, you little twerp."

"You want a ride to school, I'm leaving in twenty-five minutes. I'm not waiting for you, Holls." Carter turns to Jess. "You, either."

I pound up the stairs, careful not to spill my coffee. Twenty-five minutes is plenty of time. I thaw out in the shower, throw on jeans, a tank top, and my away jersey, and blow-dry my hair—chestnut brown, long, straight, with one stripe of electric blue. Hawks blue, bright and deep. It matches our jerseys perfectly. And, as it turns out, my dress for next Friday night's Snow Ball, Halcyon Lake's version of a Sadie Hawkins dance. It's a long-standing tradition that the girls ask the guys, which passes for feminism for some people around here.

I never should have promised Morgan and Cora that I'd go to that stupid dance. No date, no dance, I said, but Cora said she'd be my date, and the next thing I knew, they were dragging me to a boutique in St. Cloud for a dress.

But I can't worry about the Snow Ball right now. I slide a hair tie onto my wrist and am back downstairs with time to spare. I throw on my boots and team jacket, and Mom hands me a to-go mug and an egg sandwich wrapped in foil.

"Two sugars and a cream." She smiles. "The boys are already out in the truck."

"About time," Carter gripes when I get into the truck. Jesse's in the back seat, earbuds in, probably jamming out to the latest horrible pop. "What took you so long?"

I unwrap the sandwich. My stomach growls at the delicious aroma of egg, bacon, and cheddar cheese. I take a huge bite. "I'm not even late!" I say with my mouth full.

Hunter, Carter, and I are stairstep kids, all about a year apart, and Jesse's two years younger than me. Hunter's a freshman at Northern Lakes University an hour north of here. No surprise, he plays hockey for the men's team—the only one of the four of us to play defense. We were all in skates as soon as we could walk, and there was never any question about whether we would play hockey.

My brothers are more than a family. They're my teammates. And besides Morgan and Cora, Hunter's my best friend. Carter looks out for me, Jesse looks up to me. Jesse's taste in music is absolutely terrible, Carter's is only slightly better, but Hunter gets it, how important music is. Why you need to have certain albums on digital, CD, *and* vinyl. Why a person would keep their very first Sony Walkman and dozens of cassette tapes. Hunter and I can spend hours talking music or looking for decent vinyl at garage sales and thrift stores. It hasn't been the same around here since he left for school at the end of August.

"Why did we have to leave so early?" I ask Carter. "I barely had time to dry my hair."

"You would have had plenty of time if you hadn't been out on the ice this morning," Carter says without answering my question.

"Are you afraid my extra drills are going to give me an advantage and Coach will start me instead?"

He laughs. "In your dreams. I'm the captain."

"You're the *co-captain*," I grumble. "That doesn't mean you automatically start."

My phone sounds: a loud horn and the crowd cheering after a goal. A group text from Hot Sauce. I don't bother reading it but instead open my Instagram feed—a few friends from school but mostly musicians and vinyl collectors.

"What did Wes say?" Carter asks.

I shrug. "What?"

"The group text he just sent. Did you read it?"

"No."

"You are a pain in my ass. Would you read it, please?"

I do, then go back to Instagram.

"Are you going to tell me what it says?" Carter sighs.

"Oh, sorry, you asked me to *read* the text, which I did."

"Holland."

"He said tomorrow morning's extra practice is canceled.

Ice was double-booked. Why couldn't he have just told us at practice today? He takes himself too seriously."

"What is your deal with him, anyway?"

For some reason, my cheeks warm. "Why? What do you mean?"

"Why do you hate the guy so much?"

"Why don't you ask him?" I raise my eyebrows at him.

"He's not so bad once you get to know him."

"I'm sure."

"I just think it's weird," he says. "You get along with everyone. What's your beef with Wes?"

I tick off on my fingers. "He's arrogant, he's elitist, he's pushy, he's self-absorbed . . . shall I continue?"

"Just because he has a state championship medal? That's harsh, Holls."

"Why do you care, anyway?"

"Forget I said anything." Carter flips the radio on to, of course, the Power Loon, and we're treated to an early-morning Skid Row rock block. I'll have "18 and Life" stuck in my head for the rest of the day, and I'm OK with that.

Chapter Six

I FINISH MY SANDWICH AS WE PULL INTO THE SCHOOL PARKING LOT and toss the foil into a trash can on my way in. I walk down the hall toward the junior lockers and groan when I see Morgan holding a giant cluster of blue and gold balloons and Cora in her cheer uniform. Cora is the last person I would have expected to exhibit school spirit, but there you go. Never a dull moment with that girl.

"Big *G* and little *O*! Go, Holland, go!" Cora calls out on repeat, doing that weird, purposeful cheer clap on the *go*s.

I want to go, all right. Turn around and go out the way I came in. A crowd of students, including my brothers, Showbiz, and Hot Sauce, gathers in closer to see what the actual hell is going on here.

"Congratulations!" Morgan cries. "We're so proud of you!"

I shake my head as she hands me the balloon bouquet. "I didn't do anything!"

"Yes, you did," Cora chimes in. "No way would we have gotten HockeyFest without you."

I glance at her. "What, no pom-poms?"

"Girl," she says, "I am wearing a skirt and sleeveless top for you. It's *below zero*."

"Thank you?" I say.

"That's so awesome about the interview, Holland!" Morgan says.

"We'll get the broadcast for sure," Cora adds.

I sigh. I can't help it.

"Aren't you excited?" Morgan narrows her eyes with worry and pats my arm. "You don't seem excited."

We don't have time to get into it here, not this close to the warning bell.

"Well, it's a lot of pressure," I hear someone say.

Hot Sauce. I grit my teeth and whirl around. "What's that supposed to mean?"

He puts his hands up, presumably to shield himself from my verbal attack.

"I didn't mean anything by it."

"You meant *something* by it or you wouldn't have said it. Don't I disappoint you enough on the ice? Do you have to come after me at school, too?"

He flinches.

"Holland!" Morgan chides. "Be nice!"

He blows out a breath. "I guess I need to work on my delivery. I meant that I understand why you might be worried about the interview, Dutch. That maybe you were feeling some extra pressure."

"Aww," Cora coos. I glare at her.

"Thanks for your concern," I murmur. He's so incredibly irritating. I want to be angry with him for presuming to understand what I'm feeling right now.

Except for that *is* how I'm feeling right now, which also irritates me.

The warning bell for homeroom rings.

"Dutch—" Hot Sauce starts.

I cut him off. "I have to go." I turn and walk toward my homeroom, too fast, the balloons bouncing against one another behind me.

At lunch, Cora drops her tray with a clatter and sits down next to me. "Oh my God," she says. "You are never going to believe this. I heard from Miracle who heard from Matt Sullivan that Dylan Rogers got *arrested* in St. Cloud this weekend. He got in this huge brawl! At the Blue Door! He's being held on assault charges!"

This is par for the course. We come to school, Morgan and I go to our classes and, you know, learn, and Cora shares all the gossip she's collected instead of paying attention.

Morgan gasps, but it should come as no surprise that a) Dylan Rogers was at a show at the Blue Door Night Club an hour and a half south of here, and b) he assaulted someone there. For that matter, c) this is not the first time he's been arrested, even if d) it's his first since he turned eighteen a month ago. I'm kind of surprised that I haven't already heard about it.

"Who did he assault?" Morgan sounds disappointed. Showbiz, who's sitting next to her, takes her hand and brings it to his lips. Morgan and Showbiz have been dating for two and a half years. They're disgustingly cute. I don't even think he's listening to the conversation. He's simply in tune with her every mood.

"Who knows?" Cora says. She takes a sip from a giant travel mug of coffee, her constant companion. It's good stuff from Peru, where her mom's family is from, the only kind of coffee her family will drink.

She picks up a celery stick and points it at me. "Miracle also said that Jo 'Mama' Manson is going to ask your boy Hot Sauce to the Snow Ball at Coronation!"

"Not my boy. Your point?"

"You better get on that if you don't want her to beat you to it!" Cora cries.

"Um, hello? Are we not going to the Snow Ball together? The Three Amigos?"

Cora sighs. "I will make the supreme sacrifice and step aside for you and Hot Sauce."

"Where would you even get an idea like that? We hate each other. Not happening. Never in a million years."

Miracle Baxter slides into the seat next to me, thank God.

Miracle plays on the girls' hockey team, and is, honest to God, named after the Miracle on Ice. *That* Miracle on Ice, the one that happened in 1980 at the Lake Placid Olympics when the U.S. beat the Soviets. Every time I see her (several times a day), in my head, I hear the sportscaster Al Michaels saying his famous line from the broadcast, "Do you believe in miracles? YES!" Miracle's older brother plays on my team and is named Brooks, as in Herb Brooks, the coach of said U.S. Olympic squad. And I thought my household was over-the-top with this hockey business.

"What did I miss?" Miracle asks.

"I was just telling Holland that Jo is planning to ask Hot Sauce to the Snow Ball." Cora raises her eyebrows and pinches her lips together.

I shake my head and turn back to my lunch. When I look up again, Morgan is staring at me. She wipes her mouth delicately with a napkin before she says, "You know, when Wes was at your locker this morning, I thought that you two looked super cute together." She smiles.

I put down my fork. "Number one," I say slowly, tapping my left index finger with my right. "We could not have looked cute together, because we were not *together*. And I was probably scowling at him. Number two: I do not date my teammates."

"Yet," Cora mumbles.

"Number three: As I have previously mentioned, Hot Sauce and I can't stand each other. In fact, we'll probably kill each other by the end of the season."

Showbiz laughs. "No, Holls. You might kill him, but he would never kill you."

"What's that supposed to mean? He hates me! You hear the way he talks to me on the ice!"

He shakes his head. "He talks to everyone like that."

"Oh my God, you two!" Cora cries. "Stop already!"

I turn to her. "You started this! You are one-hundred-percent to blame for the utter demise of this conversation."

"Ohmygod," Cora says. "OK, fine, here's the deal. I sort of

want to ask Matt Sullivan to the Snow Ball, so I thought I would, you know, plant the seed to get you to ask Hot Sauce."

"Ohmygod is right!" I groan. "Why didn't you just say so instead of stirring up all this drama? And Hot Sauce, of all people. Just ask Matt already. Morgan can go with Showbiz, and I'll skip it. Easy."

"You are *not* skipping the Snow Ball, Holland," Morgan says sternly. "We're going with our original plan, Cora."

"Oh, fine," Cora grumbles.

"Well," Morgan says, back to her sweet voice, "I really like Jo. She's so nice. I hope he says yes."

"I guess you'll have a front row seat for the show, Holland," Miracle chimes in. "I heard she's going to ask him in the green room before Coronation."

I never expected to be voted to the Junior Court of Snow Week, the slightly less cool younger sibling of Homecoming for winter sports. But next week, I'll find myself dressed in a long black evening gown like every other girl on the Court, on display for the entire school, as the Snow King and Queen, always seniors, are crowned. My money's on Carter and Livvie MacMillan.

"Don't remind me," I mutter. "Can we change the subject? Miracle? What else do you have?"

She shrugs. "You heard about Dylan Rogers, right?" and the conversation turns back to everyone's favorite criminal.

Chapter Seven

I slide into my seat in Rieland's classroom just as the bell for last period rings. *Nothing like the last minute in journalism and in life*, she always says.

"Next week's assignments," Ms. Rieland says. "Livvie and Matt? Can you walk us through it?"

Livvie MacMillan gets up from her desk in the front row and turns to face us. She's T.J.'s twin sister and the captain of the girls' hockey team, holding steady for salutatorian, and co-editor of the *Jack Pine*, our online and print newspaper. Not going to lie, editor's my goal for senior year, too (although team captain and salutatorian? I think we can all agree that's not going to happen). The other editor—and Cora's latest crush, apparently—Matt Sullivan, also played hockey, up until last year when his mom lost her job at the paper mill and he had to pick up more hours at the take-and-bake pizza place.

"Next week's assignments," Livvie repeats as though we hadn't heard Rieland five seconds ago. "I'm heading up the social media team and Matt's got the online edition. Souma's scheduled to take photos of the pep band tonight at the arena for Miki's feature."

Matt stretches his long legs out in front of him but doesn't bother to stand. He's more chill than Livvie, and honestly?

Even though I admire Livvie for her accomplishments and drive, I'll go to Matt over Livvie with a question or problem every time.

"Holland," he says as his gaze lands on me, "you thinking a piece about HockeyFest?"

"Yeah." I glance up at Rieland, who's tapping her pencil on her giant desk pad calendar, no doubt on the date of our print deadline.

"Yeah," he echoes. "I think it should be online and print. Liv? Rieland?"

Livvie nods and turns to Ms. Rieland for approval.

"Yes, both," she agrees, her pencil now paused mid-tap. "Halcyon Lake's selection impacts a great number of students and staff. This is the biggest thing to happen in this town for years. I'm thinking full spread feature. Holland, are you up for that?"

My eyes flick from Rieland to Livvie, whose mouth has that twisty, worried look.

"Absolutely."

"Let's get something out on social media today," Livvie says. "I'm sure the TV station has posted something that we could share. Jacob, can you run with that? Be sure to put in a teaser about the feature, maybe that we'll get an insider's view from our very own Holland Delviss?"

I tune out the rest of the conversation now that I've got my assignment. My first full feature of any kind, and we go right to full spread. Not bad, if I do say so myself. Not bad at all. And while my latest story ideas have been shot down—and, let's face it, since the season started, my contributions to the paper haven't exactly wowed the crowd—a story about hockey in Halcyon Lake? Cakewalk. Child's play. Empty net goal.

Fake it till you make it.

Rieland stops me at the door after the last bell. "Holland? Got a minute?"

I'll be late for practice two days in a row. Hot Sauce is going to love this. I step back to let the last of my classmates pass by. "Sure."

Ms. Rieland, more than any other teacher, has encouraged my love of writing. She taught my freshman English class and a creative writing elective last year. She submitted a creative nonfiction piece I wrote about learning to skate on the lake behind our house to a student writing contest (which received an honorable mention) and invited me to join the *Jack Pine* staff. She played hockey in high school, too, and she doesn't miss many games, girls' or boys'.

She gets right to the point.

"What's going through your head these days, Holland?" she asks as she walks toward her desk. "Your story ideas have fallen a little flat lately, and not just the ones we talked about yesterday. I also mean some of your recently published stories. 'What I Did on My Winter Vacation'?"

"You didn't like that one? Readers eat that stuff up!" I'd collected quotes (the day of the final deadline) by walking around the cafeteria during lunch and soliciting responses to the age-old question, "What did you do over Winter Break?" Highlights included a skiing holiday in Colorado, a tour of the Warner Bros. studio in LA, and a Minnesota Wild game in Florida while visiting grandparents (that was Showbiz). Not bad for waiting until the last minute.

She shakes her head. "Regurgitated info. How much of that did you write? I'll tell you. The first sentence and the last sentence. The rest was served to you, and you served it right back."

"Well, not every quote was perfect. I had to copyedit most of them."

"Copyediting is *not* creating."

Another Rieland-ism.

"What about last month?" she asks when I don't respond. "You wrote about Snow Week, an *article*, as you call it, that copied a calendar of events from the school's website. Again, you wrote an opening paragraph and a closing paragraph. No meat. No personality. No effort. Your editors may have approved these, but going forward, that is not going to fly, and I've spoken to them about it. Since the season started, the quality of your work has slipped. And I've got to admit that I'm a bit worried about the HockeyFest article."

"Oh," I choke out, because I'm not sure what I'm supposed to say to this. "OK."

"Holland, you're an excellent writer. If you weren't, you wouldn't be in this class. You showed that with your first few assignments. Your article about the girls' soccer team at the State Tournament was excellent. You've shown what you're capable of. Let's see more of that and get you into Hartley with a strong recommendation."

I bite my bottom lip. My plan is to make it into the journalism program at Hartley University in Duluth, one of the top journalism schools in the Midwest. They're Division III and have a women's hockey team, so playing for them and scoring a full-ride scholarship wouldn't be the worst thing.

I mean, if I decide to play for a women's team.

I've been writing almost as long as I've been playing hockey. I used to fill notebooks with play-by-play accounts of games and terrible short stories about a hockey player and her three brothers who lived on a farm on a lake. In each installment, the girl, named Hope, was treated unfairly by her brothers in some way, but in the end, she always scored the game-winning goal and the brothers begged for forgiveness. In fifth grade, I produced a family newsletter, *Stories from Story Lake*, filled with compelling articles about the ice going out in spring, the birth of my goat Ozzy, reviews of old Pearl Jam and Foo Fighters albums. As soon as Mom and Dad relented, I set up my first music blog, under one condition: I had to keep it anonymous until I turned eighteen. Which was fine by me. Honestly, I'm not sure that I'll ever go public. There's something to be said for the freedom that comes with a low profile.

"Dig deep, Holland. You're going to have a lot going on with HockeyFest, so you'll need to find a way to make it all work. You're one of this school's most talented writers. Give us some heart. Like you do out on the ice."

"Heart?" I repeat. This is not the first time I've heard Rieland say this, but she's never had to say it to me. It's embarrassing. She shouldn't have to say this to me. She's right. When I'm in this room, I've got to give it everything I've got, just like I do when I'm on the ice.

She taps her fingers against her chest. "Write from *here*. From the heart."

I nod. "From my heart." I sound like a damn parrot.

"Yeah." She waves her hand toward the door. "Now get outta here so you're not late for practice."

Chapter Eight

THE LAST TIME A HOCKEY PLAYER *DIDN'T* WIN SNOW KING, SO THE story goes, a blizzard blew through Central Minnesota, dumping twenty-two inches of heavy powder and stranding the boys' basketball team (and their captain, Brett Bailey, who'd committed the offense of being crowned King) for three days in the Little Falls High School cafeteria. Two days after returning home, the Snow King broke his leg in a snowmobiling accident and was out for the season. He lost his scholarship to the University of Minnesota, married the Snow Queen, took over his dad's towing business, and lived out the rest of his days in Halcyon Lake, coaching his kids' youth basketball teams.

Well, he's still living out those days. I sit next to his oldest son in humanities.

"So." Beck Bailey leans way over and rests his arm on my desk. Like his dad, he's the very tall captain of the basketball team. Unlike his dad, however, he is not up for Snow King at tonight's Snow Week Coronation. A bunch of his teammates nominated him as a joke, but he withdrew his name from consideration. The Senior Court, male and female, will be all hockey players this year.

"So, what?" I ask, flicking his arm. He doesn't take the hint. He smells like pain reliever cream, menthol, and wintergreen.

Rumor has it, he's barely making eligibility with his GPA. How he got into this class, I'll never know.

"So, I heard that you're going to the Snow Ball with Cora. Couldn't find a date?"

I roll my eyes. I don't have the patience for this today. "Why? Are you asking? I'd *love* to go to the Snow Ball with you, Beck. Thank you so much for thinking of me!" I say in a sweet, even tone.

His eyes flicker in surprise and he turns bright red. "Um, well, I didn't actually mean—"

I raise my eyebrows. "You don't say," I deadpan and shove his arm off my desk.

It's third period. I'm hungry. I'm cranky. Almost a week has passed since Rieland told me to *write from the heart* and I've barely put down a word, from the heart or anywhere else. Last night's game went into overtime and ended in a tie. We had dryland practice this morning and my glutes are screaming.

Tonight, I have to put on a fancy black dress and act excited about being voted Snow Week Junior Royalty by my classmates. Plus, it's Decade Day, so I had to get up early to perfect my costume—and convince Carter and Jesse to dress up, too. We're the three Hanson brothers from *Slap Shot*, complete with jerseys and heavy black-framed glasses. That Best-Dressed Award is in the bag, but I'm exhausted.

My stomach growls. I need to get through the next sixty-two minutes and then I can eat. When the bell finally rings, I sprint down the hall to the cafeteria without even dropping off my books at my locker. I juggle my stuff and my tray and make my way through the line but stop short when I get to our table.

Hot Sauce Millard is sitting at our table.

In *my* spot, on the end. I'm *always* on the end. This way, I only have to share space with one other person, who should be on my left so that I have plenty of elbow room on my right. There's a good chance that Hot Sauce is going to get elbowed while I dig into today's turkey gravy with whipped potatoes.

He's deep in conversation with Showbiz and doesn't even look up when Morgan sits down next to her boyfriend and Cora parks next to Morgan. I sit, too, one over from *my* spot. Hot Sauce doesn't seem to notice any of us, least of all me.

"You do know that by sitting there, you've displaced some-one else?" I say before I shovel a rather significant amount of turkey and mashed potatoes into my mouth. I can't help the little sound of pure pleasure that escapes.

When I turn to look at him, he's looking at me, his mouth open. "Did you just *moan*, Dutch?"

"Don't call me that," I snap. "How many times do I have to tell you?"

He ignores that and goes back to my first question. "Who have I *displaced*, as you call it?"

I glance around the long, rectangular table. Our usual lunch crowd consists of mostly current or former hockey players, Cora, and Morgan. To tell the truth, there's a bit of a rotation with a few spots, besides the core group of us and Showbiz, T.J. Macks, Justin and Nik Swenson, and Miracle, who sometimes sits with Livvie and Jo and a couple of other girls from her team.

"Matt," I say.

"Matt Sullivan?" he asks, and when I nod, continues, "No big loss."

"What's that supposed to mean?"

"It means that I don't have much time for a quitter."

"He's not a quitter!"

Hot Sauce lifts his eyebrows. He reaches into his pocket and pulls out a small packet of Cholula, which he tears open with his teeth. "Oh, really? Did he not quit the team? Or am I confusing him with a different Matt Sullivan?"

I scowl as I watch him douse the turkey with the hot sauce. "You don't know why he quit."

"Don't I? I believe the saying goes something like, 'If you can't take the heat, get out of the kitchen.'" He sets the empty packet on the table.

My temper flares. How dare he say something like that? How dare he skate into town, onto our team, flaunt his championship medal, and make judgments about hardworking players like Matt? *This* is why I can't stand Hot Sauce Millard.

"That has nothing to do with it." I can't even look at him anymore. I turn back to my tray and attack the creamed corn. *You pompous, self-important piece of . . .*

"Oh, yeah?" He doesn't take the hint.

"Yeah."

"Then, please, by all means, tell me why Matt quit."

I swallow and shake my head. "It's not my story to tell." I need to shift the attention off Matt. I'm glad that Cora has been deep in conversation with Morgan and has missed the whole exchange. "What are you even doing at our table, anyway?"

"Not that it's any of your business, but I needed to talk to Showbiz."

Not my business. Ha. That's rich coming from someone who thinks it's his job to get in everybody else's business.

"You want to know who else you've displaced? You're in *my* spot." I make a point of knocking my elbow into his ribs.

"That'll get you two minutes in the penalty box," he says, and for one second, I think there's some hidden meaning to his words. It sounds *dirty*. But then: "I'd be happy to trade places with you if you aren't capable of basic table manners."

"Yes, let's," I say and stand up.

He follows, and the strangest thing happens as we switch spots. As I lower myself onto my rightful seat, he puts his hand on my back to steady me, pressing his strong fingers against me, warm and confident. I feel the heat through my Hanson jersey, a *zing* that courses all the way down to my toes.

I twist my arm behind me to smack his hand away.

He continues his conversation with Showbiz, but I ignore him and focus on my food until he nudges me.

"What?"

"Your hair," he says so quietly that I wonder if anyone else can hear him.

"What about it?" I can hardly get the words out, he's so close.

"The blue. I think it's my favorite so far, although the violet is a close second."

Violet? I haven't had a violet stripe since sophomore year. I swallow and reach for my water bottle. Empty.

"Hawks blue," he says. "It's awesome."

My *exact* words.

"You ready for your interview?" he asks. I'm glad he changed the subject.

"Don't worry about the interview," I grumble. "I won't let anyone down."

"That's not what I meant," he says quietly, and he stands up so quickly that I startle. "I have to go. See you at practice."

"See ya," Showbiz calls, then stands up himself. "I gotta take a leak." He leans over to kiss the top of Morgan's head.

"Hmmm," Cora says after Showbiz leaves, and I turn to look at her.

"Don't start," I warn.

"I'm telling you, Holland, that Hot Stuff Millard is cute."

"Hot Sauce," I mumble.

"No, he's definitely hot stuff."

"You think everyone is hot stuff, Cora," Morgan says.

"Seems to me that he was flirting with Holland, though, don't you think, Morgs?" Cora says.

"No way." I shake my head.

"He was!"

"No, not possible. Didn't you hear us? We were *arguing*. Like always."

"Mm-hmm," Cora says. "Arguing. You know it's not too late to ask him to the Snow Ball. Get in there before Jo Mama does!"

"Cora," I say with warning in my voice.

She ignores me. "You know why they call him Hot Sauce, right? He's gonna make you *sweat*."

"God, Cora. It's because he puts Cholula on everything. You saw it."

"No, no, it's because he's hot, fresh, and ready," Cora shoots back. "He'll spice up your life. He's the spice on the ice. He'll bring the *zing*."

I roll my eyes as the bell rings. We dump our trays and head out of the cafeteria.

"You're creative," I tell Cora. "I'll give you that."

Chapter Nine

AT PRACTICE, COACH WORKS US HARD. BY THE TIME HE'S GOT US doing the 15–10 Breakaway—this complicated passing and shooting drill that has the forwards trying to score fifteen goals in ten minutes—I'm *feeling* it. After my shot (the twelfth goal, right through the five-hole, wide enough for a watermelon to pass through Nik's legs), I skate over to the bench, grab a water bottle, and try to catch my breath as I lean against the boards. My calves already ache.

Hot Sauce skates up beside me, takes the water bottle, and squirts some into his mouth. "Nice goal," he says, and I snort, but before I can dispute it with evidence that Nik must have temporarily lost his mind to keep his legs that far apart, Hot Sauce launches into me. "What the fuck are you doing out there? What is this, some Sunday walk in the fucking park?"

Oh, that "nice goal" must have been sarcasm.

"I scored, didn't I?"

"You scored because the goalie had his *head* up his *ass*. You were sloppy. This isn't fucking amateur hour. Get out there and skate like I know you can. Do better. Be better."

Before I can say anything else, he skates off and is yelling at Josh, the youngest of the Swenson brothers, for slacking off and missing his turn. "You've got thirty seconds!" Hot Sauce yells. "We need one more goal. *Don't* be the guy who misses!"

I roll my eyes. I look forward to the day he calls *me* a guy so I can give him a piece of my mind.

Oh, I hate him.

But he's right. I was sloppy. And I get what he's saying to Josh. You don't want to be the guy who misses the shot and screws it up for everyone. Because if we don't get those fifteen goals in ten minutes, everybody hits the indoor track above the second sheet of ice and runs three miles.

After a two-hour practice.

When seven of us need to go home and clean up for Coronation.

But he's also being a grade-A asswipe.

Please make this shot, I silently will Josh, and by some miracle, he does.

Hunter: Whatcha doin

Me: omw to Coronation with M & C

Me: U?

Hunter: @ library.

Me: Are you coming home soon?

Hunter: Yeah Friday.

Me: THIS Friday? Like, Snow Week Friday? In two days?

Hunter: Y

Me: Don't you have a game Saturday night?

Hunter: Going back Sat morning.

Me: I don't get it. Why are you coming home for 1 night?

Hunter: Why not. R u going to Macks party after the dance?

Me: Wasn't planning on it. I've got that Fink at the Rink interview Sat.

Hunter: Fuck it. Go to the party. YOLO and all that shit.

Me: Are u coming home to go to the party?

Hunter: going to see a band in baxter. U shd tho

Hunter: Go to the party Holly

Hunter: U there?

Me: We're here. Gotta go.

I slip my phone into my backpack. T.J.'s parties are historically pretty chill, but I don't know if I can even handle chill right now. We have a game Saturday night, too, so it's not like any of us are going to get shitfaced.

Let me rephrase that. It's not like any of us *should* get shitfaced. Plenty of us will, but I won't be one of them.

I'm going to be sharp Saturday. I have to be sharp. I can't screw up. That *Fink at the Rink* interview has to be good, or the guys will be so pissed. If we don't make it to state this year, the HockeyFest game is the last shot for the seniors to get this kind of exposure.

No pressure.

Morgan parks and we hurry through the cold into school. The girls drop me off at the choir room, aka the Coronation green room. My dress—long black chiffon with a full skirt, formfitting bodice, and cap sleeves—belongs to Cora's older sister Marisol, who graduated last year and bought it when she was voted Junior Royalty. No sense in spending money when I already shelled out too much for my dress for the Snow Ball. I refused to wear her stilettos, though, so instead, I'm wearing my Van Halen striped Converse high-tops. No one can see my shoes under the skirt, anyway.

I'm one of the last to arrive. Twelve guys in suits, twelve girls in long black dresses, a Halcyon Lake tradition that dates back to the '60s.

"Hey, Holland," Carter calls from across the room, where he's standing with the other guys from the team. "What took you so long?"

I walk up to the group, relieved that I don't have to make small talk with the other girls on the junior court, girls I don't know well. "Um, a dress?"

"You look nice, Holls," Showbiz says.

My six teammates are wearing dark suits, white shirts, and blue or yellow ties, Halcyon Lake colors. There are two juniors, Nik Swenson and Luke Abbott, and the four seniors up for Snow King: Carter, Showbiz, T.J., and Hot Sauce.

"You all clean up pretty good yourselves," I say. I make an extra effort *not* to look at the grade-A asswipe.

The conversation turns to tomorrow night's game and, of course, the *Fink at the Rink* interview.

"You're not going to fuck this up for us, are you, Holls?" T.J. says, poking me in the shoulder.

"Really, Macks?" I say.

"She won't," Hot Sauce says. "She's your teammate, T.J. Have a little faith in her."

"Oh, that's rich." I turn to face him, my hands on my hips. "How about you have a little faith in me on the ice once in a while, Hot Sauce?"

"Ohhhhh!" T.J. whoops. "It is on!"

"No, it's not *on*."

"What's wrong with expecting you to always do your best, Dutch?" Hot Sauce asks. He crosses his arms, a tiny smile playing on his lips. He's not even ruffled by my outburst.

"Do *not* call me that," I say in a low—and what I hope to be menacing—voice.

"OK, you two," Carter says. "Break it up. We have to go out there in five minutes."

Even if I'd wanted to continue this conversation, Jo "Mama" Manson walks up to our group with a nervous, twitchy smile on her face, her eyebrows knitted together. She must have realized that time's ticking and now is the perfect opportunity to ask Hot Sauce to the Snow Ball.

"Hey, Wes?" She reaches out and puts a well-manicured hand on his sleeve. She's got that svelte figure-skater look about her, blond hair in a flawless bun, skintight dress bedazzled with rhinestones, which is clearly against the "plain black gown" requirement. "Could I talk to you for a sec? Um, privately?"

T.J. sniggers and the other guys turn away, uncomfortable.

Not me. I watch as Jo and Hot Sauce step over to the piano, Jo's back to me. She must have a lot to say, because

Hot Sauce watches her, that little smile gone from his face, for what feels like a very long time.

And then suddenly, he's not looking at her anymore, he's looking at me. His eyes lock onto mine from across the room for one, two, three, four seconds, before he turns back to her with a shake of his head and a shrug.

He turned her down. An unexpected, tiny thrill passes through me. I'm glad he turned her down.

More seconds pass as she straightens her shoulders and he shakes his head again. I can't tell what he's saying from this distance, but I shouldn't be watching this. I turn back to the group and wait for Mrs. Sommers, the choir director, to pair us up and lead us to the auditorium.

I feel sort of bad for Jo, even worse when Mrs. Sommers pairs us up and Jo has to walk in with Hot Sauce. She should have waited until after Coronation. What if they get crowned King and Queen? Awkward.

I'm paired up with Luke. "Ready?" he asks as he holds out his elbow to me.

"Let's do this, Liney."

If I have to humiliate myself in front of the entire town, at least it's with a teammate.

The twelve of us stand in pairs on the stage, seniors in the middle, sophomores and juniors on either side, as Mrs. Ziegler, our principal, steps up to the microphone and motions for the crowd to quiet down. After a few attempts and a few random *whoops* and a female voice that might belong to Cora yelling, "We love you, Hot Sauce," she succeeds. The pep band plays the national anthem and then the school rouser, a catchy little ditty called "Fly High, Hawks," a title that provides numerous opportunities for inappropriate lyrical liberties.

It's hot on this stage, and the lights blind me enough that I can't even tell where Cora and Morgan and Miracle are sitting out in the audience.

I can, however, see Hot Sauce, who stands to my right and slightly upstage. His stance is casual, one hand in the pocket of his tailored, perfectly fitting black suit pants. OK, fine, yes, he is hot stuff, as Cora would say, but my constant irritation with him overrides any hotness.

He turns his head to look at me as though he knew I was staring. My cheeks warm, and I hope he can't tell under these glaring bright lights. I peel my eyes away from him and instead focus on Mrs. Ziegler at the microphone.

"Thank you for joining us for tonight's Snow Week Coronation," she says. "We hope that you'll attend additional Snow Week events, including tomorrow night's home girls' basketball game versus St. Vincent's and Saturday night's boys' home hockey game against Little Falls. Friday is School Spirit Day, so be sure to wear blue and gold, and then join us Friday night at the Halcyon Days Ballroom for our semiformal Snow Ball. Tickets are still available."

She goes on to talk about school spirit, the history of Snow Week, and the value of continuing timeless, beloved traditions even as times change.

"Get on with it already," I mutter. "This dress is too tight."

Luke laughs.

"And now, without further ado, it's time to crown the Snow King and Queen, as voted by the student population of Halcyon Lake High School."

The athletic director, Mr. Handshaw, joins Mrs. Ziegler onstage and lifts the King's gigantic crown off a plush royal blue pillow on a stand. "Congratulations to Carter Delviss, this year's Snow King!"

The crowd goes wild. I haven't heard this much cheering since the pep fest for the football team when they made it to state two years ago. I mean, I knew Carter was popular, but this is sort of over-the-top. These people are way more enthusiastic than they were a year ago when Hunter was crowned King.

My brother looks a little embarrassed as Mr. Handshaw places the giant gold crown with fake plastic sapphires on his head.

"Thank you," Mrs. Ziegler says. "And now for our Snow Queen, Miss Livvie MacMillan!"

I knew it.

The crowd explodes as Mr. Handshaw crowns Liv with a sparkly rhinestone tiara.

And as my brother turns toward the newly crowned queen, puts his arm around her waist, pulls her close, and kisses her? Like, kisses the *hell* out of her? On stage, in front of God and Mrs. Ziegler, the entire student body, most of their parents, *our* parents, and quite a lot of siblings? The place goes absolutely *berserk*.

Apparently, my brother has a girlfriend. And it's Livvie MacMillan.

"Whoa, what is going on there?" Luke says. "That's kinda hot."

"Uh, gross," I say. "That's my *brother* up there."

At Mrs. Ziegler's frantic arm movements and pleas into the microphone, the noise dies down. She says a few words, something about tomorrow night's basketball game, *blah blah blah*. She spins on her heel toward the Royal Court, her face red and splotchy.

Carter stands with his right arm around Liv's waist. She's tucked up under him like she's always fit there. Mrs. Ziegler lays into them and stomps off the stage. A photographer from the newspaper takes some photos and then it's over.

We file off the stage and go back to the choir room. Everyone wants to talk to Carter and Livvie—not about their new royal titles but about how they've been sneaking around behind everyone's backs. Eventually, Mrs. Sommers kicks us all out. My parents meet us in the cafeteria for even more photos.

"Come on, Mom," I whine. "How many more pictures do you need? I have to get out of this dress."

"One more of you and Carter, OK?"

I stand next to my brother. "So, when were you going to tell us that you have a girlfriend?"

"Oh, I would have gotten around to it eventually."

"When did you start dating?"

"Right before Christmas."

"You've been dating Livvie MacMillan since before Christmas and I didn't know this? How could I not know this?"

"Come on, Holls, it's not that big a deal."

"Mrs. Ziegler seemed to think that you shoving your tongue down Livvie's throat in front of the entire town was a big deal."

Carter laughs. "Who cares what she thinks? Mom, are you done yet?" he asks as Mom swipes through the photos.

"Oh, no!" Mom says. "I forgot. One more. Holland and all the boys. Holland, you get in the middle."

Mom makes a big deal about posing me and my six teammates, with Hot Sauce and Carter on either side of me.

"Mom, really?" Carter says. "I told Liv I'd take her out for pie."

"I promise this is the last one. Boys, can you at least pretend that you're having a good time? Holland?"

I'm about to say something snarky when Hot Sauce slides his arm around my waist, his fingers pressing lightly into the space just above my hip bone. I suck in a breath at the sudden warmth of his touch. I feel his mouth against my hair, his breath hot as he whispers, "I like your shoes, Dutch," and the sensation that courses down my spine nearly sends me into orbit. I shiver, and his grip tightens.

As soon as Mom lowers her phone, I step out of his hold and sprint across the cafeteria, telling my parents I'll get a ride home with Morgan.

I can't catch my breath. I tell myself it's because Marisol's dress fits too snugly across my ribs, but I know it's more than that. Way more.

Wasting Light: A Blog About Music, Hockey, and Life
January 17 11:54 p.m.
By HardRock_Hockey
Sometimes All You Need Is a Little Flip
Now Spinning: Soundtrack from *The Cutting Edge*

Hello, Hard Rockers.

Confession: I love *The Cutting Edge*. Yes, that cheesy movie from the early 90s about a bitchy pairs figure skater without a partner and the former hockey player from Minnesota. And yes, I know in last week's post, I talked about how I don't need happy endings, etc., but I do have my favorite rom-coms. And there's something about *The Cutting Edge*.

Of course, I love it because of the hockey angle and the Minnesota connection. Doug Dorsey's cute and has some awesome one-liners and comebacks. Some of the music is awful and dated (best song on the soundtrack, hands down: "It Ain't Over 'Til It's Over" by Lenny Kravitz), but I've watched this movie so many times, those songs have earwormed their way into my heart.

Here's what I love most about *The Cutting Edge*: It's a love story, yes, and it's a story about overcoming obstacles, but it's also about a change in perspective. You know the scene when Kate and Doug do tequila shots and she gets plastered and talks about the magnets? That all they needed was a little flip? *Flip*? Yeah, you know what I'm talking about, don't deny it. Sure, she's talking about their relationship, but it's about life perspective, too. Doug was a hockey god until he got benched with an injury. Figure skating wasn't in his plan. Kate went through partner after partner. She wasn't expecting to click with this . . . this *cretin*!

Sometimes all you need is a little flip.

What does this have to do with . . . well, anything? Tonight I stood onstage in a long, black dress (it's OK, I was wearing my VH striped All Stars) with a bunch of my teammates, part of the Snow Week Royalty. It was weird and not at all something I ever thought would happen. And something else happened, too, something that surprised me, something as simple as posing for a photograph. And it got me thinking about those magnets and that little flip. Wondering if the universe is telling me that's what my life needs right now. A change in perspective. An openness to new possibilities.

Flip.

Has this ever happened to you?

HARDROCK_HOCKEY: TOP 10 ROM-COMS*

10. *10 Things I Hate About You*

9. *How to Lose a Guy in 10 Days*

8. *13 Going on 30*

7. *French Kiss*

6. *When Harry Met Sally*

5. *Kissing a Fool*

4. *Say Anything*

3. *You've Got Mail*
2. *The Princess Bride*
1. *The Cutting Edge*

*I know, right? WHAT? I have favorite rom-coms?
What's your favorite?
\m/
19

Comments

11:58 p.m.
The Princess Bride for sure is my #1. It's romantic. It's
hilarious.

> Trace
> *Reply from HardRock_Hockey*
> *12:10 a.m.*
> It's so close to number one for me, too. But.
> Hockey.

11:59 p.m.
Say Anything is the perfect movie. I kinda identify with
Lloyd Dobler, to be honest. Kickboxing. It's the sport of
the future. Haha.

> MetalManiac (Jim)
> *Reply from HardRock_Hockey*
> *12:11 a.m.*
> I gave her my heart, she gave me a pen.
> Classic.

12:14 a.m.

I love rom-coms. *Bridget Jones. 13 Going on 30.* I just recently rewatched it and I still love it. Oh, and RIP Heath Ledger. I loved *10 Things.*

> Rebekah Faith
> *Reply from HardRock_Hockey*
> *12:16 a.m.*
> I forgot about *Bridget Jones*!

1:32 a.m.

Does *There's Something About Mary* count as a rom-com?

> LizP
> *Reply from HardRock_Hockey*
> *5:45 a.m.*
> Yes, for sure.

Chapter Ten

THURSDAY NIGHT WE LOSE AN AWAY GAME 1–0, AND FRIDAY'S practice is even more brutal. A small part of me wonders if Hot Sauce feels the *zing* every time we touch, too, and if he might be nicer to me because of it. But he's disproving my theory spectacularly right now, and the only thing that's saving me is knowing that practice will be cut short because of the Snow Ball.

"Dutch!" Hot Sauce shouts after a massive fuck-up in the neutral zone on a penalty kill drill. "Snap out of it already!"

Yes, I need to snap out of it. Why am I thinking about the *zing* instead of the drill? Further evidence that I should not date a teammate, no matter how good his hand felt on my waist.

He skates toward me and I cringe.

"What the fuck, Dutch?" he shouts, so close to my face I see the flash of *pissed off* in his dark eyes.

I flinch. "Don't call me that!" I yell back.

"This isn't Peewees!" His voice is so loud and so close to my ears and damn it, why is it OK for a peer to get in my face like this? Isn't this against Minnesota State High School League rules or something?

"No, it is not!" he shouts.

"Shit, I said that out loud, didn't I?"

"Yes!"

"Stop yelling at me!" I yell. "You're making me nervous." That last part I say more quietly. No one else needs to know. And they especially don't need to know that it's not the yelling that's making me nervous, it's Hot Sauce. He's too close. He's been too close since Coronation. I can't lose the feeling of his fingers resting against my waist, his hot breath in my ear.

"I am raising my voice so that you'll hear me, Dutch. Let me help you understand the concept of the penalty kill. That's when your team is short a player because of a rule infraction, also known as a penalty. The consequence for this infraction is playing without that individual, meaning that your team is down a man and at a disadvantage—"

I cut him off. "Don't say *man*, say *player*! And I know what a penalty kill is!"

"So what was that dumpster fire just now? Keep your damn stick on the ice. I know *toddlers* who could have protected their zone better. Defend, defend, defend!"

My face is *redredredredred*.

"Sorry," I mumble.

"Don't apologize!" he yells. "Be better! Do better! I know you are better than whatever *that* was."

Between Rieland and Hot Sauce, I'm getting my fill of feedback this week.

He turns and skates away.

Not long after, Coach gives up and calls practice. Even

though I'm dreading the Snow Ball, I can't say that I'm sorry to get off the ice and away from Hot Sauce.

I'm still upstairs when the girls get here, but I'm showered and dressed and calling that a win.

Cora huffs when she sees my wet hair and holds up a sparkly purple tackle box. She flips it open to reveal tubes, palettes, pots, brushes, and sponges.

"Morgan," she orders, "go rummage around in the bathroom for Holland's foundation. I can handle the rest, but we gotta start there. Oh, and a round brush and her hair dryer, if you can find it."

She plunks me down in front of my desk, turns on the lamp, and angles the arm so that the light shines in my face. She's wearing purple—her signature color—a pale lilac shimmery shift that makes her skin glow. "Close your eyes," she says in her cajoling way, and I do. She attacks my eyebrows with tweezers.

"Ouch! Settle down there, cowboy."

"We don't have the luxury of time to *settle down*, Holland. You look so good in that dress. You can't have two caterpillars crawling across your face like you did at Coronation. You just can't."

Morgan's back from the bathroom and she tuts. "They're not *caterpillars*, Cora. Don't exaggerate. They just need some maintenance. Some TLC."

"TLC," Cora mumbles. "I'll give you TLC. *Tweeze like crazy.*"

I close my eyes and she resumes her deforestation but more gently.

"Mascara time," Cora singsongs.

"Nope, no mascara. I wore mascara Wednesday night and I ended up looking like Alice Cooper."

"I don't even know who she is," Cora says. "You have to wear mascara."

"She? *She*? What is wrong with you? Alice Cooper is a shock rocker. A *male* shock rocker."

"Whatever. I don't know what a shock rocker is, either. Mascara," Cora croons. She pulls a silver tube from her tackle box. "Good girl," she says when I don't blink it onto my cheeks. Next, she colors my lips with a deep plum that complements the rich blue of my dress, and then she starts on my hair.

The dress is fantastic. The bodice with its sweetheart neckline and wide straps hugs my curves, ending in a band of peacock feather–inspired sequins and a skirt that fades gradually to a lighter blue. It's nothing I would have chosen, ever, in a million years, but I love it.

She finishes my hair in a simple style that highlights the stripe on one side and is swept up on the other, secured with a vintage peacock hair clip, bronze with turquoise and blue stones.

"Oh, my goodness, Holland!" Morgan cries out when I stand up. "You look so beautiful!"

Cora stands back, crosses her arms, and inspects me. "Shoes," she orders, and I slip into the matching deep blue heels. "*Très bon*," she says quietly and brushes her hands together.

I turn to Morgan, who's wearing a deep red gown with a full skirt that ends mid-calf. Nothing above the knee for our gal Morgan. Her blond hair is in a complicated updo with curly tendrils around her face. Her lips match her dress.

"She got to you, too?" I ask, and Morgan nods, smiling.

"I wouldn't have it any other way," she says. She turns me to face the full-length mirror on the back of my door and my heart swells. I swallow down a lump in my throat. I look—I look *beautiful*.

"Cora," I whisper. "It's perfect."

"See? I *told* you that you wouldn't look like a hooker, o ye of little faith," Cora says as she packs up her tackle box.

My mother once again takes several hundred pictures. Carter escaped long ago to pick up Livvie, so those two won't be subjected to another of Mom's lengthy photo shoots. Lucky. Eventually, Morgan, Cora, and I leave the warmth and safety of my living room for the cold and uncertainty of the Minnesota winter and the Snow Ball.

Chapter Eleven

I WOULDN'T SAY THAT I GO INTO THE HALCYON DAYS BALLROOM kicking and screaming, but it's close. Cora and Morgan march me toward Showbiz, Matt (who caught wind that Cora wanted to ask him to the dance and was on board one-hundred-percent), Miracle, and Miracle's girlfriend, Poppy, who all hover on the edge of the dance floor.

"Whoa," Matt says. "Holy shit, you three look smokin'."

Showbiz whacks Matt on the arm. "Keep your eyes off my girl." He turns toward Morgan. "I thought you'd never get here. Want to dance, beautiful?"

Morgan beams. The lovebirds walk hand in hand onto the dance floor, and I watch them go with something like envy. But I can't fault them for finding each other, even if we were only in ninth grade when they got together. When you know, you know.

I guess.

They're everywhere, these happy couples. Cora's flirting with Matt now, and Poppy and Miracle are deep in a debate about whether the Minnesota Gophers will make it to the Women's Frozen Four this year. I turn toward the dance floor where Livvie and Carter sway and grin at each other. Even Lumberjack Lewis found a date to the Snow Ball after I rejected him—Serena Perkins, a basketball player who's about four inches taller than Lumberjack.

Ah, young love. So inspiring, so new, so spine-tingling. So glad I don't date—

"Hey, Dutch."

I whirl around. Why is he forever sneaking up on me? "Don't call me—"

Oof.

Hot Sauce is *hot*. Holy hot. Even hotter than he looked at Coronation. He's wearing a damn *tuxedo*, the top button of his shirt undone and a bowtie hanging loose around the collar like he couldn't be bothered, or like he'd already lived through ten epic Snow Ball nights. Same with his deliberately messy hair. I would like to place my hands in that deliberately messy hair and tug his face toward mine and . . .

Whoa. *WHAT?*

I swallow. "Is that how they do it in Great River?" I wave my shaky hand in his general direction.

He swallows, too. "Do what?" he asks in a choked voice, and he doesn't even bother to hide the fact that his eyes travel from the peacock clip in my hair to the tips of my sky-high heels and back up, lingering at my décolletage, until they lock with my eyes.

Uhhhh.

"The, um, disheveled formal look." I can't pull my gaze from his. The gold flecks in his eyes glimmer against the dim light from this distance. Which has suddenly become less distance. I don't know which of us moved closer or if we both did.

"Dance?"

Did Hot Sauce Millard just ask me to dance? He did. I wrinkle up my nose and take a step back so he's not so close. "Who are you here with?"

"What?"

"Your date? Who's your date?"

He smiles, like he's keeping a secret and is about to let me in on it. "I'm solo tonight."

"I suppose you're too good for all of us small people in Halcyon Lake, you and your championship medal."

His smile falters. I wait for him to shake his head and walk away or tell me to fuck off, but instead he tucks his arm around my waist, and my knees nearly buckle from the shock waves (some advance notice would be nice! For example, "I'm going to touch you now, so lock your knees and brace for impact"), and he leads me to the dance floor, and wouldn't you know it, they play "Love Song" by Tesla at *that exact moment.*

What is it with this guy and me and wretched musical timing?

And why is the DJ at a high school dance playing a power ballad that's almost thirty years old? Not that I mind. I love "Love Song," even if I have to listen to it in the middle of this fancy, old-timey ballroom that smells like my grandmother's basement, musty with mildew and memories, fake snowflakes dangling from the ceiling. Even if I am in the arms of Hot Sauce Millard, who's barely moving, holding on to me like he never wants to let me go.

But I don't hate it.

I hate that he basically called me a Peewee on the ice this afternoon. I hate that he's constantly calling me out and telling me to *do better, be better, I know you are better than this.*

"That dress," he murmurs, his head bent low so that his mouth is close to my ear, almost touching. "You. In that dress. You look incredible."

What was I saying? I shiver, and he pulls me tighter, which, I can't deny, feels amazing and scary and *right.*

Oh, no. I can't let this continue. I step back against the pressure of his arms, creating a space between us the size of Mount Rushmore.

"What's wrong?" he asks.

"Um." I bite my bottom lip and glance over his shoulder, catching a glimpse of two chaperones, my humanities teacher, Mr. Neese, and Mr. Briceño, the band director. "Chaperones. God, I hate everything about dances."

He turns and looks. "Yeah, me too. Fuck it. You want to get out of here?"

"Get out of here?"

"Yeah."

"With you."

He laughs. "Yeah."

"But we just got here."

"No, *you* just got here. I've been here for forty-five long minutes, waiting for . . ."

He trails off.

Wait. Should I leave with Hot Sauce? What will people think if they see me leaving with Hot Sauce?

He's waiting for me to say something.

"Where would we go?"

"I could eat. Pie? Are you in the mood for pie?"

Done deal. "I'm always in the mood for pie. Any food, really, but especially pie."

"It's settled, then," he says. "Shall we?"

Nope. We cannot be seen leaving together.

"Uh, why don't you go ahead, and I'll meet you outside? I need to tell Morgan and Cora."

He tilts his head, regarding me. "Oh . . . kay? I'll meet you at the coat check." He walks toward the lobby.

I'm not actually going to talk to Morgan and Cora. I move over to the dessert table (the tiny cheesecakes look delicious, but I'm holding out for pie) and count to one hundred and twenty. Then I slip out the side door.

Hot Sauce is waiting for me in the lobby. With my coat. A long black wool dress coat with gigantic white buttons that belonged to Grandma Delviss in the '60s. A coat I'm wearing for the first time tonight.

"How did you . . . ?"

"I asked the woman at the coat check."

"You didn't have my ticket."

He shrugs. "She knew you."

The attendant has got to be pushing eighty if not more. I've never seen her before. "How?"

"Hockey fan. She's looking forward to HockeyFest."

"You're full of shit."

"No, it's true." He smiles, holds out my coat, and helps me into it. "Stay here. I'll go warm up the truck and pick you up."

"You don't have to do that."

"Stay here," he says again, more firmly. "Did I mention how good you look in that dress? And with that coat? 'Short Skirt/Long Jacket.'"

He hurries away, but I swear the tips of his ears are turning pink, and now I'll have that Cake song in my head all night. *I like a girl in a short skirt and a lonnnnng jacket.*

This is not the best time of year for a formal dance, especially with a skirt this short and bare legs, but it's another one of those Hawks traditions dating back to 1965 or something like that. When I see the truck pull up a few minutes later, I push open the heavy wooden door to a blast of frigid air and hurry down the steps as fast as these heels will allow. I couldn't get away with my high-tops tonight. He meets me at the front passenger door, opening it and helping me up.

This is starting to feel like a date. Not that I would know. The closest thing I've had to a date was around the time Morgan and Showbiz got together. A mixed group of us went to the movies and a JV defenseman named Chevy Williams held my hand, and later, we fumbled our way through a first (and only) kiss that featured chapped lips (him) and braces (me).

The worst first date and first kiss ever. He must not have thought so, because he asked me out again the very next day. I told him I'd had a nice time but that I didn't think it was a good idea to date a teammate.

It's been my MO ever since.

Chevy moved a couple of months later. I don't remember the movie, but I do remember that awkward first kiss and his sweaty palm when he held my hand.

Hot Sauce doesn't seem sweaty, and I've seen him sweaty.

My cheeks warm at the thought. There's something seriously wrong with me.

"Warm up the truck" is relative, because it's still damn cold in the cab, although the air coming through the registers is warmish. And the music's good—Foo Fighters, "The Pretender." The screen reads "Wesley Millard—Barn Burner Mix." Very good indeed.

"Turn it up," I say, and he does, because we both know that "The Pretender" is a song that must be played at high volume.

He switches the song off a couple of minutes later as we pull into the nearly empty parking lot of the Full Loon Café. It's usually a popular hangout on a Friday night. Thanks to the Snow Ball, we have the place to ourselves, except for a couple of people at the counter.

Hot Sauce moves to help me out of my coat, but I put my hand up. "It's OK," I say. "I got this." I shrug out of the coat, but he takes it from me to hang it on the coatrack around the corner.

Clare, the hostess, whistles. "That's some dress, Holland," she says. "Is the dance over? Do we need to brace ourselves?"

"It's just getting started," I tell her. "We bailed."

Clare's been a hostess here for as long as I can remember, and she works at Goldilocks Hair Salon with Debbie, Hot Sauce's mom. Clare knows everyone in town, because everyone in town comes to the Full Loon for their fantastic food and "world-famous, award-winning" pie. I don't know what awards they've won, but the pie and the coffee are damn good.

"So," Clare says, leaning in, "you and Wes, huh?"

"Um, no? Why do you say that?"

She smiles. "Oh, I don't know, Holland. You in that dress, him in a tux, sneaking away from the Snow Ball?"

My cheeks warm again, thinking of him in that tux on the dance floor, holding me close. "We're not together," I say quietly. This is exactly why I shouldn't go out with teammates. "Please don't say you saw us here, OK, Clare?"

I glance sideways at Hot Sauce as he walks up, hoping he hasn't heard anything.

"Oh, OK," Clare says with hesitation. "Do you need a menu?"

I shake my head, but Hot Sauce says yes.

"Can we sit anywhere?" I ask.

"Anywhere except the porch."

Hot Sauce follows me to a booth, one far from the restaurant's front door, tucked around a corner and out of sight.

"Very intimate, Dutch," he says as he slides into the booth opposite me.

"Don't call me that, Hot Shit," I tell him. I'm suddenly very aware that I'm basically alone in a restaurant with the most frustrating, critical, irritating person I know. I exhale a long breath.

He ignores my dig. "It suits you."

"Yeah, yeah, I get it. Holland, Dutch. Clever."

He studies the menu, his brows scrunched together. I don't have to look. I'm in the mood for the Up North Nachos, a heaping platter of homemade tortilla chips and unseasoned rotisserie chicken smothered with melted Colby jack, black olives, mild salsa, and sour cream. There's a reason Cora calls me Blando Calrissian. This is about as bland as nachos can get. Of course I'll save room for pie. You're never too full for Full Loon pie.

My phone chirps with a group text.

Cora: wru? Miracle said she thought she saw u leaving with Hot Sauce n I was ha, I knew it!?

Me: Settle down. But yeah. We're at the Full Loon.

Morgan: squeeee

Me: g2g details later it's not what you think

I put my phone facedown on the table as Hot Sauce sets his menu aside.

"Do they serve all-day breakfast?" he asks. "Or do I want a burger? Anyway, yes, that's where it started. Holland. Dutch. But then I started thinking about Earl 'Dutch' Reibel. You know that name?"

I shake my head.

"But you know Gordie Howe." That's not a question. Everyone knows Gordie Howe. Mr. Hockey. Mr. Everything. Number 9.

"Of course. You play hockey, you know Gordie Howe like you know Wayne Gretzky."

"Exactly." He grins. "Or the Hanson brothers. Well played, by the way."

"Thanks. So, what about this Dutch Reibel guy?"

"If you were a Red Wings fan, you'd know Dutch Reibel. He played for them, too, only for a few years, but he was there for two Stanley Cup wins."

"OK? And?"

"His first game with the Red Wings, his very first game out of the minors, he assisted on every single goal scored, four of them. He still holds the league record for it. Well, him and Roland Eriksson, who, you know, played for the North Stars."

I nod, even though I don't know, but I have to say I'm impressed with his NHL knowledge.

"Here's something else," Hot Sauce continues. "Dutch was the only player to surpass Howe as the Red Wings' leading scorer, during the 1954–55 season, and he was fourth overall in the league. That was one of the years they won the Cup. In 1956, he won the Byng trophy."

His eyes flash as he tells me all this, the corners of his mouth upturned.

"Your point?"

"My point is that Dutch Reibel played hard. He played his heart out every single game. He's one of the greatest players in the history of the NHL, on par with Gordie Howe. Gordie fucking Howe! And the thing is, Dutch, when I think of how hard you work, how you bring your best to every game, you remind me of him."

I don't mind being compared to an NHL great, even if I've never heard of him, but I'm a little weirded out that Hot Sauce has given this so much thought.

"And what's the moral of this story?" I ask. "That even if I continue to work hard and get a bunch of assists and take out the captain for most goals scored, I'll fade into obscurity and no one will remember my name, but they'll apparently remember yours. Superstar Hot Sauce Millard. Future Mr. Hockey?"

"Are you even listening to me?" He shakes his head and sighs as the waitress comes over. "Go ahead." He nods, then looks up at the waitress.

"Oh, OK." It seems strange that he thinks I should order first, like it's chivalrous or something, but after I rattle off my usual (after which Rosemary says, "The usual. Got it," and winks at me), Hot Sauce grabs his menu again.

"I can't decide between the Twisted Sister double bacon burger with pepper jack, which is a great name, by the way, or the El Toro. Which is hotter?" He looks back and forth between me and Rosemary, waiting for one of us to answer.

"I wouldn't know," I say.

"You want the one with more kick?" Rosemary asks.

He nods. "The hotter, the better."

"The Twisted Sister, for sure. I can ask Daniel to throw a couple of extra jalapeños on it."

"Fresh? Not jarred? I like a little crunch."

"Fresh. Got it."

"Thank you very much."

Who is this boy sitting across from me in a tux, politely conversing with Rosemary and me? Where is my frustrated, impatient, insulting captain?

"The thing is, Dutch, I've been watching you play hockey now for over a year and you're *good*. You're really good. And I'm not saying that you're good for a girl, or that you're good for a girl who's playing with a bunch of guys. You. Are. Good. You're skilled and you've got a ton of power in your legs and your shoulders, you know? And your wrists. I'd never really thought about it before, how a person can effortlessly put so much grace and energy into a shot with the flick of a wrist."

Uhhhhhh.

I must look shocked, because he asks, "What? Has no one ever told you that you're talented?"

"Well, sure, but—"

His eyebrows pinch together again. "What?"

I've heard it all my life from my parents and brothers and coaches, but, I realize, this is the first time I've heard it from him. He's so quick to tell me what I'm doing wrong, every single day. Sure, I've gotten "nice shot" and "good job" once or twice, but nothing like this. I can't exactly tell him about the tiny bit of pride I'm feeling because of it.

Rosemary comes back with our meals, so I no longer need to find a way around this conversation.

"Ooh," I say, and rub my hands together as she sets down

the gigantic platter of cheesy, delicious Up North Nachos. I pick up a black olive slice and pop it into my mouth. So far, my escape from the Snow Ball with Hot Sauce is turning out . . . OK.

"This looks amazing," he says, taking the top of the toasted bun off his Twisted Sister burger. He reaches into an inside pocket in his tuxedo jacket and pulls out a packet of Cholula. Even in his tux. It's kind of adorable.

"Some like it hot, huh, Hot Sauce?" I say as he tears open the Cholula with his teeth. I'm feeling a little hot myself, wondering what those teeth would feel like on my bottom lip (where did *that* even come from?). I continue to watch as he divides the sauce over his burger and fries.

"I love it hot. Atomic Fireballs, Buffalo wings, wasabi, chile peppers. The hotter, the better. Want to try?" He picks up a fry, the tiniest bit of hot sauce on the end.

"No, thank you. I'm not really a spice girl."

He pops the fry into his mouth, and I watch him chew. I'm suddenly obsessed with the mechanics of his jaw, the strong lines and edges.

"You could be," he says. "It takes practice."

"I could be a spice girl?"

"Yes."

"With practice."

"Yeah. You didn't have that perfect backhand the first time you picked up a stick, did you?"

Hot Sauce Millard, state champion, called my backhand *perfect*.

"Someone, your dad, I'm guessing, showed you how, and then helped you get the feel of it," he continues. "How many backhands did you execute before it was second nature? Thousands, probably, right?"

"Are you suggesting that I *practice* eating spicy foods?"

"Yep."

"I don't know. I'm pretty mild."

"'Mild' is the last word I would use to describe you, Dutch. Come on, try a bite?"

I wave my hand over my plate of Up North Nachos. "This is about as spicy as it gets for me, Hot Sauce."

I pick up a chip, making sure it's got equal parts salsa, black olive, sour cream, and . . . what's this? A green pepper? That's new. Well, anyway, I like my flavors to blend. I put the whole chip in my mouth and chew.

And *holy fuck*. If Hot Sauce Millard weren't sitting across from me looking so damn hot in that tuxedo with his messy hair and gorgeous eyes (What? *Gorgeous? What is* wrong *with me?*), I would spit whatever the hell is in my mouth back onto my plate.

My flesh is burning. Searing. Flames lick my cheeks, my lips, every inch of my face from the inside out. Tears spring into the corners of my eyes, but I blink them back.

Must. Not. React.

Oh my God, the heat is shooting in every direction. To my ears, the top of my head, my *hair follicles*, down through my core, through my limbs to the tips of my fingers and my toes in their flimsy, strappy heels. My *fingernails* ache with the heat.

"Dutch? You OK?"

Blink. Blink, blink.

Nod.

"Dutch."

I try to smile, to move my lips to say something, any-thing, to in some way communicate that even though I have consumed something that the devil placed on my Up North Nachos by mistake, I am fine.

But I am not fine. A tear escapes my left eye.

"You're aware that you just ate a raw jalapeño pepper, right?"

"What?" I burst out, relieved that I haven't lost the ability to speak.

He points at one of the green peppers on my platter. "*This* is a jalapeño pepper."

Why would they do such a thing? There have never been jalapeños on my favorite nachos before. What is different about tonight?

Oh, I'll tell you what's different about tonight. The boy sitting across from me, Hot Sauce Millard, with his packets of Cholula and his "I like a little crunch." He asked for extra heat on his burger. Did that lead to an unfortunate mix-up in the kitchen?

"Are you OK?" Hot Sauce asks again. "Your cheeks . . . are a little pink. I mean, I like it. I think it's cute."

I swallow and nod.

Number one: He thinks my red-hot cheeks (pink! Ha!) are cute. Number two: I've survived. I'm a *survivor*. I have walked through flames (in more ways than one) and I would walk through them again. I may have even *liked* it—once I got past the initial shock and *pain*, I enjoyed the flavor.

"I think that jalapeño changed my life," I say.

His smile—full-on, with a single dimple on the right side of his chin—lights up the air around us.

"That's my girl," Hot Sauce says.

My girl.

What I'm feeling now is even more than whatever burned through me from that pepper.

"How about some Cholula on those nachos?" he asks.

I decline his offer, but I eat every bite of my nachos, including the seven remaining jalapeño slices, blow my runny nose so much I have to ask for extra napkins, and live to tell the tale.

"Room for pie?" Rosemary asks as she clears our plates.

"Yes!" I cry, and Hot Sauce smiles. I like it. I like this happy, smiling Wes.

I just called him Wes.

I kinda like Wes.

"Do you have . . . *Dutch* apple? Two slices?" he asks, and this terrifying, wonderful feeling that Wes likes me back vibrates through me.

"Of course," Rosemary says. She turns to go.

Wait a minute. She thinks that Wes ordered for me! Not happening.

"Wait!" I call, and she turns back to me. "I'd rather have toffee cream. And a cup of coffee with room, please."

Rosemary frowns and looks from me to Wes. "So, one slice of Dutch apple, then?"

"Two slices of Dutch apple," Wes confirms, "and one slice of toffee cream. To go, if you don't mind."

"To go?" I ask.

"To go."

Chapter Twelve

WES GOES OUT TO WARM UP THE TRUCK BEFORE WE HEAD OVER TO T.J.'s for the team after-party, and I wait by the front door with Clare and the pie.

"He's a gentleman, that one," Clare says, and I choke back a laugh when I think of some of his very ungentlemanly motivational tactics at the rink. "That whiny girlfriend he used to bring in here wasn't good enough for him."

I freeze, my fingers tightening around the to-go bag. "Who?"

"Wes's girlfriend from Park Rapids, maybe? What was her name? Gillian, I think."

"Gillian. From Great River?"

"Yes, that's it. Great River. She visited a few times after they moved here. She complained about one thing or another every single time. Her burger was overdone. Her burger wasn't done enough. Her strawberry pie had too many tiny seeds in it and they were stuck in her teeth."

I'd laugh if I weren't so surprised—and I'll admit, disappointed—that Wes has (had?) a girlfriend named Gillian. Gillian from GR. Maybe that's why he turned Jo down.

"But he doesn't bring her around anymore?" I try to sound

casual as I dig for info. I flip through a sheaf of memories from last season. Not that I've paid much attention to that arrogant state champion a-hole who lives to make my life on the ice miserable, but I think I would have noticed a girlfriend/puck bunny hanging around the locker room door.

"They broke up not long after the season started. *Last* year. She did have fantastic hair. These glossy, dark, perfect waves. Pretty, too. Classic beauty. She could have been in a Pantene commercial."

Classic beauty? What does that even mean?

"And here he is. Enjoy your pie!"

I step out into the cold night and Wes once again gets out to open the door for me.

"You don't have to do that, you know. Any of it. Open doors, let me order first, stuff like that," I say as he takes hold of my hand to help me into the truck. Again. "This isn't the Dark Ages. Or the fifties."

"Oh, I know." He closes my door and walks around to the driver's side and gets in. "I want to. Plus, I let you order first because I had no idea what to get, so I didn't want to hold you up while I deliberated."

How can I argue with that? "Still," I try. "No sense in both of us being cold after you've already been in the truck."

He laughs. "A little cold can't hurt us, Dutch. We're hockey players."

I like that he called us "us." And the Dutch thing is growing on me.

This night has taken an interesting turn.

I turn it right back.

"Tell me about Gillian."

His grip on the steering wheel tightens. After several long, uncomfortable seconds he says, "Gillian? My ex-girlfriend, Gillian? How do you even know about her?"

Ex-girlfriend.

I ignore his last question and try to keep my tone casual. Conversational. "Why did you break up?"

He barks out a laugh. "Let's just say she wasn't cut out for a long-distance relationship."

"Oh, yeah, what is it, a whole hour from here to Great River?"

"Hour and a half."

"Does she play hockey?"

"No."

"Did she play hockey?"

"No."

He's not giving me a whole lot here, but what difference does it make? I didn't know she existed until a few minutes ago.

"When did you break up?"

"Halloween. Not this past Halloween, the one before."

Halloween. Two months after he moved here. They'd only been "long distance" for two months before she gave up on him. No wonder I didn't know about her. Other than that day at Little Dipper's, I didn't see Hot Sauce much, not until the season started.

"How long had you been together?"

"Eleven months."

"What happened?" I ask, and then bite my bottom lip. "No, you don't have to answer that. I'm asking too many questions."

He's quiet for a second, and then says, "It's OK. One of my GR teammates was having a Halloween party, so I drove back to surprise her. She'd told me she was dressing up as Harley Quinn, so I bought a Joker costume with fake tattoos and everything. Turns out I was the one surprised when I found her making out with the goalie."

"Huh. It's always the goalie, isn't it?" My joke falls flat. "I'm sorry."

"Yeah. Kinda sucked, but it hadn't felt right for a while. Not since—not since I'd moved." He pauses, then asks, "What about you? What's your dating history?"

I consider this—my answer and the question itself, and the fact that this conversation exists. That Wes and I exist together in this truck on this road on this night. Dressed in formalwear. It's all a bit surreal.

"My dating history is that I don't have much of a dating history." That's all he needs to know.

"Oh," he says. "That's surprising."

"What's that supposed to mean?"

"Nothing. I mean, it's not an insult, Dutch. Geez. It's that . . . I . . ."

He trails off and I turn to look at him. I can't be certain in the darkness of the cab, but I think *he's blushing*.

I turn away quickly and look out the window instead. I

don't need an answer. Nope. Nope. Nopity nope. Don't need to know.

We pass a sign that reads CASS COUNTY.

Wait a minute.

"Where are we going?" We're way north of town. Great. I knew there was no way he was capable of being nice to me. This was all a ploy to transport me to some run-down shack in the snowy backwoods of Cass County and murder me. No one will look for me here, but eventually a hiker will find my cold, lifeless body in a shallow grave long after the season's over. I'm going to miss the HockeyFest game.

I'd like my gravestone to read, *She had a perfect backhand.* Well, except that I plan to be cremated and have my devastated brothers scatter my ashes in the lake behind our house just before it freezes over. While wearing Hanson brothers jerseys.

"You'll see," he says.

Oh, that's not ominous at all.

A few minutes later, we turn at a sign that says A-FRAME RESORT & RECORD SHOP in swirling script, and bump our way down a rough, icy driveway.

I've lived in Halcyon Lake my entire life. I've played at the smallest, dumpiest arenas you can find all over central and northern Minnesota. I've eaten at small-town diners, slept at run-down twenty-unit motels with pink toilets. But I have *never* heard of the A-Frame Resort and I sure as hell haven't heard of the A-Frame Resort & *Record Shop* or I would be basically living here, even if it is an hour from home.

The resort consists of a large cabin (A-frame, of course) at the edge of the driveway and a few smaller cabins close to the lakeshore. Those cabins seem deserted, but the big cabin is lit up and cozy, which makes me suspicious.

"Where are we?" I ask. I don't even know which lake this is.

He looks at me, mouth open in disbelief. "Are you kidding me? You don't know about the A-Frame?"

I shake my head.

"But—but you love music."

"Yep."

"But you've never been to the A-Frame." It's not a question. It's a sad statement.

"Correct."

He grins, and there's that dimple again. "C'mon, Dutch. You are in for a treat."

Chapter Thirteen

Wes gets out of the truck. I open my own door and get out before he makes it around to my side, but that doesn't stop him from placing his hand firmly on my back as we move across the icy, uneven driveway. I can feel the jolt even through my heavy coat.

"My dad and I found this place a few years ago," he says as he guides me around a slick patch. The freezing wind coming off of whichever lake this is bites into my legs and poor feet. "It's legendary in the used vinyl world—well, at least in the vinyl Midwest. The summer I got my permit, my dad and I went on a big record store road trip all over Minnesota and Wisconsin. This was our first stop."

"Sounds awesome," I say, "but is it even open? On a Friday night in the dead of winter?"

"Nance knows we're coming."

"Who's Nance?"

As if she heard her name, a woman who must be Nance opens the door and waves. "Get your butts in here, kids," she says.

"We brought pie," Wes says, and she pulls him into a hug.

She's wearing a Black Sabbath T-shirt. Her straggly brownish-gray braid falls past the waistband of her black jeans, and she's got heavy metal tattoos across both arms. First impressions are everything. I love this woman.

And I also insta-love her record shop, which takes up the entire front room of the house—bin after bin of albums with dividers labeled in slanted black marker. Behind the cash register are a simple wooden staircase and an open door to a kitchen.

I scan the first row, see that I'm in the rock section, and dive in.

"You must be Dutch," Nance says with a laugh.

I look up. "How do you know that? It's Holland, actually."

"Wes told me he was bringing his friend Dutch for a visit." That's acceptable, I guess. She reaches out her hand and I shake it. "I wasn't expecting a gorgeous girl, but that's Wesley for you. Full of surprises. I'm Nancy."

Gorgeous, huh? Yeah, Nance and I are going to be good friends.

"Nice to meet you. Thanks for opening up for us."

"Well, who can say no to Wes?" Nance laughs again. She's got a nice, friendly laugh.

"Dutch can," Wes says. "She says it plenty. You could learn a lot from her."

Rude. I don't give him the satisfaction of a response. "How long have you had this store?" I ask. "And what lake are you on?"

"I've had the resort for ten years, and I opened up the shop about seven years ago."

"*Seven* years? *Seven* years and I'm just finding out about you?"

"Best-kept secret, I guess. That's Settlers' Lake, west shore."

"Settlers' Lake? We're that far north? Like, Settlers' Corner?"

Nance nods. "I'm about five minutes from Settlers' Corner. I grew up out here but followed my rock-and-roll dreams to LA. When my husband died, I decided to come home. So, I bought the resort."

"I thought for sure that Wes was driving me out to the middle of nowhere to either kill me or have me killed." I raise my eyebrows at Nance and she howls with laughter.

"Have a look around. I'll be in the kitchen sharpening my knives." She pats Wes on the shoulder as she walks past. "I like her."

"Oh my God, how did I not know about this place?" I ask again. I start flipping through the bin—AC/DC, Aerosmith, Aldo Nova, Alice in Chains . . . "Ooh, look, a 2010 import reissue of Alice in Chains on *MTV Unplugged.*" I slide the record out of the sleeve and inspect it under the bright lights, then look up at Wes, smiling. I can't help myself. This place makes me *happy.*

"Dutch," Wes says, and he swallows hard. "Do you . . . you like Alice in Chains?"

He looks like he wants to say something else. His eyes shift from me to the record in my hands.

"Yes," I answer quietly.

Yes, and I think I might actually like you.

I like his passion for hockey and the filing cabinet of stats and NHL history in his brain. I like that we have similar taste in music.

I like *this* Wes, the one who drives forty-five minutes to bring a slice of pie to a woman who lives in a record store on a lake.

I return the album to the bin. Flipping through the rest, I can think only of the boy standing so close—my *captain*—and how *that* makes *this* a *bad* idea.

"Find anything you like, Dutch?" Nance asks.

We've joined her in the kitchen, where she's set out the pie on three plates.

"Plenty." I looked at the Rock section and skimmed through Soundtracks. "I'll have to come back. I might even need to book a cabin and make it a weekend."

Nance chuckles. "Have a seat and eat this delicious pie. You spoil me, Wesley."

I like that she calls him Wesley.

I move around the table to the spot where my toffee cream pie sits. As I do, Wes steps to the side and pulls out the chair. I give him a look.

"Your throne, m'lady," he says, and winks.

Smart-ass.

He sits down next to me and digs in. A little chunk of apple drops from the fork to his bottom lip and he stretches out his tongue to flick the apple into his mouth. A rush of *feeling* drenches me. I am *lusting* after Hot Sauce Millard and his tongue.

Oh, shit, my thoughts are starting to read like porn-iterature.

"Shoot, I almost forgot," Nance says, standing up. "I found that book I was telling you about. The Led Zeppelin one. Let me grab it for ya."

She gets up and goes back out to the front room, where, I notice only now, low bookshelves are tucked along one side of the slanted wall. She rummages around and swears. "Where the hell is it now?"

I smile, pick up my fork, and shove a bite of pie into my mouth. The slightly lopsided slice has mostly survived the trip intact, partly thanks to the subzero temperatures. I slip my feet out of my shoes and sigh with relief.

"How's your pie?" I turn toward Wes and stop chewing.

He's not eating. He's staring at me, and he's smiling. A small smile, but it's there.

"What?"

He shakes his head. "You surprise me."

Heat creeps up into my cheeks, all the way to the tops of my ears. I turn back to my pie. "Is that a good thing?"

"That's a very good thing."

Nance comes back in and sets the book in front of Wes. "Here we go," she says.

I peer at the title: *Hammer of the Gods: The Led Zeppelin Saga*. "Oh, I've read that," I say. "It's good."

As we finish our pie, Nance starts telling us about the last time she and her husband saw Robert Plant in concert.

"No way," Wes says. "My dad was at that show."

He runs a hand through his spiky, messy hair and drops

it to his lap. Then he reaches across the space between us and places his hand on my leg just above my knee. I can't breathe. He moves his index finger in a small circle, slowly, slowly, electrifying me.

"I wonder if I still have that album," Nance says. I've lost my place in the conversation. I have no idea which album she's talking about. "I'll go upstairs and check."

Wes pulls his hand away as Nance walks around the table and out to the staircase but grabs mine as soon as we hear footsteps on the stairs. He stands and pulls me up.

"Come on," he says. "Let's wait out front."

"What album is she looking for?" I ask. I'm surprised at how breathless I sound.

"Mmmm?" Wes replies. He's staring at me again. The smile has faded somewhat. He leads me into the front room.

I want to kiss him. I want to lean him up against *Rock A*, where he first learned how much I love Alice in Chains, and kiss him.

He tugs my hand and we move to a more secluded corner of the room, home to the *Soundtracks* bins. Earlier I found a rare, must-have copy of the soundtrack to *This Is Spinal Tap*, still in cellophane, that will be more than worth the drive back up here when I have some money. He stands, facing me, then drops my hand, puts both of his on my hips, warm and steady and electrifying. Terrifying.

I close my eyes.

Everything has slowed down.

"Dutch . . ."

I want to capture this moment and the way he says my name and bottle it, wear it around my neck, against my skin, close to my heart.

He smells so good, like the icy air outside and campfire and pine and something else, shampoo, maybe. I slowly, deeply inhale his scent as he moves closer, closer, and I open my eyes for one beat, and his eyes are wide open, gazing at me, as he leans in, slowly . . .

I hear footsteps on the stairs and startle. Wes steps back, drops his hands. But he's still looking at me, his deep, dark eyes locked with mine. When Nance steps into the room, I look away first.

What was I thinking?

"Well," Nance says, "it's not upstairs, so it must be down here somewhere."

"That's OK," Wes says, and his voice sounds a little strangled. "We need to go, but I'll come back soon, and we can look for it, OK?"

Nance nods. "It's been a pleasure, Dutch. Come back with Wes sometime, why don't you?"

I nod, too, unable to speak.

"OK, then," Wes says, pulling me gently to the door, "see you soon."

Chapter Fourteen

Wes doesn't say a word as he opens the passenger door and helps me in. He starts the truck and only lets it warm up for about thirty seconds before turning around and heading down the long driveway. He's not as careful or slow, and we jostle roughly along the gravel road. He doesn't turn the music on, and it's so quiet, so cold, so dark.

"Thank you for bringing me here," I say quietly. "That place is . . ."

Amazing. That place is amazing. There are a few used bookstores in Brainerd with minimal vinyl selections, but you have to drive to St. Cloud if you want a shop with any substance. But this! This is practically in my backyard!

He takes his eyes off the road for a split second to look at me, that longing back in his dark, flashing eyes.

Is he thinking of our near-kiss against the bins? Because I can't stop thinking about it. What his lips would feel like against mine. Warm and soft. How I want him to pull over and put the truck in park and lean over and kiss me.

I could tell him to do it. *Pull over*, I could say, nothing else, and then I'd lean in and kiss *him*. My heart pounds, thinking that, but I can't, I can't, I can't. Stop, stop, stop. I inhale a sharp breath.

He smells so good. Like winter. The scent of him has settled all around me, like something physical, like a dusting of snow.

No, I shouldn't think about how good he smells, either.

"That place is amazing." I finally finish my sentence, my voice shaking. I'm shaken. "I love it. And Nance. She's great."

"Yeah," he says. Quiet. "Dutch? You—well, I think that you're amazing, too. Can we—would you—tonight's been—shit."

"What? Tonight's been shit?"

He mumbles, "I'm terrible at this."

Wes reaches across the small space between us, puts his hand lightly over mine, tentatively, a question. Currents travel from his skin to mine, a low buzz. I bite my lower lip and allow his hand to rest on mine for the briefest of moments, commit the feeling to memory, before I slip my hand from underneath his.

He sucks in a breath, reaches that hand to turn on the radio, and exhales another swear. We are now at the mercy of the Power Loon. I only hope they don't play "Every Rose Has Its Thorn." I don't know if I will be able to resist if Wes starts singing.

Oh, shit, I'm terrible at this, too. I don't know how to like a boy when I shouldn't like him, or how to stop liking him, or how to let him down. I don't know how to act after we've escaped our lives for a little while, away from our friends, away from expectations, and now it's time to return to reality.

"Wes." It's not lost on me that this is the first time I have ever called him by his real name to his face. "I—" I stop myself before I apologize, although I am sorry that I will miss out on those feelings that course through me when he's close, when he touches me. "We can't."

I wait for him to say something, but he doesn't. Maybe he's not embarrassed by my rejection. Maybe I've misread everything that's happened tonight.

But I know that I haven't. I felt it. And I know he felt it, too.

Neither of us speaks, not for a very long time, not over the car dealership ads and chatter from the deejay, not over the Rolling Stones or Bon Jovi or Jimi Hendrix.

"Why not?" he finally says, and it's been long enough, at least half an hour of classic rock and no talk, that at first, I'm not sure what he means.

Oh, yeah. That.

"Dutch?"

The sound of his voice, the nickname he's given me, tugs at something deep inside me. "Wes," I begin, but my voice cracks. I clear my throat and start again. "Tonight's been fun. I mean, we haven't argued at all, not once. I didn't think that was possible. But, uh, *this*—" I wave my hand around between us. "Well, uh, *this* can't happen."

"This." It's not a question.

"Right. This."

Please, please, please don't ask me to explain.

"Do you mean holding my hand? Spending time with me? Going out on a date with me? Because I'd like to take you out on a date. A real one. Not just making a grand escape from a school dance." He seems to have regained his ability to string coherent words together.

All of the above.

"Yes."

"Oh." He pauses. "Because we don't get along. You don't like me."

"No, that's not it," I say before I can stop myself. Super. I basically admitted that I like him. Wes Millard. I like Wes Millard. My cheeks burn and I'm so glad he can't see them in the dark. "It's that—I sort of have this rule about dating teammates."

"That's a real thing? *That's* the real reason you turned down Lumberjack?"

I snort. "No. I turned down Lumberjack because he's an arrogant, self-absorbed . . ."

Before tonight, I would have said the same thing about Wes.

I am more terrible at this than I thought.

"I—I appreciate the offer. But—"

Wes cuts me off. "Save it."

Uh, he's so irritating.

"I don't date teammates, OK? I wouldn't want anyone to accuse me again of being a *distraction* for the poor boys. Especially the captain and leading scorer."

"What? That's the stupidest thing I've ever heard."

"OK, then how about this? Do you remember the first thing you ever said to me? 'Don't ever think anyone is going to give you a free pass because you're a *girl*. You have to *earn* it.'"

He looks at me for a flash of a second, his jaw tight. "Dutch—"

"No, you know what? It's fine, I don't expect you to understand what it's like for me. You've had everything handed to you from the moment you scored your first goal. I can't say the same."

"Dutch—" he tries again, but I hold up my hand to stop him. I've said enough. Too much.

I turn to look out the window, watch the lights and the houses until we finally, finally round the corner to T.J.'s street, lined with vehicles, cars crammed into his driveway.

"You can park in Morgan's driveway." I say it with more confidence than I feel. "Fourth house on the left, the one with the giant wreath. They won't mind."

He pulls into the driveway and puts the truck in park but doesn't switch off the engine.

"Well," I say, like we didn't just have the most awkward conversation ever, "thanks for everything. I'm staying at Morgan's tonight, so you don't have to give me a ride home or anything."

I'm out of the cab and walking as fast as I can in these stupid heels toward the MacMillan house and a crowd I can hopefully disappear into.

Chapter Fifteen

My plan is to walk into the party and find Morgan and Cora, hang out and socialize with our classmates without incident or drama, have some snacks and a Coke, and avoid Wes. After a little while, Cora and Morgan and I will go to Morgan's, where we'll eat popcorn and ice cream and scare ourselves shitless with episodes of *Ghost Adventures*.

I find Morgan and Cora right away, in a room off the kitchen watching *Friends*, the one when Ross wears leather pants. Miracle and Poppy sit on the couch in the living room, holding hands. They've changed out of their fancy dresses and are wearing matchy-matchy Gophers women's hockey jerseys. Carter and Jesse are probably here somewhere, and Hunter said he might stop by after his concert.

Luke's in the kitchen. "Hey, Liney," he says, "you want a drink?" He rubs a hand over his chest. There's a dark, damp blob across the front of his gray Hawks hockey T-shirt.

I shake my head. "Um, no? Are you drunk?" I lean in close and sniff. He smells like sweat and some sort of sweet, boozy cocktail.

"Maybe. What can I get for you? Livvie said me and my friends can have the good stuff, and you, Holland, are my friend." He throws his arm around me and pulls me into the kitchen.

"My friends and I."

"Not *your* friends. *My* friends. C'mon."

"No, really, I'm good."

"C'mon," he says again. "Lighten up a little."

I shrug off his arm. "I don't really drink. Plus, I've got that interview tomorrow."

"Oh, God, the fucking interview. I wondered how long it would take you to bring that up."

"Well, you don't have to be such an asshole about it!"

He laughs. "I'm not trying to be an asshole. I'm trying to get you to loosen up and stop worrying about that interview. It's all over your face."

I raise my eyebrows at him.

"Yep. You look like you just got kicked in the cojones."

"I don't have cojones, Luke."

"Of course you don't have cojones, although you play like you do."

I shake my head. Luke is pretty crocked, but that's no excuse.

"Luke, you can't say shit like that. It's sexist."

He ignores me. He opens the fridge and rummages around, bottles clanking together. "Liv's got some girly wine coolers or some shit in here."

Oh my God. I cannot allow this. "Girly? What the fuck, Luke? Are you saying that men can't drink wine coolers? Only women? Or that women only—"

"Are you talking to me?" He cuts me off as he emerges triumphant with a bottle of something orange. "I heard you were hanging out with Hot Sauce tonight. No wonder you're stressed out. This'll take the edge off, I promise. Just have one. It's cool."

I groan.

"What's up with that, anyway?" Luke asks. "He putting his biscuit in your basket or what?"

"Luke!"

He lifts my hand, opens my fingers, puts the bottle against my palm, and closes my fingers around it. "I'm just giving you shit. I know you hate the guy. It's a party. Chill the fuck out."

"'Chill the fuck out,'" I mutter as he walks out of the kitchen.

I haven't seen Wes since I left him in the truck in Morgan's driveway. For all I know, he didn't bother to come in after all. But I don't care, right? I can't let it bother me. My decision. Good decision.

I look down at the bottle in my hand. Harding's Classic Screwdriver. Natural Orange Flavor.

To drink or not to drink—also my decision. Why not? Maybe if I drink this, I'll forget that I left the dance with Wes and people are talking shit about it. Exactly what I *didn't* want to happen. Can't hurt to try. The interview isn't until tomorrow afternoon, and besides, what's one screwdriver in the grand scheme of things?

I twist open the bottle, take a sip, toss the cap in a nearby trash can. Not bad. I can handle this. I take another long swallow—OK, maybe a third of the bottle—and feel a rush of warmth deep in my belly. I let the sense of calm wash over me and walk out into the living room. And right into Wes.

"Dutch. What the fuck. I leave you alone for twenty minutes—" He takes hold of my arm and tugs me around the corner into an empty alcove lined with bookshelves.

"Hey! Cool your jets! I had *one sip*—"

We both stop, and he looks at me with those damn gorgeous chocolatey eyes, and I want to step into them, the deep, rich pools. I want to get out of this house where I have to share the same space as him, because that space is shrinking, making it hard to breathe. Because the space isn't small enough, we're not close enough.

He takes the bottle out of my hand and holds it up. "One sip, huh?"

OK, nearly gone. There's maybe, uh, one sip left.

"I should take you home," he says.

First, I think, *Like hell you should*, and then I think, *Yes, please.*

And then I think that I would like Wes to touch me, and I remember the warmth that coursed through me, the *electricity*, and I close my eyes to capture it again. I think again about what it would have felt like to kiss him, and I bite my lower lip.

Wes makes a strangled, choking sound and my eyes fly open.

"Great," he says. "You've got a pretty good buzz going."

"No, I'm not buzzed," I say, but when I think hard about

it, I might be. There might be a bit of fuzz around the edges.
I laugh. One drink. One drink and I'm buzzed. What a light-
weight. I try to remember the last time I had a drink. I'm not
much of a drinker. My training is too important. So, let's see.
Last summer, Hunter's going away party. At T.J.'s house. *This*
house.

I straighten my spine. "I'm not buzzed. Don't you ever
drink, Hot Sauce?"

"Not during the season."

I sigh. "Me, neither."

Wes snorts. "Is that right? What made tonight different?"

You. You made tonight different.

I shrug. That's the only answer he'll get. "I was just on my
way to find Morgan and Cora. I'm staying over at Morgan's
house, remember?"

"Fine. It's late. Find them and go home. The interview is
tomorrow and—"

"That fucking interview!" I yell, cutting him off. Now I
sound like Luke. "I can handle the fucking interview."

Wes grits his teeth. Then he takes a deep breath. "You are
the most frustrating, argumentative—"

"Oh, really? You should talk!"

He groans. "Just go to Morgan's. And promise me you
won't drink again this season, OK? You're too important to
the team, Dutch."

"Half the team is completely shitfaced. Why aren't you
getting on anybody else's case? What a load of double stan-
dard bullshit."

"How do you know I haven't?"

I huff. "Speaking of shitfaced teammates, Luke just asked me if you were putting your biscuit in my basket. That kind of shit is exactly what I don't need!"

He rubs a hand over his face. "Take some ibuprofen and drink a ton of water. You can't be hungover for that interview tomorrow."

"There you go again, telling me what to do."

"You are impossible," he says.

"*You* are impossible," I bite back.

A senior volleyball player named Logan walks past the alcove and glances in. I'm about to sigh in relief that she didn't acknowledge us when she doubles back and throws her arms around Wes's neck. "Wes! I haven't seen you in forever!" She smiles and squeezes him closer.

"Hey. Logan. Long time, no see." He smiles.

Uh-uh. No way.

"Um, excuse me?" I say, and she looks at me with surprise before stepping away from him and out of the alcove.

"That's not fair," Wes says in a low voice, his frustration with me dissipated.

"What's not fair?"

He leans in close, and I can smell his wintry, smoky, delicious scent. "You. Acting like that."

"Like what?"

"Like you . . . like you . . ."

"What, Wes? Spit it out."

"Like you like me. Like you have some claim on me. You

don't want me to be your boyfriend because I'm your captain, but you get pissed when another girl gives me a hug. You can't have it both ways."

That stops me. He's right, of course. I can't have it both ways. My decision. Good decision.

He's so close. Close enough that I could move a fraction of an inch forward and find his lips with mine, pull him down to me, my palms pressed against his cheeks.

"I wish—I wish I'd kissed you at the record store," I whisper.

He shudders, and a rush of breath escapes him.

Oh, fuck. I shouldn't have said that.

"Dutch," he says, and nothing more.

No, I shouldn't have said it.

"I'll go," I whisper, but I don't move right away, not yet, breathing him in, not ready to leave this tiny pocket of what might have been.

Chapter Sixteen

Cora and I are already settled in on the huge sectional in the Fillmores' living room, *Ghost Adventures* on the giant TV, when Morgan brings in bowls of microwave popcorn.

"So," Cora says, "Holland. Hot Sauce. Spill."

I roll my eyes and turn my attention to the show. "Which episode is this?"

"Nice try," Cora says. "Twin Bridges Orphanage. Now spill."

"Oh, that's a creepy one."

"All the episodes are creepy," Morgan says as she sits down, her face twisted in a grimace. Last time we watched this episode, she cried when she heard about the cruelty those kids endured. She yawns.

"You will *not* fall asleep," Cora yells at her. "Look at Zak's biceps. That will keep you awake."

I snort. Cora *loves* the host of this show, Zak Bagans. If she could drop out of school and join the *Ghost Adventures* crew, she would. Morgan's more of a Zac Efron girl. We saw *The Greatest Showman* three times in its two-week run at the little theater downtown. Zach Parise of the Minnesota Wild is more my style.

"Tell us!" Cora cries.

"Fine. Wes and I bailed on the dance, we ate at the Full

Loon, we looked at some used records, and we ended up at the party. End of story."

"Ha!" Cora bursts out. "Bullshit, end of story! I saw how he was looking at you!"

"Yeah," I said, "if looks could kill, right? Same old, same old."

"No." Cora shakes her head. "Something happened."

"You called him Wes," Morgan says quietly.

"Ohmygod, you're *right*!" Cora leans forward and spills a few kernels of popcorn. Morgan's fuzzy cockapoo, Cosmo, appears out of nowhere to scarf it up, then shakes his whole body, head to toe, tags jingling.

"Come here, Cosmo," I call in a high voice, holding out my hand. He comes over to sniff me but sticks his nose in the air and leaves when he realizes I'm not offering popcorn.

"Don't use the dog as a distraction," Cora says. "You've never once called that boy by his real name before."

"Where were you looking at used records? There's no record store around here," Morgan adds.

"Um, the A-Frame? Up near Settlers' Corner?"

Morgan's eyes go wide and Cora shrieks.

"Skip to the good part! Did you kiss him?" Cora yells, and Morgan shushes her.

"No."

"But you wanted to!"

I shake my head a little, but a jalapeño-like heat crawls up my face from my neck.

"Why didn't you kiss him?" Morgan asks.

I can only shake my head again, my voice trapped in a tight little ball.

"Oh, sweet child o' mine," Cora singsongs, "you *do* like him."

I throw up my hands and find my voice again. "So what if I do? It's not like I'm going to do anything about it. I can't go out with one of my teammates, *especially* the captain. That's my rule. Plus, I mean, it's not like it's official or anything, but when I made the team, Coach sort of—well, he sort of suggested that I don't get involved with any of the guys. It could get really weird, you know?"

"Your rule is stupid," Cora says, "no matter what Coach says. He can't tell you who to love."

"I don't *love* him, Cora. Drama, much?"

"But, Holland," Morgan says in her gentle way, "you like him. And he likes you back, right?"

"Yeah." The word swooshes out of me.

"So why don't you go for it?" Cora asks. "Who cares about your stupid rule?"

"It's not a stupid rule. Enough people already say I shouldn't be allowed to play on the boys' team. What would they think if I started dating the *captain*? I can't let anyone think I'm getting special treatment."

"Anyone who thinks you're getting special treatment doesn't have eyes in their head. Or doesn't know anything about hockey," Cora says. "*I* don't know anything about hockey, and I can tell that you skate circles around those goons."

"Why don't you at least give it a chance?" Morgan asks softly.

I shake my head. "Nope. No way. Not with HockeyFest coming up. The interview's tomorrow—"

"Stop with the interview!" Cora yells. "Look, your little rule is admirable. Whatever. However, when's the last time you went on a date? Sweaty Chevy? What, two years ago?"

"Longer," Morgan says. "It was right after Showbiz and I started dating. Two and a half years ago."

"Christ. That's a long time. Little chicken, you need to go get your man."

"People are already saying stuff. Well, one person."

"So take a page out of Carter's book and keep it a secret. Don't tell Coach or your teammates or anyone. Well, tell us, of course."

"Cora!" Morgan cries. "That's dishonest."

"Is it, though?"

I sigh. "Look, it's just not a good idea right now. Can we drop it?"

"She said 'right now,' Morgan," Cora says. "There's hope!"

She may believe there's hope, but I do not.

"I want to hear what's going on with you and Matt. Enough about Wes."

"Wes," Cora says, and shakes her head. "She keeps calling him Wes."

HARDROCK_HOCKEY: WHAT MIGHT HAVE BEEN PLAYLIST

1. "Every Rose Has Its Thorn"—Poison
2. "Love Song"—Tesla
3. "Short Skirt/Long Jacket"—Cake
4. "The Pretender"—Foo Fighters
5. "My Own Worst Enemy"—Lit
6. "Blurry"—Puddle of Mudd
7. "Through Glass"—Stone Sour
8. "Little One"—Highly Suspect
9. "Everlong"—Foo Fighters
10. "Angels/Losing/Sleep"—Our Lady Peace
Bonus: "Spice Up Your Life"—Spice Girls

Chapter Seventeen

MY HEAD HURTS.

From one screwdriver, five-point-nine percent alcohol by volume.

It could be worse, I guess. While Cora and Morgan and I watched *Ghost Adventures*, I drank bottle after bottle of water. I didn't sleep much, thinking about every single time Wes touched me. Remembering the weight of his hand on my leg, my waist, my hips. *Through* my clothes. I'm branded.

We wake early, and Morgan's mom makes us breakfast—raspberry and cream cheese–stuffed French toast (a *Top Shelf* recipe, of course) and bacon—and that helps, too. And coffee. Lots of coffee.

At home, I take the longest shower in the history of showers. I shave my legs and pits, because, hey, I'm going to be on TV, not that anyone will see anything other than my uniform and gear. I dry my hair and use this weird torture device Cora sent home with me to create wavy curls. "The wave maker is the new flat iron," she'd told me, assuring me of its no-fail operation. I have to admit, she was right. I suppose, then, since my hair looks so good—especially the stripe—I shouldn't skip makeup.

Someone knocks on my door as I'm blotting my pale pink, shimmery lip gloss. Hunter pokes his head in.

"What happened to your face?" he asks, and I throw a used cotton ball at him. It lands several feet short of the target. He bursts out laughing.

Hunter's got hockey hair for days. Chestnut like mine, but with a natural, regal wave that sweeps back from his face and touches the tops of his shoulders. The epitome of *flow*. The envy of his teammates.

"How was the show?" I ask.

"Killer. You'd love these guys. Kinda reminded me of Chevelle. I picked up their vinyl and the lead guitarist came out to the merch table after the show and signed it for me."

"Cool."

"I went to T.J.'s party after but Hot Sauce told me you'd already left. He seemed pretty cheesed about something. What's his deal?"

"How should I know?" I snap.

"Settle," Hunter says. "I didn't come in here to get bitched at. I came in to tell you good luck on your interview."

My irritation deflates. "Sorry."

"I wish I could be there for it, but I've got to get on the road. Coach wasn't super happy that I was coming down here last night, so I can't be late."

"Thanks."

"So, if you can't tell me what's up Wes's craw, why don't you tell me what's up yours?"

"Nothing is up my *craw*, thank you very much."

"Bullshit." Hunter comes into the room and shuts the door behind him, then moves a stack of books and my team jacket off my desk chair and sits down. "Come on, Holls, I wasn't born yesterday. You've got that look."

I snort. "Which one?"

"The one you get when your brain won't shut off and somebody needs to remind you to breathe."

At that, I let out a long exhale.

"See what I mean? What are you twisting in knots in that brain of yours?"

"How much time do you have?"

"Not much. But I can guess. You've decided that you're solely responsible for your team getting that broadcast, so you've piled that stress on top of all the other stress you're already feeling."

"Yeah, that's part of it."

"Look, Holls, you're an awesome hockey player. Everybody knows it. You're on that team because you deserve to be."

"Many people disagree with you there."

"Such as?"

I point to the curling newspaper clipping. "Big Don, for one."

"You've still got that stupid letter up there?"

"Pete and George, too."

"So, a bunch of old-timers."

"Yeah."

"What did they say?"

"The usual. I'm an embarrassment. A liability because

hockey isn't safe for girls. That I'm taking a spot that right-fully belongs to a boy."

"You know that shit's not true. And since when do you care what a couple of old-timers say?"

"Oh, I don't know, always?"

"Bullshit. That's bullshit. You gonna let them take up all that real estate in your head, Holls? You gonna let those idiots move in and put their muddy feet up on your coffee table and tell you that you're less than somebody else? Haters gonna hate. You've already spent too much time worrying about them. Time to kick them to the curb."

"Easy for you to say."

"I know it's never been easy for you. But I also know that you're not one to back down from a challenge. Don't let Pete or George or especially Big Donnie mess with your head."

He stomps over to my bulletin board, grabs the yellowing newspaper clipping, rips it from beneath the thumbtack, and crumples it up.

"Hey!" I lunge for the paper, but he lifts it high above his head.

"No. Done. You are done with this bullshit."

"Hunter. Give it back."

"Why? So you can continue to torture yourself?"

"No!" I shout. "For motivation."

"Oh, for Christ's sake. Find a healthier motivation. Listen to some Metallica or something. Read the comments on your Facebook fan page."

"I have a Facebook fan page?"

He grins. "Nah, I'm just giving you shit. Look, I gotta go. But about that interview? Just be yourself, tell your truth, and that interview will be a walk in the fucking park."

"Oh, sure, no problem."

"Look." He walks to the door. "Holland. Give yourself a break, but whatever you do, don't fuck this up. See ya."

I give him the finger and he laughs.

Give myself a break.

If only it were that easy.

I look at the blank space on the corkboard.

Doesn't matter. I still know every single word.

Chapter Eighteen

ALTHOUGH TEMPS HAVE WARMED SLIGHTLY, IT'S STILL BARELY ABOVE zero when I catch a ride to the arena with Carter.

I can't remember the last time I was this nervous. Tonight, more than any other night, I've got to prove myself. I've got to show Jason Fink and his *Fink at the Rink* viewers that Halcyon Lake is worth their vote. My insides flip again as we pull into the arena parking lot, already nearly half full. They flip right back when I see Wes leaning against the concessions counter talking to Molly and Darla. I scurry past, hoping he doesn't notice me.

My interview is scheduled during the third period of the JV game, but until then, I need some time alone. The far end of the bleachers is pretty much deserted, most of the small crowd of spectators favoring seats nearer the blue line. I sit at the very top corner of the stands, hopeful that no one will notice me over here.

I should have expected that Wes would find me. After last night's awkward car ride and lecture, Wes is the last person I want to talk to right now.

"Haven't you said enough?" I ask as he sits down. Too damn close. And then, to make matters worse, he hands me a cup of coffee. With a metal straw.

"Hello to you, too," he says. "I'm fine, thanks for asking. And you?"

"I didn't ask."

"You're mad."

"You're observant."

"I've got a gift for you from Molly. Well, the straw's from Molly. The coffee's from me."

I put both hands around the cup to warm them. "Thank you," I say, because even if I am irritated with him, I don't want to be rude. Also: coffee.

"I talked to Luke," Wes says. "I basically ripped him a new one for what he did."

"What did he do?"

"The booze? The screwdriver you were drinking?"

"He didn't force me to drink it. I'm a big girl. I make my own decisions."

"He convinced you, though, that it would take the edge off? Right?"

I shrug, take a sip of coffee through the metal straw. Just how I like it. Two sugars and a cream. He pays attention. "Maybe."

"Dutch." Soft. Warm.

I know he's looking at me.

I can't look at him. I can't. If I do, if I look at those warm brown eyes, filled with concern, I'll remember how his hand felt on my leg, how I would have kissed him if Nance hadn't come back downstairs, how I told him that I wished I had.

If I look at him, I'll think about how hollow I felt in his truck on the ride back to town, after I told him, *We can't.*

"Are you OK?" he asks.

"Why do you ask?"

"Because I need you to be OK."

"Oh, *you* need me to be OK?" My tone is sharp. "Why? Are you worried we won't get the broadcast, too?"

"You know what, Dutch? For once, I wish you'd stop only seeing me as your captain and realize that I'm your friend. It's OK for us to be friends, right?"

I ignore this. "What do you mean, you need me to be OK?"

He doesn't answer right away. Still, I don't look at him. Finally, he takes a shallow breath and says, "Part of it is that I need you to be OK for our team. I need you to be on top of your game and go out there and show everyone what you can do. And yeah, part of it is that I need you to kick ass on that interview today so that we get the broadcast. But mostly, I need you to be OK because I care about you, and I don't want to see you worried or upset."

Then his hand is on my back, and he's running it up and down my spine, gently but deliberately, and my body hums with sensation. My thoughts slow with his touch, my anger at him dissipates.

"I'm OK," I tell him quietly after a long moment, hoping that he won't hear me, that he'll keep touching me. I crave the contact, any touch.

"You sure?"

I nod.

He stops rubbing my back and runs his hand through his messy hair, and I miss the warmth, the hum of his touch.

"Dutch, when you go down there for that interview, I want you to remember that you're talented and you work hard and you deserve to be on this team every single day. When you're on the ice, you're—you're this force. Powerful. Smart. You're one of the best, Dutch, and all you have to do is tell your story. The rest will take care of itself."

Finally, I turn to look at him, and I'm surprised when I *don't* find concern in his eyes. Or frustration. I see pride there. He's proud of me.

"You look ready," he says. "You look like you're ready to shake off the dust of this little town and go conquer the world."

"Amazing what a little mascara can do."

He turns away. "I'm serious. Be you, Dutch. Don't try to be someone you're not. Don't do this interview for anyone but yourself."

We watch the action on the ice for a few minutes, not saying anything else. My little brother hops over the side of the bench on a line change, even though the door is open. He doesn't make the landing, though, and falls flat on his ass. I snort. Wes groans.

"For the love of all things holy," he murmurs.

"Wes?"

"Yeah?"

I swallow down the emotion that's threatening to spill over, my gratitude for his belief in me, my worry, my need to feel close to him. "Thank you," I whisper.

For a long moment, Wes says nothing. Then he stands. "Second period's almost over. See you after the interview."

Chapter Nineteen

I STAND AGAINST THE PLEXIGLASS, IN FULL PADS AND UNIFORM. I hold my helmet and play with the straps while Jason Fink, tall and lanky with curly red hair, asks me inane questions that I'm sure won't stay that way. I've seen enough of his *Fink at the Rink* features. He'll dig.

"How old were you when you started playing hockey?" he asks.

"I started skating at three and joined my first team at five."

"Have you always played on a boys' team?"

"Yes. I've got three brothers. I've grown up playing with them and their friends, and I've only ever played on a boys' team. When I was younger, there were a couple of other girls until there was a girls' team in town, but no one consistent."

"Why did you stay on the boys' team?"

"I wanted to be with players I already connected with. And it's the only thing I know."

Fink pauses, then says, "Some people might say that you think you're too good for the girls' team. Is that true?"

I take a deep breath. I've been expecting the conversation to turn down this path. I'm ready for it.

"No, I don't think I'm 'too good' for the girls' team. I've played with the boys my whole life. Trying out for the boys' team was the logical next step for me. I'm very lucky that my high school athletic department was receptive to the idea, as well as Coach Giles, Coach Edwards, the rest of the coaching staff, and my teammates. I would hope that any girl in any high school would have that opportunity if that's what she wished to pursue."

Fink nods at me, his eyes crinkled in thought. "What about your teammates? Your *male* teammates? Do they feel the same way?"

I shrug. "I've played with most of these guys for a long time. They've never treated me differently because I'm a girl. The coaching staff, the fans, my teammates all hold me to the same high standards as any other player. If anyone personally feels like they don't want a girl on their team, I don't know about it. I can't control how someone else feels, but I can control how I feel and how I react to situations. I feel honored to be able to play the game with a group of such high-caliber, dedicated players."

"You wouldn't feel honored to play on the girls' team?"

"I didn't say that." A flutter of nerves makes its way from the pit of my stomach up to my throat and lodges there.

"But you feel that the girls' team doesn't have the same high-caliber pool of talent, so your talent would be wasted there?"

"I—I didn't say that, either," I stammer. "And that's not a fair question. The girls on that team are skilled and driven."

"So why don't any of those girls play on the boys' team with you?"

This guy is past the point of annoying. I don't care for his leading questions—it's like he's trying to back me into a corner so I say something I don't mean. I won't let him get the best of me.

My heart pounds as I answer his question as best I can. "I can't speak for the girls on the team. I can only speak for myself. I earned my place on the boys' varsity team, and that's where I intend to stay."

The minute the words come out of my mouth, I wish I could take them back. I meant to sound confident and persistent, and instead I came off as arrogant and condescending. Great.

He changes tack, thank God. "Your parents must be very supportive, what with four kids playing hockey."

"Absolutely. They've encouraged me every step of the way."

"Your dad, Marcus Delviss, led the Halcyon Hawks to the state tournament twenty-five years ago this March. I'll bet he's your biggest fan."

"He's one of them, for sure. I'm grateful for my parents' support and their belief in me."

"And your brother Carter," Fink continues, "captain this year, is following in the footsteps of your oldest brother, Hunter, who was also captain of this team and now plays for Northern Lakes University. Those are some pretty big skates to fill."

"*Co-captain*," I say. "Carter is *co-captain* this year."

Fink ignores me. "And what about your younger brother, Jesse? Where does he fit into the equation?"

"Jesse's a Delviss. He's been skating as long as he could walk, like the rest of us. He plays JV. Jesse's very talented, and I'm sure he'll be captain one day, too."

"Does it bother you that your dad, your two older brothers, and predictably your *younger* brother will all wear that captain's *C*, but your jersey will go without?"

"What are you saying? That I can't be the captain of my team because I'm a girl?"

"Well . . ."

That gets my hackles up. "That's ridiculous. The captain role is a leadership position, determined by a vote of your peers. Male, female, doesn't matter, as long as you're a strong leader, as long as you remember what that *C* really stands for—caring, courageous, consistent."

"So, you'll be throwing your hat into the ring next season?" Fink asks, his lips twisted into a smirk.

"Watch me."

And once again, I want to kick my own ass for saying something so stupid.

"You heard it here, folks. Will ambitious, driven Holland Delviss earn a captain's spot on next year's varsity boys' team? Stay tuned. In the meantime, Holland, I would imagine that it's been challenging for your brothers over the years to see you in the spotlight, especially now."

"I wouldn't say that I've been in the spotlight, exactly."

"You don't think you get extra attention because you're a girl?"

"Are you suggesting that people have treated me differently because I'm female?"

"Of course they have."

I'm getting hotter. "I work hard to get the puck in the net.

That's what wins games. The fact that I don't have a penis makes exactly zero difference."

Fink nearly chokes. "Jesus," he says under his breath, then recovers. "You don't think that your opponents have treated you differently? You don't think that maybe someone has made a move to check you and lightened up because you're a girl?"

"Do you think that those same opponents don't look at my brother Carter, who's basically a brick shithouse, and think, *I'm not going to mess with that guy*?"

The guy behind the camera chuckles.

"OK," Fink says, "let's loop around to a different topic. What about college? Are you planning to play in college?"

"I hope to study journalism and communications at Hartley University in Duluth."

"Have you considered broadcast journalism, Holland?" he asks. "I'm impressed with your poise. The phrase *grace under fire* comes to mind."

"I play hockey, Mr. Fink," I say. "I'm trained to respond quickly and instinctively in high-pressure situations."

"Will you play hockey?" he asks again.

"I'd like to, yes."

"For the women's team at Hartley?"

"Yes."

"You aim to play women's hockey in college, but you don't want to play on the girls' team now."

"I'll try out for the team, yes. There are no guarantees in life, however, as we know."

"Seems a bit insulting, don't you think?"

Here we go again. "Insulting to whom?"

"Other female athletes. Women in general."

"No," I say. "It's not uncommon for a girl who plays on a boys' team in high school to go on to play women's collegiate hockey. So, I don't find that insulting at all. I do find this line of questioning insulting, however."

He sighs, the camera guy laughs again, and I'm pretty sure most of my interview is going to end up on the cutting room floor.

"I heard you were a spitfire," Fink says, then slips back into sportscaster mode. "HockeyFest Weekend is coming up before we know it, when the Halcyon Lake Hawks will face off against the Freeley-Simmons-Hammond Vikings on the recently renovated Hole in the Moon outdoor rink downtown. What about HockeyFest are you most looking forward to, Holland?"

An easy question. Thank all the hockey gods and Saint Sebastian, patron saint of hockey players.

"The game, of course. The opportunity to showcase an awesome community that values and appreciates the sport of hockey."

"And maybe an opportunity to prove that you're a valuable member of the team and worthy of the captain's spot?"

"That's my goal for every game."

"Any last words?"

"Yeah," I say. *"Refuse to lose. Whatever it takes."*

Coach calls me into the guys' locker room for a pregame pep talk while Archie, the arena manager, clears the ice after the JV loss.

"This is it, people," Coach says almost reverently. "We've got Twin Cities media here tonight. Holland's already filmed her interview. Jason Fink may want to ask a few of you some questions as well. My advice is to remember who you are. What you stand for. What this team stands for. Don't get cocky. Don't tear anyone else down to make yourselves look good. Not anyone on this team, or the opposing team, or even the other HockeyFest teams vying for broadcast."

No one says a word. The guys almost seem subdued. I'm not sure what this feeling is, but it's not the usual pregame excitement.

"I saw Holland's interview. I want you all to know that she represented her team beautifully tonight," Coach says, and I startle a little. I didn't even know he'd been nearby, and my mind spins with all the things I said that I shouldn't have, all the ways my words could be twisted and misconstrued. "She acted with integrity and respect for every single player in this room, and a few outside of it. You should be very proud of your teammate, and I believe that you owe her a debt of gratitude for her efforts tonight, whether we're awarded the broadcast or not."

Showbiz, standing next to me, grins and gives me a little nudge with his elbow.

"Now it's time to think about the game," Coach says. "Go out there and play your hearts out, like you do every game."

We huddle up in the center of the locker room, hands in. All in.

"On three," Wes yells, and Carter counts it off.

"*Refuse to lose. Whatever it takes*," my teammates and I yell.

When I step out onto the freshly cleared ice, a few spots still streaked with water, I'm fueled by every emotion I've felt today.

My first shift, I come off the bench and connect with a pass from Luke, catch the goalie off guard, and, with a graceful flick of my wrist, send the puck flying high into the upper left corner of the net.

Whatever it takes.

Chapter Twenty

LATER THAT NIGHT, MY PHONE BUZZES.

Wes: Great game tonight. You were ON. ALL IN. Proud of you.

My heart flutters with excitement and confusion and promise, all of it. Wes is proud of me.

In my head, I text him: *Every time I'm near you, even though you irritate the hell out of me, I feel this connection, this electricity, and I'm not sure that I hate you anymore.*

In reality:

Me: Thanks. Same to you. Nice goal.

Wes scored the game winner in the third period, three minutes and forty-one seconds left on the clock and the game tied at three.

Another buzz. A video.

I click to download, and it takes a while, but eventually I've got it. I rotate my phone for a better view. The video is somewhat out of focus and unsteady, but I can tell it's at the arena, in the hallway in front of the guys' locker room. I see Wes and Fink and the cameraman. The camera shakes and

I hear his little sister's voice: "Mom, I got this." The shot zooms in.

To Wes. Still in full gear, his helmet tucked under his arm. His dark hair is damp and hangs in his eyes. He's smiling, cheeks flushed; clearly, the clock has run down, and we've just won the game. Off camera, I hear:

"I'm here with Hawks co-captain Wesley Millard, formerly of the state championship Great River Thunder. This is your second year here in Halcyon Lake, your second year playing with a female on the squad. How has that impacted your level of play, Wes?"

Even though I can see only the top half of him, I can tell he's shifting his skates back and forth underneath him as he speaks. "Truthfully, I was apprehensive at first. But since my first practice with the Hawks, it's clear how much Holland contributes to this team. Maybe not in points, but in positive attitude and determination. She's got a lot of skill, yes, but really? I think I admire her most for her grit, and not just because she's female. How many people do you know who would basically put themselves in the line of fire like this every week? She makes me want to be a better player."

The film shakes again and then the video stops, and my breath shakes, too, for a few seconds.

I lean back against my pillows, my phone in my hand, trying to think of a response. What can I say that will adequately describe to Wes how I'm feeling right now, how much this video means to me? Even if the TV station takes the film and twists it around and makes it seem like Wes can't stand being in the same arena as me, I've got the raw footage. I've got the proof. I watch the video again.

Maybe I made a mistake, telling Wes I couldn't date him. Maybe Morgan's right. Maybe Wes and I could make it work.

Maybe.

My buzzing phone jars me from my thoughts.

Wes: Dutch you there?

Life is short, I think. *Take the shot.*

Me: ♥

Me: Thanks for that. And for before the interview. I needed to hear it.

Wes: I mean every single word.

His next text is a YouTube link. I laugh before I even click. This is going to be good. And it is. Survivor, "Eye of the Tiger." I watch, mesmerized by the cheesy lights and cinematography as the guys in the band walk down the street in time to the powerful beat of the drums. Then I search for something equally cheesy and wonderful to send in return.

It's a few minutes before he responds. He must be watching the entire video, Europe's "The Final Countdown," one of my all-time favorites.

Wes: The lead singer is so pretty. His makeup is A+.

I snort.

Me: His makeup game is better than mine. In fact, he's prettier than me.

The little bubbles that indicate he's replying start and stop, start and stop.

Me: I'm not fishing for a compliment if that's what you think.

Bubbles. Bubbles.

Wes: I think you're much prettier than that guy.

He sends another link. Guns N' Roses, "Paradise City," where the grass is green, and the girls are pretty. Clever.

Another text arrives before I finish watching the video, so I switch back over to messages. Another link. Metallica, "Enter Sandman."

Wes: Sweet dreams Dutch.
Me: You are sick.

Bubbles. Then the bubbles disappear.

My finger hovers over the keyboard. It would be so easy to tell him, to type those words that have settled into the back of my mind: *I don't think I hate you anymore. Maybe I was wrong. Maybe we could do this.*

Me: Off to never never land. Good night.

Chapter Twenty-One

THE INTERVIEW AIRS TWO NIGHTS LATER. MY GRANDPARENTS JOIN us for my favorite dinner: turkey with mashed potatoes and gravy, green bean casserole with the little crunchy onions, and chocolate espresso cake for dessert. My contribution to the meal is a sweet and spicy cranberry relish made with cayenne pepper for a little kick. No one expects this from me, but everyone seems to love it. Carter even foregoes gravy for the relish on his second helping of turkey.

Wes would love it, although it might be a little mild for his taste.

Grandma volunteers Jesse and Carter to do the dishes, Mom makes popcorn, and the rest of us settle into the living room to wait for the interview. The minutes tick by. I sit on my hands to keep from biting my nails to the quick. There's a crash from the kitchen, Carter mutters, "Shit," and a few minutes later, Jesse and Carter come in bickering about who dropped the casserole lid.

"You two," Dad says. "Zip it and sit down. It's almost time for your sister's fifteen minutes of fame."

"She'll be lucky if she gets five," Jesse says as he plops down on the floor in front of the ottoman and leans against it.

Carter sits next to me on the couch. "Hey," he says quietly, "you breathing over there? Deep breath, Holls."

"I'm fine," I say, but my voice shakes.

"Give me three deep breaths."

I take a breath for the count of four, hold it for a beat, then exhale for a count of six. And then I do it twice more. Sometimes I like to crank up Foo Fighters really loud and release all my pent-up, negative feelings, and sometimes I like to meditate. Both work.

Mom comes in with a tray of bowls filled with salty, buttery popcorn, but I shake my head when she offers. For once in my life, I'm too wound up to eat.

The weather guy wraps up the forecast and the camera cuts to the female anchor. "When we come back," she says in that poised, television personality voice, "Jason Fink of affiliate station KSPL takes us to the fifth and final HockeyFest Minnesota location, a quaint resort town north of Brainerd, where he met with a Rotary Club dedicated to their community and a spunky young lady determined to prove she's worth her salt."

Carter snorts and Jesse doubles over with laughter. "Spunky young lady?" he gasps out. "Oh my God, oh my God."

"Shut up, Jess," I mutter. My phone buzzes.

Morgan: I'm at Cora's and we're watching the interview with her parents!
Cora: DYING. DYING. The BEST teaser in the history of broadcast journalism.

Me: Consider this the biggest eye roll in the history of eye
rolls, Cor.

I slip the phone back into my hoodie pocket, but not half
a minute later, there's another buzz.

Wes: EOTT

I screw up my face in confusion, and a few seconds later,
he sends another message, like he knows I don't understand.

Wes: Eye of the tiger, get it?

Ah, yes.

Me: Excuse me, I'm very busy. I'm a very important person here
about to watch a very important interview I recently filmed.
Wes: No matter what happens, remember . . .

I wait.
And wait.
No bubbles.
Finally, bubbles.
Bubbles.
I click on the link. Papa Roach, "Born for Greatness."
The long, resonant opening notes burst from my phone
as the video plays, and I scramble to silence it as Grandma
shoots me a look.

Carter elbows me. "What's that about?"

"What do you mean?"

"Did Wes send you that?"

Heat creeps up my neck and into my cheeks. "Why would you even say that?"

"Oh, I don't know, because he plays it during warm-ups every single day?"

I'm saved from having to respond as the furniture store commercial ends and Mom shushes us.

"Tonight, we have a very special report coming to us from our affiliate in the Twin Cities. One local town finds itself in the spotlight as they prepare for HockeyFest Minnesota, an annual event that showcases five cities across the state. This year, Halcyon Lake has been selected to represent the Central region, and recently, KSPL sports reporter Jason Fink visited to find out what makes Halcyon Lake special."

The report begins with a wide shot of the snow-covered park at Hole in the Moon and moves in toward the stone wall surrounding the rink and the warming house. Jason talks about the history of the rink, the Rotary Club, and how they raised funds for the renovation.

"Come on," Jesse mutters. "Get to the good stuff."

"Hey," Grandpa says, sticking out his chest a little. "This *is* good stuff!"

As Coach Giles predicted, Fink, on hockey skates in the middle of the rink, interviews a couple of cute little Mites ("I love playing hockey!" one of them squeaks out from behind the cage of his helmet) and a Squirt, a girl, her long blond ponytail streaked with turquoise.

"Who's your favorite player?" Fink asks her.

"Holland Delviss," the girl says with certainty. "She's so awesome."

Carter nudges me, and Grandma says, "Oh, sweetie!"

My cheeks warm again. I tuck my hands under my legs and lean forward a little.

Fink now stands at the glass in the arena. "Holland Delviss is something of a local legend around Halcyon Lake. She and her three brothers have skated as long as they could walk—only natural when your father, Marcus Delviss, led the Halcyon Lake Hawks to the high school team's only state championship appearance *ever* and *won*. Grandfather Grant Delviss also played hockey in his day, was a longtime president of the town's Blue Line Club, and, as Rotary president, had a hand in the Hole in the Moon renovation.

"But what sets Holland Delviss apart? Holland plays for the boys' hockey team. In fact, she's *always* played on a boys' team."

The scene cuts to a shot of me from Saturday night's game, skating across the blue line, taking a pass from Luke, and firing it toward the net. The goalie stops it with his stick, the puck bounces out toward me, and I swat at the rebound. Really? They couldn't have filmed my goal?

"Three words to describe this young lady: determined, driven, and spunky."

Carter snorts again.

The screen fills with a montage of photos of me through the years, mostly in hockey gear, mostly with my brothers. "Mom!" I say. "Really?"

She shrugs. "What was I supposed to tell them? No?"

"Shush," Grandma says again. "I can't hear the interview."

The voiceover explains my hockey history. How I've always played with the boys. Then the camera focuses on me, standing up against the glass, and the conversation turns to my thoughts on the girls' team.

Fink: Some people might say that you think you're too good for the girls' team. Is that true?

Everyone in the room stills.

Me: No, I don't think I'm "too good" for the girls' team. I've played with the boys my whole life. Trying out for the boys' team was the logical next step for me. I'm very lucky that my high school athletic department was receptive to the idea, as well as Coach Giles, Coach Edwards, the rest of the coaching staff, and my teammates. I would hope that any girl in any high school would have that opportunity if that's what she wished to pursue.

The scene jumps to Coach Giles standing outside the door of the boys' locker room.

Coach Giles: No one affiliated with this team has any issue with having a female player on the roster. Holland's been a great addition to the team. Day in, day out, she's out there working hard, constantly training to improve her game, setting an example for the younger players. She steps out on that ice with integrity and determination every single game, and she lives that way off the ice, too. She's a real go-getter.

Grandpa chuckles—yes, actually chuckles. "'A real go-getter,' huh, Holland?"

Back to me.

Fink: What about your teammates? Your male teammates? Do they feel the same way?

Me: I've played with most of these guys for a long time. They've never treated me differently because I'm a girl.

Cut to a shot of me and Wes on the bleachers before the game, sitting away from our teammates but definitely close to each other. How in the hell did they get this footage? How in the hell did we not notice someone filming this? I feel Carter's eyes boring into me, but I will not turn to look at him.

Fink (voiceover): Wesley Millard, co-captain of the Halcyon Lake Hawks and formerly of the state championship Great River Thunder, has played with Delviss for two years. I asked him to share his feelings about having a female on the squad.

Cut to Wes after the game, the interview from the video he sent.

Wes: Truthfully, I was apprehensive at first. But since my first practice with the Hawks, it's clear how much Holland contributes to this team. Maybe not in points, but in positive attitude and determination. She's got a lot of skill, yes, but really? I think I admire her most for her grit, and not just because she's female. How many people do you know who would basically put themselves in the line of fire like this every week? She makes me want to be a better player."

"'She makes me want to be a better player,'" Jesse mimics. "Barf!"

"Holy shit!" Carter says.

"Carter! Language!" Grandma and Mom say at the same time.

He nudges me. "Is there something going on between you and Hot Sauce?" He sounds completely, one-hundred-percent incredulous.

Like I couldn't have something going on with Hot Sauce? Does he think Hot Sauce is too good for me?

Oh my God, no, stop.

"Don't be stupid."

Carter's face appears on the screen again.

Carter: I've played hockey with my sister my whole life. It's weird when she's not out there with us.

Fink: Do you think her talents would be wasted on the girls' team?

Carter: Uh, well, I guess. In pick-up games and stuff, she smokes those girls.

Oh. My. God.

"Carter!" I elbow him in the ribs. "What the *hell*? And what's your *girlfriend* going to say about that?"

"She agrees with me."

Me: The coaching staff, the fans, my teammates all hold me to the same high standards as any other player . . . I feel honored to be able to play the game with a group of such high-caliber, dedicated players.

Fink: You wouldn't feel honored to play on the girls' team?

Me: I didn't say that.

Fink: But you feel that the girls' team doesn't have the same high-caliber pool of talent, so your talent would be wasted there?

Me: I—I didn't say that, either. And that's not a fair question. The girls on that team are skilled and driven.

Fink: So why don't any of those girls play on the boys' team with you?

Me: I can't speak for the girls on the team. I can only speak for myself. I earned my place on the boys' varsity team, and that's where I intend to stay.

"Oooh," Jesse says loudly, "Snap!"

Carter reaches over and whacks him across the head. "No one says 'oooh, snap,' you dork."

"Carter! Jesse! Quiet!" Dad says.

Fink speaks over more footage of me during the game: *What about college? Are you planning to play in college?*

Me: I'd like to, yes.

Fink: For the women's team at Hartley?

Me: Yes.

Fink: You aim to play women's hockey in college, but you don't want to play on the girls' team now.

Me: I'll try out for the team, yes. There are no guarantees in life, however, as we know.

Fink: Does it bother you that your dad, your two older

*brothers, and predictably your younger brother will all wear
that captain's C, but your jersey will go without?*

The camera focuses on my face, how my eyes narrow and
my lips pinch together before I reply.

*Me: What are you saying? That I can't be the captain of
my team because I'm a girl? That's ridiculous. The captain
role is a leadership position, determined by a vote of your
peers. Male, female, doesn't matter, as long as you're a strong
leader, as long as you remember what that C really stands
for—caring, courageous, consistent.*

*Fink: So, you'll be throwing your hat into the ring next
season?*

Me: Watch me.

My mom sucks in a breath, and Grandpa chuckles again.

"Crap," Jesse mutters.

The camera focuses on Fink at the Hole again.

*Fink: You heard it here, folks. Will ambitious, driven Hol-
land Delviss earn a captain's spot on next year's varsity boys'
team? That remains to be seen. Will the Halcyon Lake game be
the televised HockeyFest Minnesota spotlight game? That's up
to you. Voting is now open. Visit our website to watch all five
features and vote for your favorite.*

And that's it.

Dad lifts the remote from the arm of the recliner and
clicks the TV off. He clears his throat.

"Well," Mom says as she stands and begins to collect
glasses and popcorn bowls, "that was—"

Jesse interrupts. "Captain, Holland? Are you serious? I

can only imagine the crap I'm going to get about this at school tomorrow," he grumbles.

I stand up. "Look." I take a deep breath. I have no idea what to say. Because even though I hadn't considered being captain before I said it, why not? Who says I can't? But I'm tired. Tired of this day, tired of defending myself, explaining myself, validating myself. "Hey, at least they edited out the part when I talked about not having a penis or when I called Carter a brick shithouse."

Carter bursts out laughing, Grandpa and Dad both try to hide their smirks, and Mom shakes her head.

"Holland, do you have to be so crass?"

"Most days, yes," I say.

Jesse stands up and gives me a light shove. "You are such a drama queen, Holland," he says, but he can't hide his smile. "Nice interview. But they should have interviewed me. I'm the best looking."

I step over to my grandparents on the love seat and kiss each of them on the cheek. "Good night. Thanks for coming over to watch with us."

"I'm proud of you, honey," Grandma says.

"So proud," Grandpa agrees. "You've done your team *and* your town proud."

I snort. "Oh, I'm sure they'll love that captain comment."

"Well, we all say things we don't mean when we're under pressure," Grandpa says, and I can tell that he's not kidding.

"Grant!" Grandma cries, swatting him on the arm. "Why would you say she didn't mean it?"

"Well, now, that would be a little out of the ordinary, wouldn't you say? If they gave the captain position to you instead of a boy who's worked hard to earn that role?"

My own grandfather!

"What about me?" I ask. "Haven't I worked just as hard? Am I not as deserving?"

"Old-timer," my dad says to Grandpa, "you should quit while you're ahead."

"He's not ahead!" I say. "He's wrong!"

Grandma stands up and gives me a side hug. "Sweetheart, we're going to go so you kids can get your homework done. Don't listen to your grandfather. He's old and set in his ways."

"I'm not that old," Grandpa grumbles. He stands, too, and kisses me on the cheek. "I'm not saying you don't deserve the position, honey. I'm only saying it would be rather unusual for that to happen."

"Well," I say, "that doesn't mean it *can't* happen."

"I'll give you that."

I roll my eyes. "Gee, thanks for the vote of confidence, Gramps."

My phone buzzes as I'm walking up the stairs, and then again, several times.

Hunter: u kick ass call me when u have a sec.
Morgan: OMGosh, Holland, that interview was amazing! So proud of you!
Cora: Glass ceiling smashed WTG!

Wes: You rocked that interview. You are a total badass.

I'm happy to hear positive feedback from my brother and the girls, yes, but that text from Wes sends a rush of warmth through me. I try to tell myself that it's only because I'm proud that my captain took the time to compliment me, but I know it's more than that. It takes several minutes for me to think of a suitable response.

Me: Thanks again for the pep talk beforehand.

His response comes only seconds later.

Wes: ANY time. I mean it.

I settle in to finish my homework and try to forget about the interview and how, in parts of it, I sounded like an arrogant asshole. A couple of hours later, my phone buzzes again, and I tell myself I deserve a break. It's Wes again.

Wes: Quick, turn on the Power Loon.

Then he sends a link to a video. I'm too lazy to get up to turn on my radio, so instead I click the link: Poison, "Every Rose Has Its Thorn." I can't help the grin that spreads across my face as I remember the night that Wes sang along.

Before I finish the first video, he sends a link to another.

"I Remember You" by Skid Row. And less than a minute later, another, "Sweet Child o' Mine" by GNR.

Then:

Wes: you're on my mind fwiw

This time, I respond right away. I wish that I didn't have to study so we could have another '80s glam metal video battle. I wish that I could text with Wes late into the night.

Me: FWIW, that's worth a lot.

Chapter Twenty-Two

"So, *Captain*," Justin says to me the next morning between second and third periods as we walk toward my locker. "That *Fink at the Rink* interview provided some *fascinating* insights into your personality. And ambitions."

I groan. "Slacks. Stop."

"And what did Coach say that day? About your interview? That you'd 'represented your team beautifully'? 'Acted with integrity and respect'?" He laughs.

"Shove it, Slacks."

Morgan and Cora are already at the locker bank. I spin my combo, pop my locker open, and stuff my books inside.

I turn back to Justin. "I did all of those things. I never once disrespected anyone on our team."

"Potato, potahto. What about the girls?"

"What about the girls? Are you saying I disrespected them?"

"*I'm* not saying it, but I've heard rumblings."

"From?"

"Please stop fighting," Morgan says.

"We're not fighting, sweet cheeks," Justin tells her, then turns back to me. "Jo Mama Manson, for one, and Lakesha Smith, for two."

I roll my eyes. Lakesha is the other starting defense with Jo on the girls' team.

"What did they say?"

"Lakesha said someone needs to knock you off your high horse, and Jo said she's sick and tired of your holier-than-thou attitude."

"Oh, for the love," Cora says. "I'll show her holier-than-thou."

As much as I don't want any of this to bother me, it does, but I would never let Justin—or anyone—know.

"Did they really say those things or are you creating drama, Slacks?" Morgan asks, and I love her for taking the words right out of my mouth.

"Can't it be a little bit of both?" he replies with a devilish grin. "Fine. Yes, they actually said those things."

"I can't control how someone else feels," I murmur. "But I can control how I feel and how I respond to situations." I repeat the line from my interview that didn't make the final edit. Too bad. I'd love for a few hundred people to hear it.

And I'd love to believe that I have that kind of control over my emotions, which at the moment are worn a bit thin.

"Oh my God, how very Zen of you, Holls." He smirks. "All of Coach's deep breathing and meditation and shit must be working for you."

"Gotta go." I pull a notebook out of my locker and slam the door shut. "See you all at lunch."

This conversation—along with rude comments like, "Your

hair looked surprisingly good, Holland. Did someone, like, *style* you?"—has put me in a bad mood.

When I sit down next to Beck in humanities, he says, "Saw you on TV, Delviss. You looked super hot."

"Shut up, Bailey."

"You've got balls, I'll give you that."

Not this again. "What's that supposed to mean, I've got *balls*?"

"Oh, come on, you know. Playing hockey with the big boys, telling everyone you want to be captain next year. That takes guts. Balls. Gonads."

"I see. So, for someone to do something gutsy, she needs *balls*? As in, testicles? Meaning that someone without testicles is inherently less courageous?"

"Aw, crap," Beck mumbles. "It's just an expression. Chill out already."

"I will not chill out. It's *not* just an expression. Shit like that is demeaning, Beck, whether you mean it to be or not."

His face flames. "Geez, Holland, I'm sorry. I didn't realize—"

"Well, now you know." I turn to face forward as Mr. Neese clears his throat and introduces the old PBS video we're about to watch on the building of French cathedrals in the twelfth and thirteenth centuries.

I concentrate on the patterns and lines and splendor on the screen and try to forget about the interview and Jo and Lakesha and anyone else who's found new fodder for their arguments against me. I try to forget about my disappointment, my anger, my ideals.

My teammates—besides my beloved, snarky Justin—don't seem to be bothered by the interview, and I grasp on to that knowledge with both hands. I get a couple high fives in the lunch line, Luke tells me he thinks the broadcast is in the bag, T.J. makes a crack about me being captain next year, and that's about it.

I can't get Jo's comment out of my head, though. Even three deep breaths aren't going to clear *that* from my cluttered mind. But a talk with Miracle might. I catch her before she sits down.

"Hey, got a minute?" I ask.

"Always." She's got her hair in pigtail braids—hers are short, not even down to her shoulders, but it's something all the girls on the team do on game day, along with wearing their jerseys. "What's up?"

"Jo and Lakesha are pretty pissed at me, huh?" No sense beating around the bush.

"Well, you gotta take that with a grain of salt," Miracle says. "I mean, for one, you got interviewed and they didn't. Two, I mean, look at you, you're playing on the boys' team and they're not. No matter what you say, that does kinda make us look bad."

"It's not like either of them tried out."

Miracle ignores that comment and continues. "Three, you and Wes disappeared from the Snow Ball and showed up at T.J.'s party together hours later."

"We didn't show up *together*. And what does that have to do with it?"

"Uh, yeah, you did. Jo asked Wes to the Snow Ball, remember, and he said no? He shows up to the dance without a date, but then he leaves with you. And then the party. So, yeah, Jo's not feeling a whole lot of love toward you right now, Holls."

I groan. "But—but there's nothing going on between me and Wes!"

"Maybe not. But I wouldn't worry too much about Lakesha and Jojo or anyone else. They'll get over it."

"Wait, what do you mean, anyone else? Are other people talking about me?"

Miracle smiles. "Yeah. *I'm* talking about you. I'm telling anyone who asks that I respect your decision to keep playing with the boys and you killed that interview. Do I wish you played for us? Hell, yes. We could use a sniper like you."

"Sniper!" I laugh. "That's a stretch."

"Don't sell yourself short," Miracle says. "You got this, Holls."

"OK," I say and take a deep breath. "Thanks, Mir. I feel at least nineteen percent better."

She laughs, and we head to our table.

Wes sits down with his tray seconds after I do. "Hi, Dutch."

"Hi." I watch out of the corner of my eye as he tears open a packet of Cholula with his teeth and shakes it over his cheeseburger—pepper jack, of course. I think about his text from last night, that I was on his mind. My cheeks heat.

"You want one?" He waves the empty packet.

I shake my head. I don't feel hungry anymore. I feel a little nervous and awkward and maybe even shy. What is that about? Blech. I'm acting like an insipid, lovestruck ninny. All these emotions today. It's exhausting.

Wes and Showbiz talk about HockeyFest and the interview. I tune them out.

Until he elbows me. "Right, Dutch?" he asks.

I look up from my untouched lunch. "What?"

"Awesome, right? How your interview turned out?"

"Oh, yeah, awesome."

I don't want to talk about the interview anymore, not even to Wes. I stand and make up some excuse about forgetting that I needed to talk to Rieland.

"Holland!" I hear Morgan cry out behind me, and then Cora, "She's not *eating*?"

Ms. Rieland doesn't hide her surprise to see me.

"Holland," she says and sets her sandwich down on a paper towel on her desk. "I'm glad to see you. I wanted to touch base with you about how your feature is coming along."

"Yeah," I say, "not great. But that's not why I'm here. I mean, it sort of is, but it isn't."

She tilts her head to one side. "I'm not sure what you mean."

I sink into a desk in the front row. "Did you happen to watch the *Fink at the Rink* interview last night?"

"I did. I wouldn't have missed it."

"Why didn't you lead with that, like everyone else in the school?" OK, maybe a small exaggeration.

"Do you want to talk about it?"

"I guess."

"OK, would you like to start, or should I?" She smiles. For being such a stickler about deadlines and going to print, blah blah blah, Rieland can be very understanding. And intuitive.

"Go ahead?"

"I was impressed by your on-screen presence, first of all. Were you nervous? It seemed like you felt right at home."

"Ha! That's part of the problem. Maybe I'm getting too comfortable in that arena for my own good."

"Your answers were thoughtful and well delivered. You were respectful to the existence of the girls' team without discrediting your own team, or anyone else."

"Not everyone agrees with your opinion," I say.

"Of course not," she says, like I should know this already. That's kind of a thing with journalism, I guess. Sometimes you present the facts from both sides. Sometimes you express your opinion, knowing that others won't share that opinion.

"They don't have to be so rude about it."

"Do you feel bad about what people are saying?"

I bite my bottom lip, wondering if I'm overreacting. "I mean, I don't feel good about it. And it's only one or two people, but . . ."

"Holland, do you want to tell me what's going on? Everything you say here is confidential, unless someone is hurting you, and then I'm mandated to report it. You know that, right?"

I nod.

Can I trust Rieland? Lately, nothing I say or do is good enough for her. She's always pushing me to be better, do better.

Huh. When I think about it, she's an awful lot like Wes.

She's young, only a few years out of college. She played hockey in high school, so she may have some insight.

"I know," I finally say. "OK. I'm pretty sure that it will come as no surprise to you that I don't give two shits about what most people think."

One perfectly groomed eyebrow tweaks up slightly, but other than that, she gives no reaction. I continue.

"But, I don't know, this feels really personal. Like, lately, with HockeyFest coming up, and everything with the interview, the stuff people are saying really bothers me. It's messing with me."

"In what way?"

"I feel like every day I have to go out there and prove to myself and the team and everyone, really, that I can do this. That I still deserve to be there. Especially now. Because I put my foot in my mouth and said I thought I was good enough to be captain." I bark out a bitter laugh. "I know I am. I'm good enough. It's just harder to believe lately, with all the negative stuff on constant repeat in my head. I don't know how to let it go."

"So, sounds to me like you've got to figure out a way to let go of all that negativity. Think it through, Holland. What's your plan?" Another catchphrase. Go to Rieland with a problem, and she might give you some advice or insight, but she's always going to throw it back to you, guaranteed. *Figure it out. Work through it. You'll find your answer.*

What's my plan? I don't have one, except to do what I do every day. Keep moving forward. "Get through today? Get through practice, and our games this week, and then I'm going to get through HockeyFest. Probably spend a little extra time on the lake. It's kind of my happy place."

She nods. "One day at a time, one game at a time. I like that plan. My happy place has always been the weight room. I figure, if I can tackle that, I can tackle anything. You want to know my personal motto? 'I can do hard things.' I've proven that I can get through a challenge, so I can do it again. I'd say the same for you."

It's a simple motto, but it's a good one, and she's right. I've done a lot of hard things. Maybe I *can* do this, too.

"Where did you grow up?" I ask.

She smirks. "I grew up in Riverview, and you know how they love their hockey there."

I nod. The high school at Riverview, a close suburb of Minneapolis, has more than its share of state championship trophies from across the decades. At least the boys' team does.

"Ours was one of the first girls' high school hockey teams in the state," Rieland continues. "A lot of families welcomed the opportunity, but just as many resisted the change. You'd think it would be a no-brainer, right? Title nine, twenty-first century, in a suburb with one of the most progressive voting records in the Twin Cities. This is a city that had banned plastic bags before most people even knew they were a problem, but nobody better mess with River-view's hockey tradition."

"So, wait, before you had a girls' team, where did the girls play? I mean, were girls able to play on boys' teams?"

She shakes her head. "It wasn't prohibited. Official policy welcomed girls to try out, but that's usually as far as they got. Once you aged out of the youth programs, options were limited. You could open enroll to a school with a girls' program, or play recreational, or hang up your skates. Riverview is not a wealthy suburb. Most of the girls could barely afford to play as it was. Open enrollment or a traveling team weren't really viable options for those girls. So, when I got close to aging out, my parents and a few others started a campaign for a girls' team. It got pretty ugly."

"Huh. I guess I've taken a lot for granted."

"Maybe. It's all a matter of perspective. You're lucky that there's enough interest here to sustain both teams, and that, for the most part, people support your decision to play for the boys."

The warning bell rings; the lunch period is almost over. I stand up.

"Are you OK, Holland?" she asks.

"I guess. What choice do I have?"

She stands up, too, and smiles. "You could always write about it, you know. That might bring some clarity."

Her suggestion stirs something inside me. Maybe. Maybe I could write about it.

"Thanks, Rieland," I say. I lift my hand in a half-assed wave and step out into the hall. I check my phone as I walk to my locker.

Wes: Everything OK?

Wes: Where are you? I can come find you.

Wes: Dutch, you OK?

Wes: Dutch.

Wes: OK I'm officially worried.

I tap out a quick message.

I'm OK. Talk later.

His response comes within seconds:

Whatever it takes. x

Was that x a typo or intentional? Do guys even do that, use x and o? My heart feels tight. Gah, all these feelings today.

I close my locker door and hustle to get to English before the final bell.

The x must have been a mistake.

Today varsity practices at Hole in the Moon to get the feel of the rink before HockeyFest. Wes is his usual charming self:

"You think you can slack off now that the interview is over? No! Now you have to work *harder*."

"You got bricks in your skates today, Dutch? *Skate*, damn it."

And my personal favorite: "This little black rubber disc?

It's a *puck*. Puck, meet Dutch. Dutch, meet our new best friend, Puck."

I'd like to tell him what he can do with our new best friend Puck.

Even though I say nothing, he must see the flash of indignation and resentment in my eyes, because he locks his gaze and grins.

"I know you're dying to tell me where I can shove that puck." He leans in, both hands on the top of his stick. "You are my favorite little fireball."

He turns and glides away.

"Bite me!" I call after him, and he skates back to me.

He's so close, and I shouldn't have said it, and I'm suddenly very, very afraid. He's so close that I see him raise his eyebrow through his cage.

"Name the time and place," he says, and smirks before skating off again.

Maybe the x wasn't a mistake.

Oh, shit. I'm in trouble.

We're sloppy. Maybe it's the ice, playing outside, the pressure, whatever, but we cannot get our act together today. Coach calls practice early and sends us back to the arena to run it off.

Perfect. It's just what I need to work out everything that's twisted and knotted up in my head. I'm the first one up to the track. I slip my headphones on, find Wes's Barn Burner Mix on my music app, and run through the confusion.

WESLEY MILLARD—BARN BURNER MIX

1. "Thunderstruck"—AC/DC
2. "The Pretender"—Foo Fighters
3. "Runnin' with the Devil"—Van Halen
4. "Crazy Train"—Ozzy Osbourne
5. "Welcome to the Jungle"—Guns N' Roses
6. "The Day I Tried to Live"—Soundgarden
7. "In Hiding"—Pearl Jam
8. "For Whom the Bell Tolls"—Metallica
9. "Kickstart My Heart"—Mötley Crüe
10. "Dragula"—Rob Zombie
11. "Chop Suey!"—System of a Down
12. "Toxicity"—System of a Down
13. "Epic"—Faith No More
14. "The Red"—Chevelle
15. "Master of Puppets"—Metallica
16. "In the End"—Linkin Park
17. "Immigrant Song"—Led Zeppelin
18. "Wish You Were Here"—Incubus
19. "You"—Candlebox
20. "Seek & Destroy"—Metallica
21. "Down with the Sickness"—Disturbed
22. "You've Got Another Thing Coming"—Judas Priest
23. "Rainbow in the Dark"—Dio
24. "The Otherside"—Red Sun Rising
25. "Cemetery Gates"—Pantera
26. "Walk on Water"—Thirty Seconds to Mars
27. "I Will Not Bow"—Breaking Benjamin
28. "The Mountain"—Three Days Grace

Chapter Twenty-Three

THURSDAY NIGHT, WE HAVE THE GOOD FORTUNE TO PLAY THE TINY, terrible Wellspring-Settlers' Corner consolidation team, a school with a program so small it can't even support a junior varsity squad. That means that Coach calls up a handful of guys from JV to dress for our game: Lumberjack, Max Reynolds, Lakesha Smith's little brother Evan, and Jesse.

The mood is light and upbeat as our side of the scoreboard ticks higher. Wellspring-Settlers' Corner starts to get sloppy and they pull a bunch of penalties. We score on nearly every power play and even make a couple of short-handed goals. I assist on our second and third goals and score the fifth. Once we've racked up the score six–nothing, Coach sits most of the seniors and works the JV guys into the rotation.

Big Mick, the announcer, uses our nicknames in his scoring summaries, and the crowd gets into it, chanting "Hot Sauce" and "Six-Four" and even "Showbiz," who plays defense and scored from the point on a power play. This feels good, especially after Tuesday's practice at the Hole. It's just us, the ice, some crappy opponents, and the game, with none of the HockeyFest pressure or weirdness.

At 10–0, with three minutes left in the game and another

Wellspring-Settlers' Corner penalty that puts us at an advantage, Coach calls a time-out.

"Go easy on 'em, OK?" he says. "As much as it pains me to say this, try to keep the puck out of the net."

Jesse, who happens to be sitting next to me on the bench, mumbles, "Aw, come on! I haven't gotten my point yet."

I roll my eyes.

But he goes out on the power play, scores on a spectacular breakaway, and gets his ass chewed by Coach when he comes back to the bench.

That's also when Big Mick christens him with his new nickname.

"Heeeeeeeeere's your Halcyon Lake Hawks scoring summary. Scoring unassisted, his first goal of the season, number 52, Jesse 'Jet Skiiiiiiiiiiiiiii' Delviss."

The crowd goes nuts, and Coach shakes his head.

Later, after having to listen to "Jet Ski" on the ride home go on and on about tonight's awesome game and how easily he scored that goal, I take a long, hot shower and settle in with a big mug of Mom's *Top Shelf* Almond Joy hot chocolate and a night of catch-up reading for English.

But I can't stop thinking about Wes. I'm so conflicted. I like him, but I can't like him. I have a rule. I do not date teammates. I can't break my own rule.

I set aside Margaret Fuller's *Woman in the Nineteenth Century* and pick up my phone.

Me: Tonight was really fun. 🏒

I wait.
And wait.
Finally, bubbles.

Wes: Sorry studying for a big physics exam tomorrow

Carter's studying for the same test, so at least I know he's not lying.

Me: It's OK. Good luck on your test. Night.

I'm so chicken. Why didn't I say something like, *I can't get you out of my head. I miss you. Maybe we could make this work?*

I don't watch my phone to see if he's responding. I set it on my nightstand and pick up my book again. The phone buzzes before I've read one (lengthy) paragraph.

Wes: Sorry I can't talk tonight but do you want to listen to music together? Power Loon? 🦆

That is absolutely the cutest thing anyone has ever said to me. A grin spreads across my face as I reply.

Me: You realize that emoji's a duck, right, not a loon?
Wes: Closest I could get.

Me: That is ducking adorable.

I walk over to the boombox on my desk and flip on the radio.

Tesla. "Love Song."

The song is almost over.

He heard "Love Song" on the Power Loon and wanted me to hear it, too.

Bubbles. Bubbles.

No bubbles.

Bubbles.

Wes: You are ducking adorable.

The rush of heat and tingles that sweeps through me? That must be what they mean by "swoon." I'm ducking swooning for Wes Millard.

I fall asleep listening to the Power Loon and thinking about my captain.

Chapter Twenty-Four

Saturday.

Two weeks, five games till HockeyFest. This afternoon, we're back at Midview, against LaPierre. I sit next to Wes in the stands while we watch JV take another beating. The peaceful, easy feeling from the other night when we stomped all over Wellspring-Settlers' Corner has disappeared, and I'm on edge. I bounce my leg up and down, press my fingers against the sweat along my hairline, and hope that Wes can't hear how loudly and quickly my heart's beating.

Why am I nervous? The game? Sitting this close to Wes?

Is it HockeyFest? Voting closed last night. Coach said we'd hear by Monday if we got the broadcast. You'd think in this digital age, they'd be able to calculate a few votes in a matter of minutes, not days.

"How was your physics test?" I ask Wes.

"Good, I think."

"Good."

Bounce bounce bounce bounce bounce.

"What's wrong?" Wes says in a low voice. He doesn't look at me, doesn't take his eyes off the action on the ice.

"Why do you ask?"

He puts a heavy hand on my knee to steady me and I nearly jump out of my skin from the voltage.

"What's wrong, Dutch?" he asks again, pulling his hand away, still looking straight ahead.

He feels it, too.

"I don't know," I admit. "Something's off."

"Besides Utecht's goaltending?"

"Ha ha. Yeah."

"Want a Fireball?" He reaches into his pocket and pulls out a piece of wrapped candy. I hold out my hand so he'll drop it into my palm and I won't have to touch him again. Touching is too much. I unwrap the little devil and pop it into my mouth.

"Do what you gotta do to work through it before the puck drops."

"Yeah, OK."

"You want to walk?" he asks, pointing up. "I, uh, I can keep you company."

I follow his gaze to the track above the rink, then look at him.

His eyes. His eyes get me every time.

I give a tiny shake of my head. "We can't."

"Why not, Dutch? No one's paying any attention. No one cares."

I can't answer. The candy has reached its peak of hotness and my eyes water. I open my mouth and pant a little. He smiles as he watches me.

"But they do," I say. His smile fades.

"Why does it matter?"

"Because, Wes. I don't want to give anyone a reason to say I haven't earned my place on this team."

"But you're already playing. You've already earned your place on the team, and you prove every game that it was the right decision. So what does it matter?"

"It matters. We probably shouldn't even be sitting together right now. When they showed that clip in the interview, when we were in the stands before the game, Carter asked me if something was going on between us."

"Did you tell him there is?"

"Wes."

"Well, there is. I know you feel it, too, whether you like it or not."

Oh, I like it, all right.

I don't say anything for a minute. I don't look at him. My best course of action is to ignore his comment. Finally, I say, "I forgot my headphones." I crunch the candy, now a plain jawbreaker, the heat dissipated. "I can't walk a track without music."

His next words are so quiet, I need to strain to hear them. "So, it's fine for you to flirt with me over text, but it's not OK for me to want to spend time with you in real life?"

"Wes, come on."

"No." He stands up. "Forget it."

My heart cracks a little as he walks away.

❅ ❅ ❅

After JV's ugly loss, Coach calls the varsity squad into the JV locker room. We cram into the small space, surrounded by waves of ripe sweat and disappointment.

"Sorry that your game didn't go the way you planned, boys," Coach says, "but about five minutes ago, I got a call from Mr. Handshaw. Jason Fink called him personally this afternoon to let him know that the votes have been tallied."

My stomach drops. Oh, God. This is why I've been so off today. This is the reason behind that awful sense of foreboding.

I blew it.

We didn't get the broadcast.

Acidic saliva fills my mouth. I think I'm going to be sick.

"Team, congratulations. Halcyon Lake not only received a record number of votes but won by a record margin. Our story blew the competition away, and the game next Saturday will be broadcast statewide. There's also a fairly good chance that we'll be picked up by a regional or national network."

My stomach drops again, this time out of relief. Justin grabs me around the knees and lifts me high into the air while our teammates cheer and whoop.

"All hail Queen Holland!" he says. "Fuck, yeah, girl!"

"Shit, Holls, you did it," Carter says. "You did it. You got us the broadcast!"

Wes stares at me with his genuine, vibrant smile, and I'm so relieved to see it after our last conversation. His eyes say everything I'm feeling: *There are too many people in this room. I wish it could just be the two of us.*

Chapter Twenty-Five

EVEN WITH THE GOOD NEWS ABOUT HOCKEYFEST, THE ODD FEELING doesn't completely go away, and I annoy the piss out of my teammates with my jitters.

"What is *wrong* with you?" Justin says about halfway through the first period. "Are you three-quarters high off nothing or what? You are marshing my mallow here with all this nervous energy."

"What?"

"Calm the fuck down, Princess. You are amped up like Bennie and the Jets over there."

"What are you even talking about?"

"Whatever's got you all a-jitter, you need to take it down a couple of notches. You are messing with my mojo. What's your problem, anyway? You got us the broadcast. All your hard work is behind you."

I shake my head, stand up, and move closer to the door for the shift change.

"Skate it off!" Justin yells as he follows me out.

The ice is fast tonight; the play on the ice is faster. These guys are good, and the back-and-forth wears me down quickly. Our shift is underproductive and Coach signals for a change. I catch my breath and drink some water once I get back to the bench, but I don't sit. I can't. The nervous ball of energy in the pit of my stomach grows. Whatever this is, some sort of uneasiness about the game or residual worry about the broadcast, I'm annoyed with my own self.

Breathe.

I move to the opposite end of the bench from Justin so he can't yell at me for not sitting, for bouncing up and down while I wait for our next shift. With how fast this game is moving, and how long it's been without a whistle, our turn comes way more quickly than any of us expect. I follow Luke and Justin out into the fray, and there's finally a whistle when one of the LaPierre players knocks the puck into the backside of the net.

We line up for the face-off. The player across from me, number 9, gets a little too close for comfort, jabs at my skates with his stick. Nothing I can't handle, but I've got my eye on this guy.

Luke wins the face-off and we easily maneuver into their zone. Number 9 is on my ass, though. He won't leave me alone, jostling and hassling me even when I don't have the puck. I throw him a tiny, nearly unnoticeable elbow in the ribs.

"Bitch," he hisses.

I pivot and skate off, but he follows and hooks his stick around my calf, hard enough that I lose my balance and go down. Idiot. The ref blows his whistle.

"Two-minute minor, hooking, number 9, LaPierre," the announcer rattles off.

Wes comes off the ice and immediately starts yelling at me. "Did that asshole say something to you?"

"What?" Why is he yelling at me? "Why are you yelling?"

"Because I'm pissed! What did he say to you?"

"He called me a bitch, Wes," I snap. "It's nothing I haven't heard before. Let it go."

"No, I will not let it go. Fuck!"

Coach yells for Carter and Wes to get back on the ice, even though Wes just came off a shift.

"Power play," I tell him and point to the ice. "The best thing you can do right now is score on them."

The five guys on the power play unit pass the puck around, working toward the perfect setup. Time ticks down on the clock. They can't blow this player advantage.

"Shoot the puck," I mutter under my breath, and a heartbeat later, Carter cranks out a slap shot that's off by millimeters. The puck *pings* against the post and skids into the net.

The guys on the bench jump up in their excitement, bang their gloves against the ledge. LaPierre's back to full strength, but our power play line stays out on the ice. Less than fifteen seconds after the face-off, Wes comes around the net from behind and stuffs the puck for a second goal.

Two–nothing and I've been avenged.

I wish it had been me doing the avenging.

Chapter Twenty-Six

SOMETIME DURING THE GAME, THE SNOW STARTED. I'D GOTTEN A weather alert on my phone on the bus ride to the game but hadn't read past "snow expected." I mean, this is winter in central Minnesota. We pretty much always expect snow. But by the time we trudge through the foot of snow in the parking lot to the bus for the ride back to Halcyon Lake, the weather alert changes to "blizzard warning."

I take the first open seat up front, right behind Coach. After Coach's debrief, which was subdued even with a shutout victory and the news about the broadcast, I settle in with earbuds and my postgame chill-out playlist and fall asleep. Turns out to be a decent little power nap, because it takes us nearly an hour on slick roads to get back to the arena.

Where we then have to dig out the vehicles that are buried by wet, heavy snow. Carter clears the snow from the driver's side door and climbs in while I take the scraper and begin to shovel the snow off the windshield and hood.

"Jess, start clearing off the back window," I tell my brother, who's standing around doing what he does best—nothing.

"You have the scraper," he whines.

"Use your glove. It's freezing out here and I'm getting

pelted in the eyeballs by ice chunks falling sideways in the sky. Get your ass moving!"

"Yeah, yeah," he mumbles and shuffles through the drifts of icy snow, some up to his knees.

Carter turns the key and the engine makes the sickest, weakest *weoah weoah* sound I've ever heard. "Oh, shit," he says.

Beside us, Wes fires up his big, shiny, new black truck (covered in snow, but still). The truck rumbles to life, and for a moment, I let myself think of the night of the Snow Ball and the A-Frame, those tenuous moments in his truck, listening to the Barn Burner Mix, and I wonder how things could have been different between us.

Good decision, I assure myself for the four hundredth time.

A gust of wind shoots icy snow into my face. I swipe at it with a wet mitten as Wes steps so close to me, I can almost feel the heat and energy pouring off him.

"Hey," he says and takes the scraper from me. "No sense in doing that if the truck won't start. Why don't you and Jesse go inside while Carter and I try to figure this out? Send Archie out to help, would you?"

I should give him some shit about the big tough men solving the problem while the women and children go inside, but I'm too damn cold. I nod, teeth chattering. Jesse speeds toward the building, but I'm careful as I shuffle my way across the parking lot, slipping in some places, the ground covered with a thin layer of ice underneath the snow.

If they ever get the Suburban started, it's going to be a fun drive home.

❄ ❄ ❄

I stand in the arena vestibule and peer out through the smoky windows. The snow's coming down so hard, I can barely see the streetlamps, let alone the Suburban or Carter and Wes. Jesse's behind me, pacing, his headphones on as usual.

"Will you stop?" I say. "You're making me nervous." Now I know how my teammates must have felt with my jitters tonight.

This day keeps getting longer and longer. I take a deep breath. I'll be fine once we get home and I'm in my pajamas, safely snuggled under heavy quilts in front of the fire with a cup of hot chocolate and a plate of monster cookies. Until then, I'll white-knuckle the trip home, if County Road 27's even open.

My phone rings. I walk over to the closed concession stand and lean on the counter.

"Hey, Mom." I called her earlier to let her know we'd gotten back safely—and to report the dead Suburban. She and Dad had left the game early and made it home before the worst of the storm hit.

"Hi, sweetie. Are you still at the arena?"

"Yeah. Carter and Wes are out in the parking lot with Archie, trying to jump the Suburban. Might be a losing battle, though. I can't even see them from the front door."

Mom sighs. "I called the Lakeside Inn and the Halcyon House. They're full. Could you stay at Cora's?"

"They're out of town this weekend."

"Do you want Dad to drive back into town to pick you up?"

"The roads are terrible. No way is he driving back into town tonight. But I don't think the truck is going to start. Maybe Archie will let us crash here."

"You are *not* staying at the arena," Mom says.

I'm hearing it in stereo.

Wes stands next to me, completely covered in wet, icy snow, even his eyelashes. The cold air radiates off him and I shiver. He peels off his balaclava and blinks a few times. Before I know what I'm doing, I reach a hand to one of his red, damp cheeks, like ice to my touch.

What *am* I doing? I start to pull my hand away, but Wes is too quick. He latches on to my wrist. Now I'm sure my cheeks are as red as his.

"The Suburban's toast," he says. "But you're not staying here tonight. You can crash with me. Come on. My truck should be warmed up by now."

He releases my wrist and walks away.

"Who was that?" Mom is saying through the phone. I'd forgotten about her. Shoot. "Someone who lives in town?"

"Wes Millard. He said we can stay with him. I have to go. I'll call you when we get there, OK?"

Archie and Carter have come inside now, too.

"You kids got a place to stay tonight?" Archie asks, the *s* on the end of "kids" more like a *c* than a *z*. Archie's in his late fifties, with shaggy salt-and-pepper hair and cheeks permanently red from the cold. He's worked at the arena as long as I can remember.

"They're coming home with me," Wes says, and I feel like a stray.

I grab my gear and follow Jesse and Carter out to Wes's truck, the heater blowing warm air, the snow cleared away. He's careful as he maneuvers around the few cars left in the parking lot, including the dead Suburban, and makes his way across downtown.

Wes seems to be in complete control of his truck, of the road, of the snow coming at the windshield horizontally. But still, I'm relieved when we pull into the driveway of the little blue rambler fifteen minutes later.

Wes's mom, Debbie, has frozen pizza ready for us when we walk in the door. Basic toppings, pepperoni and sausage, that my brothers and I scarf down like we've never seen food before. Mom's most-pinned pizza recipe on Pinterest is chicken, artichoke, and blue cheese, and she makes it at least twice a month. I'm sure that someday I'll appreciate her gourmet tendencies and the fact that she taught me how to properly use all kinds of knives when I was five, but tonight, I'm all about the cardboard crust, the cheesy goodness, and the grease.

A yellow Lab walks into the kitchen while we're eating, makes the rounds to sniff at our legs, and plunks down on my feet. The dog is warm and heavy and solid.

"Oh, nice doggie," I murmur. "What's your name?"

"Tallie," Wes replies for the dog. "Short for Metallica."

I look across the table at Wes and grin. "That is—that is adorable."

"Adorable?" he scoffs. "There's nothing *adorable* about the greatest metal band ever."

"Except that you named your *adorable* dog after them." I reach down to scratch behind Tallie's ear, and she makes the cutest growly sound. "*Ducking* adorable."

Wes coughs. "She likes you," he says after he recovers, pride lacing his words. I'm not sure who he's proud of, the dog or me.

"Could you two please shut up?" Jesse asks. "I'm trying to eat here, and this conversation makes me want to barf."

"Your playlists make me want to barf, Bieber," I volley back, and Wes laughs.

Our jeans are soaked. Wes finds the guys sweatpants to change into, and they head down to the basement, where Wes's mom has made up beds on the couches and a gigantic recliner. I shake my head when Wes suggests I wear something of Debbie's. She's about a half foot shorter than me, and tiny.

"I'll be OK," I tell him. The heavy, wet denim clings to my legs, cold and uncomfortable. I shiver.

"Let me find something," he says and disappears down the hall to his room again. While I wait, I look at the ornaments on their colorfully lit Christmas tree, tucked into a corner of the living room next to the fireplace. Many of the ornaments are handmade and hockey-related, several wooden hockey sticks and skates, smooth and glistening in the lights. I like that they still have their tree up, weeks after Christmas.

When Wes comes back a few minutes later, he's got a green Minnesota North Stars hoodie and a pair of black sweatpants with the orange Great River Thunder logo down one leg.

"No way," I say and cross my arms.

Wes grins. "The last of my Thunder apparel. I saved these for posterity. They're a couple of years old, so they won't be so huge on you."

I point at the logo. "I cannot wear those."

"You can't wear those wet jeans. You'll get sick."

"I won't get sick from wet jeans. I might get sick from having to wear *those*."

He laughs, and I like his laugh. I like being in the same room as Wes and having an actual conversation rather than texting back and forth. I like spending time with him.

But this is *not* flirting.

We're friends.

I change into his stupid sweatpants. They're soft and worn and even though they're too small for Wes, they're way too big on me. I pull the drawstring tighter and roll the waistband. I bring the fabric of the sweatshirt up to my nose and breathe in.

Good. So good.

Wes has joined Carter and Jesse in the basement. He's sprawled out on a beanbag chair on the floor with a video game controller in hand. When I come down the stairs, he turns to look at me, a grin across his face.

Must. Resist.

I ignore him and the boys and curl up on the bed Debbie has made for me. Carter stretches out on the long blue sofa, and Jesse's got the recliner, but I get the sleeper sofa on the other side of the wide room, which she's piled high with quilts and pillows. I burrow under them, safe and protected from the raging storm outside and the one in my heart. I try to read *Woman in the Nineteenth Century*, but the warmth of the quilts lulls me to a sleepy, dreamlike state, not quite out, the video game noise and the boys' chatter a comforting backdrop.

My last thought before I fall asleep in Wes Millard's basement is that I've never been so grateful for a blizzard.

Chapter Twenty-Seven

"HEY. HEY, DUTCH."

My eyes pop open. I shake my head, disoriented. It takes a few seconds for me to realize that I'm still in Wes's basement, which would explain why he is standing over my bed calling my name. Carter and Jesse are still lounging in front of the TV on the other side of the room, now playing *Madden.*

"What? What time is it? What's wrong?"

"Nothing's wrong."

I'm so confused, and tired, and more than a little grumpy about being woken up *for no reason*, apparently.

"Then why did you wake me up? I was sleeping, you realize?"

"It's only, like, nine o'clock. And I'm bored."

"You're bored."

"Yeah." He sits down on the edge of the sofa bed. "Your brothers have started an epic playoff reenactment that could take hours. Let's go watch a movie."

"A movie?"

"Is there an echo in here? Yeah. Come on."

I probably could have slept for an entire day, but I can't deny that the idea of watching a movie with Wes, presumably without my brothers or his little sister, Jilly, appeals to me. I shouldn't let it, but I'm too tired to fight it.

"OK."

"OK. Good. Come on, let's go upstairs."

"Hey," Carter calls, not looking at us, as we walk past. "Don't even think about messing around with my sister, Hot Sauce."

Jesse snorts. "Good one," he says.

Oh, lord. I scurry up the steps ahead of Wes, my face hot. He mumbles something to the guys, but I don't hear it, and I don't want to.

When he said upstairs, I thought he must have meant the living room, but he walks through it and into the long hallway that leads to the bedrooms. I hesitate. The main level is quiet and dark except for a light above the sink in the kitchen and the multicolored, flashing LEDs on the Christmas tree.

"Dutch? You still with me?" he asks in a quiet voice, almost a whisper. I suppose Jilly's in bed already.

"Are we—where are we watching this movie?"

"My room." He says this like my heart should not be pounding or my hands sweating like I just scored on a breakaway.

"Oh. Right."

I follow him, second door on the left. Tallie sneaks in behind us and jumps on the bed before he closes the door slowly and without a sound.

His room is neater than mine, the bed covered by a thick red-and-black buffalo-plaid comforter. Posters of hockey players, some of them signed and framed, cover the walls. There's a half-empty canister of Atomic Fireballs on top of a stack of hockey books on his desk. A framed photograph of the Thunder's state tournament team hangs above his desk, and the medal is in a plexiglass case next to it.

I search for Wes in the photo, and when I find him, I reach out to touch my index finger to the glass. He looks so young here, barely sixteen. A wild grin lights up his entire face.

"Wow," I say. "What a moment." I turn to look at the real Wes and see that same wild grin.

"Yeah," he agrees. "It was something. Could turn out to be a once-in-a-lifetime thing."

"I hope not. Do you think we've got a shot at state?"

"Maybe." He shrugs. "We've got a lot of natural talent on the roster. It's a matter of working as a team, keeping the momentum going, not letting ourselves be intimidated by the big guys, you know?"

"Spoken like a true captain."

He shrugs again. "That's my job."

A tall bookcase takes up one wall, filled with photos and wood carvings of ducks and birds and books. He reads! Real books! Hardcovers, paperbacks. *Clapton: The Autobiography. High Fidelity* by Nick Hornby. *Room Full of Mirrors: A Biography of Jimi Hendrix.* Lots of Stephen King.

My eyes fall to the bottom shelf. His vinyl collection. Four feet of albums.

"Holy shit, Wes." I drop to the floor and sit crisscross applesauce, tilting my head to read the narrow spines. Pink Floyd, Led Zeppelin, the Beatles, Matthew Sweet, an entire section of Chris Cornell—solo, Soundgarden, Temple of the

Dog, Audioslave. Tallie walks over and lies down, her head on my knee. I scratch behind her ear. "Wait. Al Hirt? Herb Alpert and the Tijuana Brass? Why all these trumpet players?"

Wes laughs. "I inherited my grandfather's collection. He liked trumpets. Some of it's really good."

"Forget the movie. Let's listen to music."

He reaches out his hand to pull me up. "Another time."

I hesitate before taking his hand, but when I do, I'm rewarded with the now-familiar electricity that passes between us. And a smile from Wes.

I wish there could be another time.

He grabs a couple of remotes, leaps onto his neatly made bed, and pats the spot next to him. "What should we watch? Let's see what we've got." He turns on the TV and streaming service and clicks to RECOMMENDED FOR YOU. "*Mystery, Alaska*? *The Princess Bride*?"

Two of my favorites. Two very different movies in style and content. "You pick."

"You're my guest, Dutch. You choose."

"*The Princess Bride*."

"As you wish," he says in a terrible British accent.

Uhhh, he's so perfect.

"Come on, don't be shy. Make yourself at home."

He must not realize that sitting next to him on his bed is going to send me into shock. I lower myself onto the bed and lean up against the pillows. I leave about a foot of space between us.

Space that says I should *not* be in his room, I should

not be thinking about the things I'd like to do with him on this bed.

Tallie moves into the space and snuggles in, her nose on my shoulder. I curl my arm around her and stroke her floppy, velvety ears.

"Lucky dog," Wes says as the movie begins.

Not five minutes later, Tallie jumps down and whines at the door. Wes gets up, too.

"Be right back," he says before opening the door and following Tallie out.

I pause the movie. When he returns, his cheeks are pink from the cold and there are a few snowflakes in his dark hair. He's alone.

"Where's Tallie?" I ask.

"She's no longer invited," he says as he settles back in against the headboard and pillows. He doesn't leave as much space between us, and I can feel the chill of his skin from the few minutes he spent outside.

Somehow the space becomes smaller and smaller as the love story of Buttercup and Westley plays out.

And disappears completely the moment Wes slips his arm around me, tucks me in close, and I rest my head on his chest, breathing him in as Inigo Montoya fights the six-fingered man who killed his father.

He's warm and comfortable, his breaths steady, rhythmic. We fit together perfectly, and my heart gives a little lurch. The moment doesn't feel real. We're tucked away inside that pocket again, where real life doesn't exist, where I don't have to worry about what the old-timers think, what our team-mates might say about us. Luke's drunken comment at T.J.'s party. Coach's warning.

"This is OK, right?" he murmurs.

I clutch at the fabric of his shirt. "Sure," I say, my voice strained. "I mean, we're friends, after all."

Friends. That's all.

When the movie ends, I slip out of his arms and leave the room, not saying a word, feeling his eyes on me even after I've closed the door and gone back downstairs, where my brothers are playing the Super Bowl.

Chapter Twenty-Eight

I WAKE EARLY, THE LIGHT FROM BEHIND THE BLINDS A MUTED BLUE. The basement has a heavy, musty boy smell to it. Jesse snores. Carter's still sleeping, too, his bare feet sticking out from under the tangled quilts.

I'm toasty and comfy and could stay in bed all day, listening to the howling wind and blowing snow, but I could also eat something. My stomach rumbles and makes the decision for me.

Jilly makes breakfast, which consists of toaster pastries, cereal (with or without milk, my choice, she says), and fruit cups.

"Sorry I don't have something more substantial," Debbie says as she pours me a cup from the Mr. Coffee. "I didn't make it to the grocery store this weekend."

"This is perfect," I say. I add a splash of milk and sprinkle in some sugar from the dispenser on the table.

Tallie comes in and sits on my feet. We've never had pets, other than the chickens and goats and barn cats. One summer, we "boarded" a pig that I, of course, named Wilbur. Besides Cosmo, my dog experience is limited. Tallie seems to love me, though.

I peel back the plastic on a cup of pears and dig in. "We're so grateful that you had room for all of us. Staying at the arena would have been terrible. Have you heard the forecast? Is it supposed to snow all day?"

Jilly scoots onto the bench next to me with a plate piled high with steaming toaster pastries that smell like strawberry jam. "Yeah," she answers for her mom. "We could get another foot of snow!"

"Really? Another foot?"

Debbie nods. "Yes, they're saying ten to twelve inches on top of the ten we've already gotten. Twenty-seven is still closed, but it sounds like roads should be drivable by early evening, even with all the snow."

"I hope we get a snow day tomorrow," Jilly says.

Debbie laughs. "Enjoy this one! Worry about tomorrow tomorrow."

"Today's not a snow day! Today's Sunday!"

I take a sip of coffee. Part of me wants to go home to take a long, hot shower and change into my own clothes, but another part of me wants to stay here, watching movies in Wes's bedroom, dressed in his sweatpants, for days.

Wes's stepdad, Tim, a Crow Wing County sheriff's deputy, comes into the kitchen in jeans and a Green Bay Packers sweatshirt. He kisses Debbie, hugs Jilly, and pours himself a cup of coffee.

"What time did you get home last night, Daddy?" Jilly asks.

"I rolled in around two. Roads were terrible. Hey, Holland, how's it going? You kids have everything you need?"

"Yes." I don't know Wes's stepdad well, and with his work schedule, he's not often able to make it to games. But when he's there, he's loud and proud. "Thanks for letting us stay last night."

"Glad you didn't try to make it out to Story Lake. The evening might have had a much different ending."

He sits down next to Jilly and breaks off a corner of her toaster pastry. I like Wes's family.

"I did a load of laundry last night and tossed in your and the boys' wet clothes, Holland," Debbie says. "Everything's clean and dry if you want to shower and change back into them."

"Oh, that was so nice of you," I tell her. "I'd love that."

When I come back out to the kitchen a half hour later in my familiar, comfortable jeans and Hawks hoodie, Wes sits at the farmhouse table next to Jilly, a game of cards between them.

He looks up from his cards to me, and his face falls. Why does he look so disappointed to see me?

"You changed," he says simply.

Oh.

"I kinda liked you in my old sweats."

My face heats up.

"Wes," Jilly says, "your friends are staying all day, right?"

"Not safe to drive," he says, "so I guess they don't have a choice."

"Tonight, too?" Jilly asks.

"If the plows can't clear the roads, then yes." Wes looks at me when he says that last word.

Yes.

So much weight in three little letters.

I try to ignore the little thrill that passes through me.

"Mom says she thinks the roads will be clear by dinner."

"Well, then, we'd better make the most of today," Wes says and stands up, tossing his cards onto the table. "Dutch, you up for a little fresh air?"

"Um, I guess?" I'd expected a lazy snow day in front of the Christmas tree and the fireplace, catching up on my English reading. But why not?

"Can I go?" Jilly asks. "Where are you going? I want to go with. Can I?"

"Not this time, Rocket," Wes says and tugs on one of her pigtail braids.

"Where *are* we going?" I ask as Wes motions me to follow him to the laundry room, where he finds me snow pants and a parka that are only a bit too big.

"We're going to rent Jilly a movie."

I laugh. "Rent a movie? What is this, nineteen ninety-six? Can't she just stream a movie?"

He shakes his head. "Not since Mom caught her watching *The Breakfast Club*. Let's just say she lost some privileges. Now it's DVDs only, and since we got rid of most of them before the move, we're regulars at Third Street Rental."

I stop. Third Street Rental, the shop that old-timer George runs with his sister.

"Uh, no, I've changed my mind."

"No," he says firmly. "No way. You're going."

"No." I can be firm, too.

"Dutch."

"Wes."

"You're going."

"No, I'm not."

"I will not let you put your life on hold because of what one guy thinks."

"Little dramatic, don't you think? Put my life on hold? So I don't want to go to the video store. Big deal. Nobody died. And also? It's more than one guy."

"Little dramatic, don't you think?" he echoes. "That you'd rather miss out on the most amazing popcorn experience on the planet than have to face a guy whose opinion doesn't matter?"

"Don't bring food into this! That's not fair!"

The corners of Wes's delicious-looking lips quirk up. "Fine. You'd rather miss out on a walk in this beautiful snowfall with *me* than have to face a guy whose opinion doesn't matter?"

"*Fine,*" I snap. "Let's go. You are impossible."

"*You* are impossible," he says, but he's laughing. "I love arguing with you almost as much as I love playing hockey with you."

I suck in a breath and pretend that he didn't let the *l* word slip. Twice. While talking about me. I mean, not the *l* word *about* me, exactly, but close enough.

The garage is still blocked by drifts of snow, so we suit up in the living room and leave through the front door. We make a path where the sidewalk would be, down the driveway to the street. The plows must have come through at some point, but it's impossible to keep up with the snowfall.

At first, we walk in silence, except for the *swish swish* of our snow pants as we shuffle through the snow and Wes's occasional chuckle. When we reach the park, I stop, delighted by the line of pine trees, their branches weighted down with heavy, glittering snow.

"Oh, so pretty," I say. "I love winter. It's my favorite season. I can't imagine living anywhere but Minnesota."

"You're planning to go to college here, right?" he asks. "Hartley?"

"Yes. Hopefully I'll get in."

"Duluth, huh? You must *really* love winter."

"What about you? Have you figured out college yet?"

He gives me a look. "You know I'm going to Northern Lakes, right?"

Wes got a full ride to play hockey for NLU. "Everyone knows that. I mean, what do you want to study?"

"Oh. People don't really ask me that."

"Are you serious?"

"I'm a hockey player, Dutch. Nobody cares about anything except how many points I have on the season."

Anger flares up inside me. "Well, that's bullshit. They should. You're smart, and not just book smart. You've got common sense. You're a problem solver. That's what makes you such a great captain."

I clamp my mouth shut before I say more and start

again in the direction of the video store. I've already said too much.

"I want to study exercise science and go to graduate school for physical therapy."

"Wow," I say. "How did I not know this about you?"

He laughs, and it's tinged with bitterness. "See? No one ever asks."

"I'm glad I did," I say quietly.

For a few minutes, neither of us speaks. I breathe in the cold, fresh air, tinged with that dirty, wintry exhaust smell. I listen to the high-pitched whine of snowmobiles, to the scrape of a shovel as someone clears their sidewalk.

"You think I'm a great captain?" he says finally. There's no teasing, no arrogance in his words.

"The best I've had," I say. It's true. *My captain.* "Ever."

That shuts him up again, and we're quiet for the last block to the yellow Victorian that houses the video store. We walk up three wooden steps, recently brushed clear, and stomp the snow from our boots on the front porch before we step inside. Inside my chopper mitts, I cross my fingers that George won't be working.

No such luck.

"Wes!" George calls from behind the counter. He's wearing a Halcyon Hawks hockey hoodie. How appropriate. "How's it going, Cap?"

"Hey, George," Wes says. "I was worried you'd be closed with this weather."

"Nah," George says. "I live upstairs, so I might as well open. Besides, what else am I going to do on a day like this?"

I look around. There's one other person in the store, a kid who looks about twelve, in full-on snowmobile gear, looking at video games. And George's sister, Rollie (real name unknown, at least to me), is in the popcorn room.

Third Street Rental's claim to fame is not its wide selection of DVDs, video games, and even VHS tapes that are a big hit with the summer cabin crowd, but rather, the gourmet popcorn. One whole room houses row after row of canisters with every popcorn flavor imaginable. Buffalo Chicken. Dill Pickle. Pumpkin Pie. Salted Caramel. They make the popcorn fresh every day during the summer tourist season but not quite as often during the winter months, so the selection is smaller.

I decide I'll escape to the popcorn room, but as I take a step toward it, Wes catches me by the sleeve.

"George, you know Holland, right? Holland Delviss?"

Is it my imagination, or does George stiffen a little behind the counter? His lips pinch together in a slight frown. Not my imagination, not one bit.

"Well, sure, I know all those Delviss kids."

Yep, that tone is definitely frosty compared to the warmth and love that oozes from him when he's addressing his Cap. *My* Cap, thank you very much.

I give George a tight smile. "All those Delviss kids love the popcorn here! Excuse me." I move into the popcorn room while Wes and George chat about the chances that the roads will be cleared before our game on Tuesday night.

"Hi, Rollie," I say. She's a character, that Rollie. Her long gray hair is twisted up in a bun and tucked into a fluorescent lime hairnet. She's wearing a black tank top with a giant white screen-printed feather. A tank top! In the middle of a blizzard.

She nods and dumps a fresh batch of caramel corn into the bin. Then she scurries into the kitchen behind the counter. I don't know that I've heard her say more than five words. Ever.

I find my favorite flavor, Bacon & Brown Sugar. I stick the tongs in for a sample, even though I already know I love it and will buy a bag to bring home. It doesn't taste quite as good with the sour taste in my mouth from my exchange with George.

"Check this out," Wes says as he comes up behind me.

Close behind me. My sour feelings melt away with his closeness. Who cares about a grumpy old man who makes popcorn and doesn't like the girls' hockey team or the girl on the boys' hockey team? Not me. Wes was right.

"New flavor." He points at a canister and I squint to read the handwritten label.

Hot Sauce.

"Are you kidding me? They named a *popcorn flavor* after you?"

He beams. "Not only that, I helped develop it!"

"Shut up."

"It's true. Go on, try it."

I do. I grasp a kernel with the tongs and drop it into my hand, inspecting it before popping it into my mouth. It's Cholula, that's for sure. It's smooth, hot, but not too hot.

Wes watches me with that familiar grin, and his dimple flashes. "You good? No emergency?"

I beam, too. "I've been practicing!"

He laughs. "I've never known you to back down from a challenge."

"I want my own popcorn flavor. What do I have to do to get my own popcorn flavor around here? What did *you* do?"

"Well, they love me."

"I've been coming here for years! Why don't they love me?"

Wes reaches across me to take a sample of Caramel-Cheddar. "They love you."

I point my thumb in George's direction. "Clearly, George does *not* love me."

"How could they not love you? Everyone does." His cheeks go a little pink.

"Not that shithead from LaPierre last night."

"Do guys talk to you like that a lot? Opponents?"

I nod. "Yeah. I mean, not a lot, but every so often. Don't players say shit to you?"

"Yeah, but it's different."

"How is it different?"

"I don't feel threatened by some dipshit shooting off his mouth."

My eyes go wide. "But I should?"

"Look, Dutch, I'm not saying this because I think you're helpless or you need protection or anything like that. I'm saying it because it's reality. Right or wrong, fair or not."

"I can handle it, Wes."

"I didn't say that you couldn't. But I want to know if it happens again. Promise me that you'll tell me if something else happens."

I nod.

"Say it, Dutch." His deep brown eyes lock with mine. "Promise me."

He's so serious, and his concern sends a wave of something unrecognizable through me. Something that scares me and something that I want to investigate all at once.

"I promise."

Satisfied, Wes grabs three bags of popcorn—Hot Sauce, Caramel-Cheddar, and Bacon & Brown Sugar, like he can read my mind—and we move into the DVD room. It doesn't take long to pick out two movies for Jilly—*Tangled* (my choice) and *Go Figure* (his), a Disney Channel movie about a figure skater on a hockey scholarship.

Wes pays for our spoils and I offer to carry the bag. George says good-bye to Wes but acts like I'm not even in the room. Oh, well. I'm going home with popcorn.

"Jilly hasn't stopped talking about you since the interview," Wes says as we make our way across the snowy sidewalk. "She asked Mom to put a blue stripe in her hair, and this morning while we were playing cards, she drilled me with questions about you."

"Why?"

"You're kidding, right? Every female hockey player in this town wants to be you, Dutch."

I snort. "Every female hockey player under the age of thirteen, maybe."

"That's a lot of girls looking up to you."

I grimace. "That's a lot of pressure."

"Nah," he says. "You're amazing, and now the rest of the world is finding out, too."

"Thank you," I mumble. I tuck my chin down into the parka as far as it will go.

We walk in silence again for a few minutes, until we get to the park with its beautiful line of snow-covered evergreens, where Wes stops, almost in the exact spot we stopped before.

"Hang on a sec," he says.

I wait for him to continue, to tell me whatever's on his mind. I wonder why we've stopped here when we're walking into the wind now and it's so cold. We could be having this conversation in the kitchen while we divvy up the bags of popcorn.

"Look, Dutch . . ." He starts, then falters. He sighs. "Last night—well, I had a good time with you. Watching the movie."

I nod. "Me too." Too good.

"I should have—shoot." He shakes his head and looks upward for a second before his eyes lock with mine again. "Dutch. Do you remember, uh, when we were at the A-Frame? After we had pie? And then at T.J.'s party when you were drunk and—"

"I was *not* drunk."

"OK, when you were buzzed, and you told me that you wished that you'd, uh, wished that you'd kissed me?"

I look away, up to the tops of the trees, heavy with snow. "Yeah," I say quietly. "I'm sorry. I shouldn't have, not after what I said in the truck."

"But did you mean it?"

I turn to look at him again, his rich brown eyes wide with anticipation, hope.

"I meant it. But it would have made things harder."

"Why? Why does this have to be hard?"

"What do you mean?"

He moves his hand in the air in the space between us. "*This*. You and me. Being friends or whatever we are. I like you, Dutch. A lot. The time we spend together—it's the best part of any day. I like being with you as much as I like playing hockey. And playing hockey with you—it doesn't get any better than that."

"Wes—"

"Hear me out. I want to spend as much time with you as I can, Dutch." He reaches for my mittened hands, clasps them within his, and brings them to his chest. "We're good for each other. I know that you see it, too. And I get it. I understand why you don't want to date a teammate, especially me. But whatever bad stuff you think would happen, I don't know—it doesn't have to be like that. I want to give this a shot. Us. We deserve that." He smiles. I want to carry his smile tucked deep into my pocket.

I close my eyes and breathe in the cold air.

Maybe. We *are* good for each other, even though he irritates the hell out of me most days. Maybe Cora was on to something when she said we could keep this to ourselves for a while. Like Carter and Livvie.

I think about last night, how we fit together so perfectly, how comfortable I felt in his arms while we watched *The Princess Bride*.

Maybe we can make this work.

"I like spending time with you, too, Wes. On and off the ice. Well, on the ice you're kind of rude, but . . ."

He laughs quietly. "It works, doesn't it? You bust your ass every single day."

"I'm scared, Wes. It feels like people are constantly watching my every move, waiting for me to screw up or quit the team or—I don't know. And you're my captain. I'm not supposed to . . . to . . ."

"Who says you're not supposed to?"

"Wes, come on. Everyone? Well, everyone except Cora and Morgan."

"That so?" He grins. "Don't be scared."

"Easy for you to say."

His eyes lock with mine, his gaze now serious and intense, sending shivers through me. "Do you want to give this a shot? Can we try?"

I blow out a long breath. "On one condition."

He groans. "You're killing me, Smalls."

The Sandlot. His taste in movies is almost as good as his taste in music.

"If we—if we do *this*—" I wave my hand between us like he

did. "If we do this, we have to keep it to ourselves, like Carter and Livvie did. We can't let anyone know, at least for a while. Is that OK with you?"

He doesn't answer right away, his eyes searching mine. I wonder what, exactly, he's looking for.

"Yes, yeah," he says slowly, "if that's the only way you'll give us a shot, Dutch. We can keep this to ourselves for now."

"OK. But remember, you're my captain. No special treatment on the ice. OK?"

"Easy. I can keep my roles separate."

"Your roles?"

"Your captain and your boyfriend."

I swallow. My boyfriend? He's calling himself my boyfriend?

"But I can give you special treatment off the ice, right?" He grins.

My face heats and I nod.

"Do you remember, at the A-Frame? I believe I had my hands on your hips. Like this."

He drops my hands and places his on my hips, and yes, even though he's wearing thick gloves, and I'm covered by snow pants and a parka, I'm instantly warmed by his touch as the current passes through me.

And then he crushes his mouth against mine.

And, *Oh*. Wow. A cascade of electricity rushes through every cell of my body. It's a fast, searing guitar riff. The exhilarating rush of a breakaway. A burst of fresh, cold, pure winter air. All my favorite things in one perfect moment as he tugs me even closer, as I part my lips and he slips his tongue inside my mouth. He tastes sweet, like caramel and chocolate.

I'm on fire. Hot Sauce is so, so hot.

I'll take this kind of special treatment any day of the week.

The bag of popcorn and DVDs falls to the ground and I reach up and put my arms around his neck, trying to get closer, closer as I taste him, as he nips my bottom lip, as he breathes out so I can breathe him in, like the Foo Fighters song, as his lips move up my jaw to my earlobe, as I murmur his name and smile, as his mouth finds mine again, crushes against me, tangles up in me, tangles me up.

Whoa.

I hear the swooshing sound of snow under tires and I jump back from him. Even though we're bundled up, I worry that someone will recognize us.

"You see? That's the kind of thing I'm worried about. We're in the middle of a public park!"

Wes reaches out a gloved hand and places it on my cheek but doesn't make a move to kiss me again. "Then let's take this somewhere private."

I pick up the bag and brush the snow off. He grabs my free hand as we continue down the sidewalk toward his house. I'm too stunned—*I'm holding hands with Hot Sauce Millard*—to make casual conversation. After we trudge up the driveway, he drops my hand to enter in the code on the keypad. Someone has cleared the driveway and sidewalk, but the drifts are starting to pile against the house again.

"Wait," I say. "Don't go in yet."

I wade through the snow in the front yard toward the fence.

"What are you doing?" Wes asks.

"I want to see this up close."

I shuffle along the mural, back and forth, from winter to spring and back again. Blooming flowers and green grass. A father and a daughter on a rowboat fishing on the lake, the sun sparkling on the surface. Orange and red and brown leaves along the shoreline. A group of hockey players on the frozen lake. Wes waits for me there.

"This is amazing," I say. I'm a little out of breath, from our walk, our kiss, the cold. "Who painted it?"

He tilts his head. "You really don't know?"

I smile and shake my head. "No. I mean, I know it wasn't here before you moved in. Your mom or Tim, maybe?"

"No," he says. "Look closer. Look at the players."

I take a step toward the fence, and my gaze falls on each of the hockey players.

One of them has a long brown ponytail with a thin violet stripe.

She's me. With a violet stripe.

I turn to look at him, my eyes wide.

"You painted this?"

He nods.

"Wes, it's so good. I had no idea you were an artist."

"There's a lot you don't know about me, Dutch," he says.

I turn back to the winter scene, reach out and brush snow

off. "When?" I ask, my throat tight. I try to think if I ever saw it as a work in progress, but I only ever remember seeing it finished. "When did you paint this?"

"Last fall. I finished this scene the day after Thanksgiving. We got three inches of snow the next day."

"Last fall," I repeat. "She's me."

It's not a question.

He nods, his eyes narrowed, brow furrowed. "Yeah," he says slowly.

"But you don't like me. *Didn't* like me. Why did you paint me on your fence when you didn't like me?"

"Dutch," he says in a low voice, but he doesn't continue.

He painted me in his mural. My heart soars and aches at the same time.

We've wasted so much time. I don't want to waste any more.

"We should go inside," he says after a few seconds.

I touch the girl with the violet stripe one more time before following Wes across the yard.

Chapter Twenty-Nine

ONCE WE'RE IN THE GARAGE AND HE'S PUSHED THE BUTTON FOR THE door to come back down, he leans in, kisses my ice-cold cheek with warm, soft lips, and slowly moves to the corner of my mouth, so tenderly and with so much possibility, I have to close my eyes to believe it.

"Come on," he whispers.

We stomp the snow from our boots in the garage before stepping into the laundry room and stripping off our cold, wet things, hanging them over the utility sink, the washer, the closet doors, wherever we find space.

"I was beginning to worry," Debbie says as we walk into the kitchen. Now that we're back at the house, I'm self-conscious, apprehensive about the kiss(es). Wes must feel the same, because he stands about ten feet away from me. "Tim got called back to work," Debbie says. "I heard on the news that there have been seven hundred and fifteen car accidents in Minnesota in the last twenty-four hours."

She's stirring something on the stove, and Wes leans over to inspect it.

"Tomato soup," he says. "This the good stuff?"

Debbie nods.

"You want me to make grilled cheese?"

"Sure. Holland, why don't you give him a hand?"

"I don't know, Mom," Wes says. "Holland's a professional here. I don't want to embarrass myself."

I snort. "The *daughter* of a professional. What are the boys doing?"

"Still playing video games."

I scoff. "It's like they've never seen a game console before today."

Wes hands me a loaf of swirled pumpernickel-rye, a stick of butter, and a knife, and I set to work while he slices and seasons tomatoes. We don't talk as we work together to make a stack of perfectly browned, gooey sandwiches. Of course he sprinkles his with Cholula before he grills it, but I shake my head when he offers it for mine.

"Baby steps, remember?" I say.

We bring everything over to the kitchen table and call the boys. Jesse slurps his soup and picks the tomato out of his sandwich. Wes and Carter talk shop. We've got a home game on Tuesday night, so even though I secretly hope for another snow day tomorrow, I know that life will soon return to its regularly scheduled programming.

Jilly tells stories of school and friends and skating lessons.

"At first, I thought I'd like to be an Olympic champion figure skater. But then Wes got me a pair of hockey skates for my birthday when I was five and took me skating a lot and taught me a bunch of stuff, and I fell in love with it, you know?"

I nod, my mouth full. There's nothing better than bread. Except toasted bread with gooey melted cheese and peppery tomato. At Wes's kitchen table. I take a drink of ice water and swallow. "Yes, I know exactly!"

She nods, too, very serious. "I thought you would. I saw your interview, and you were awesome! Anyway, hockey's my thing now. But I'm not very good, so I play on a girls' team." She looks away, like she's embarrassed by this fact.

"I'll bet you're fantastic if Wes is teaching you everything he knows," I tell her with enthusiasm. "Just because I play on a boys' team doesn't mean it's the right thing for every girl. And it certainly doesn't mean that girls' teams aren't just as good. Minnesota has some amazing women's college teams that have won national championships."

"Oh, yeah," she says. "I like the Bulldogs."

"Me too. And did you know that there will be seven Minnesotans at the Olympics next month on the U.S. women's hockey team? Maybe when you get a little older, if you think you'd like to try out for the boys' team, you can, but you don't need to decide now. You've got time."

Jilly looks back over at me, the smile returned to her face. "Yeah, I guess you're right."

"Keep practicing. When you fall down, pick yourself back up. Keep moving forward. That's the main thing. Ask for help if you need it. The rest will take care of itself."

Debbie sits across from me and smiles, first in Jilly's direction, then at me. "Thank you," she mouths.

I startle a little when I feel Wes's hand—and the now-familiar voltage that goes with it—on my knee under the table. He gives a little squeeze, and then it's gone. For the rest of the meal, I wait for him to do it again, to touch me again. I crave it. It doesn't come.

When we're finished eating and Debbie stands to clear the table, Carter stops her. "Let Jesse and me do some of the work," he says.

"What?" Jess whines. "We're in the middle of a game! Plus, we already cleared the driveway while Wes and Holland were out playing in the snow."

Wes coughs and tries to cover it by lifting his water glass to his lips.

His full, soft lips. I now know what it's like to kiss those lips, to feel those lips brush against my cheek.

"Show some gratitude and respect," Carter says with irritation. "You are getting on my last nerve, and there won't be a game if you don't start pulling your weight around here, you lazy shit."

"Carter, language!" I say, since Mom's not here to do it, and Jilly snickers.

"I've heard it *all*," she says. "Have you met my brother?"

Her brother stands and puts a hand around my elbow, gently, to pull me up. "Thanks for cleaning up, guys. Come on, Dutch, I want to show you something."

I'm sure that vague comment won't arouse suspicion. I roll my eyes and follow him downstairs, through the big family room, and into a small workshop around the corner that smells of sawdust and metal shavings, paint and turpentine.

"Hi," he says after he slides the pocket door closed.

"Hi. So, what did you want to show me?"

"Uh, this?" He hooks his fingers into the belt loops of my jeans and tugs me close. He leans in. "This."

He presses his lips to mine with a groan. "Jesus, Dutch," he mutters, moving his mouth from mine and kissing my neck. I turn my head for better access.

"You're so strong," he says between kisses. "So confident. I mean, you're beautiful, too, but your confidence, I gotta say, is really sexy."

Pretty sure there's nothing I don't like about this boy.

I pull his face back up to mine. I kiss him fully and deeply, my mouth bursting into flames as his tongue slips into it. He presses against me, and I feel the hum of his moan. His hand slips under my shirt, his index finger tracing a line across my stomach, and I laugh against his mouth at the sensation.

"Is this OK?" he whispers.

"Mm-hmm."

"Would it be OK if I—if I moved my hand up—uh, higher?"

Oh, my sweet lord.

"Yes, please." My voice cracks. I feel the corners of his lips turn up in a smile.

His hand moves up, up, so slowly, so deliberately, and I'd love to give him a little nudge to move things along, but I let him take his time, relishing the feel of his touch, the current passing through every cell of my body. After what feels like a triple-overtime, he finally trails a finger along the top curve of one breast, slips his hand inside the lace, and I'm flooded, floating, flying.

More, more.

"OK?" he asks again.

More than OK. So much more than OK.

He laughs.

"Did I say that out loud?" I ask, and he laughs again.

I'll never get tired of that laugh.

This weekend has been strange and wonderful and the perfect escape from reality. Things are so off-balance right now. But with Wes, all that fades away. HockeyFest. The old-timers. The *Jack Pine* feature I need to write. The asshole at yesterday's game.

"Dutch," he murmurs, sending jolt after jolt of electricity down my spine, into my toes. "Let's go out on a date. A real one, where I pick you up at your house and take you out to dinner and kiss you on the front porch when I drop you off."

I nuzzle my face into his chest. Here, in his basement workshop, the house blanketed by snow, we can be together without scrutiny. Here, we're Holland and Wes. We're not the captain and *the girl*. I inhale for four.

"Please?"

Exhale for six. I can do this. We can do this. I nod.

"Is that a yes?"

I lean my head back and meet his gaze. "Yes."

He grins, bright and beaming. "Have you ever eaten at the Chinese Lantern in Brainerd? Let's go there."

The Chinese Lantern is one of Brainerd's oldest restaurants, with intricately designed red-and-gold carpets, lanterns, and decor throughout the dining room, the walls covered with signed photographs of the owner posing with visiting celebrities and public figures. He especially loves to pose with hockey players at all levels, college and NHL and Olympic. When we were Squirts and Peewees, it was a team tradition to eat there any time we had a tournament in Brainerd or Baxter to gush over the latest pictures. My family still eats there a couple of times a year.

"I haven't been there for months. That'll be fun."

"Everything's more fun with you, Dutch."

"Brainerd's good," I say. "No one will see us together in Brainerd."

"Oh, right." He pauses. "We're keeping this under the radar." He doesn't sound thrilled, but he kisses me again, this time a light brush against my lips.

I leap away when I hear pounding footsteps on the stairs above us. I slide the door open as quietly as I can and walk over to the sofa bed.

"Where were you?" Carter asks as he flops into a beanbag chair and picks up a controller.

"Bathroom."

"Hmm. Where's Wes?"

I shrug. "His workshop?" I say as carelessly as I can as Wes comes around the corner holding a rough wood carving of a hockey player, arms and stick upraised.

"I found it," Wes says, stopping when he sees Carter and Jesse. "Oh, hey."

"Wow, did you make this?" I ask.

"Yeah, my uncle has been teaching me. He gave me all his wood carving equipment."

"The ornaments on the tree, too? The skates and the sticks?"

"You saw those?"

I nod. "You're so talented," I say quietly. "Painting. Wood carving. Gourmet grilled cheese. Gourmet popcorn, for that matter."

He shrugs and nods his head in my brothers' direction. "Nobody really knows about this. It's a good way to unwind, you know? I listen to music and carve."

"I hate to interrupt this artistic love fest," Carter calls, waving his phone in our direction, "but I got a text from Dad. Twenty-seven is open and he's on his way to town. Wes, can you give us a lift to the arena?"

Chapter Thirty

WE GET HOME IN TIME FOR DINNER, COMFORT FOOD, SHEPHERD'S pie, and after I scarf down three helpings, I retreat upstairs to replay every moment I spent with Wes at his house over the last twenty-four hours. School's already been canceled for tomorrow, another five inches forecasted overnight.

Cora calls, digging for details.

"Your text messages were *cryptic*, Holland. I want to know what's going on."

"Nothing's going on. Blizzard. Roads closed. Slept in the Millards' basement. With my *brothers* in the same room. What could possibly happen?"

I don't tell her what we've decided, how Wes has planned a date to the Chinese Lantern. If we're keeping this to ourselves, that means I can't tell the girls or Hunter. And there's a part of me that wants to keep it close, my own, for a little while longer.

Instead we talk about the hit I took at the LaPierre game, and she's not satisfied until I tell her that I'm bruised and stiff but not in pain. Next, I call Morgan and have essentially the same conversation with considerably less snark and much more empathy.

I text Wes early Monday afternoon.

Me: Want to watch Spinal Tap with me? I'm procrastinating on my Jack Pine article.

When he doesn't respond right away, my mind starts to spiral with possibilities, all of them negative. *The Princess Bride*, the walk in the snow, our first kiss, that hot make-out session in his workshop, all a dream. My imagination. Or worse, a mistake.

How will we make this work? How will I be able to keep my hands off him? How will we possibly keep this from our teammates? From Coach? Carter already suspects something's going on and has for days.

An hour later, I still haven't heard back, so I watch *This Is Spinal Tap* on my laptop. When it's over, I figure I've procrastinated long enough on my article, so I open a new document and jot down the easy stuff: *who, what, where, when, why,* and *how.*

I get stuck on the *why,* hung up on everything that's happened since the interview. Jo Manson and Lakesha Smith. The LaPierre player calling me a bitch. Grandpa telling me I shouldn't even consider taking the captain spot from another player, a male player.

What a mess.

I text Wes again after dinner: **You there?**

Nothing.

I delete the last paragraph of my article and try again. I write about the history of Halcyon Lake hockey and a few things about the rink renovation. Then I call Grandpa to talk about the renovation. I've heard these stories a hundred times, but it gets him talking and keeps my mind off Wes. Grandpa provides a couple of good sound bites and I get back to work on the article.

My phone buzzes as I'm finishing up my closing paragraph, and I'm surprised to see that it's after ten.

Wes: Sorry, I took Rocket out to skate at the Hole today and then I fell asleep. Did you watch it without me?

My heart feels tight when I think of him teaching his little sister how to play hockey, when I think of him sleeping on top of his buffalo plaid comforter, Tallie snuggled up next to him.

Me: Yeah. You're a good brother.
Wes: Is it weird that I miss you?
Wes: Can I call you?

He doesn't wait for an answer.

"Hi."

"Hi, Dutch." Music to my ears. "Tallie misses you, too. She's been sleeping on my bed with her nose pressed into your pillow."

He asks what I've been doing all day and I tell him about the article, that I'm worried Rieland's going to rip it apart, worried that my half-assed attempts at journalism won't be enough to get into the program at Hartley.

"How old were you when you started writing?" he asks me.

I give him the abbreviated version of my long history as a writer. "When I started working on the *Jack Pine* this year, I thought I was so experienced and worldly because of my blogging experience. Rude awakening doesn't even cut it."

"Blog?" he asks, and I could kick myself.

Other than Hunter and my parents, no one knows about the blog. Not even Carter or Jesse.

"Oh, ha, yeah, this music blog I write sometimes. No big deal."

"Oh," Wes says. "I thought you meant you helped your mom with her blog or something."

"No, no." I laugh uncomfortably. "Nothing as big and official as that."

It's not only that I made a deal with my parents to keep the blog private. The thought of Wes reading my work—especially about music—sends me spinning with nerves. I can't wrap my head around it, why it's so important to me that he doesn't think I'm a hack.

"Well," he says, "if you write like you handle a puck, you've got this. I know you feel like you're under a lot of pressure right now with this and HockeyFest, but if anyone can do it, you can. Now, get back to work."

I tell him good night and pull my laptop closer. I'm rereading the last paragraph I wrote when my phone buzzes again.

Wes: Night Dutch

He sends a link to the Foo Fighters' "Big Me" video, the parody of those goofy Mentos commercials, Dave Grohl's hair in twin pigtail braids.

Concentration and motivation are officially lost as I search for meaning in the bizarre lyrics.

Wasting Light: A Blog About Music, Hockey, and Life
January 29 11:33 p.m.
By HardRock_Hockey
Big Me: A Search for Meaning
Now Spinning: Foo Fighters, *Foo Fighters*

Hello, Hard Rockers.

The last couple of weeks have not been conducive to blogging. I'm doing a lot of writing for school and I'm doing a lot of skating, but I've neglected the blog. Sorry about that. I'm heavily involved in an event that's happening in town in a few days, and that's taking up a lot of my time. Along with . . . other things . . . my time and my mind space.

Anyway, tonight I'm inspired to write about a song from my favorite band, Foo Fighters: "Big Me," the fourth single from their 1995 self-titled debut album. I watched the video for "Big Me" a couple of hours ago (thanks, 17) and suddenly found myself down the rabbit hole of really old online forums, overanalyzing the lyrics and trying to figure out why this particular song on this particular night after this particular conversation. I mean, it's a long story. I'll spare you the details.

Verdict: I have no idea what this song is about.

Do we ever know what's going through a songwriter's head? I suppose in some cases, yes. We know that Paul McCartney wrote "Hey Jude" for John Lennon's son

Julian when his parents were divorcing. We know that Gordon Lightfoot's "The Wreck of the Edmund Fitzgerald" is about . . . you get the idea.

But that's the cool thing about music and lyrics. The songwriter blends inspiration with emotion to *create* meaning. The end user blends personal experience with emotion to *find* meaning. I hear the lyric "But it's you I fell into" from "Big Me" and it may mean something completely different than what Dave Grohl meant or what my brother thinks when he hears it.

Songwriting isn't black and white.

Life isn't black and white.

Life is kind of like one big search for meaning. We look for answers and try to make sense of the world around us. You need a decent soundtrack for that shit.

HARDROCK_HOCKEY: TOP 10*: FOO

10. "Wheels"

9. "Walking After You"

8. "Long Road to Ruin"

7. "Learn to Fly"

6. "My Hero"

5. "Times Like These"

4. "Something from Nothing"

3. "These Days"

2. "Everlong"

1. "The Pretender"

*Selection and rank were nearly impossible tasks. I love you, Dave. You, me, Xcel Energy Center, October 18. See you then.

Tell me, what's your favorite Foo Fighters song?

\m/

19

Comments

11:37 p.m.

Why don't you have any songs from the new album on this list? PUT IT ON THE TURNTABLE.

> Hunter_Not_The_Hunted
> *Reply from HardRock_Hockey*
> *11:39 p.m.*
> You mean the album that you gave me for Christmas that "accidentally" found its way into your suitcase when you went back to school? The one that you've conveniently forgotten every time you've come home since?

11:42 p.m.

Fuckin' A, man, I love this post. Sometimes you just gotta do the hard shit in life. But such a hard question, dude. How can you pick one favorite Foo Fighters song? I mean, I don't think it's physically possible. But if forced at gunpoint or something, I gotta go with "Monkey Wrench."

> MetalManiac (Jim)

Reply from HardRock_Hockey
12:03 a.m.
Good one. Seriously, this was so hard.

12:05 a.m.
It's you I fell into.
        Hot_Sauce_17

Chapter Thirty-One

TUESDAY, GAME DAY. I DON'T SEE WES UNTIL LUNCH, WHERE HE HAS found a permanent spot at our table—on my left, of course.

"Hey," he says as I sit down, his hand on the back of my jersey. "Did you get my message?"

"Do you mean the message on my blog?" I ask quietly, glancing around to see if any of our friends are paying attention to our conversation.

"Yes."

"How did you find me?"

"This newfangled thing on the world wide web called Google."

"Very clever." At this point, I suppose if anyone hears us, they'll assume we're talking about music (which we are) or bickering as usual.

He turns to me and smiles as he opens a packet of Cholula and pours it over his soft-shell beef taco, then opens another. He holds it out to me and raises one eyebrow. "Want some of this?"

He's killing me.

"Sure," I say and grab the packet. I sprinkle a few drops

and hold it out to him, hanging on for a second before he takes it from me. His pinky dips down and strokes the underside of my hand and I almost gasp from the shock of his touch. I let go and he dumps the rest over his taco.

"What the what?" Cora says. "Did you just put hot sauce on your taco over there, Blando Calrissian? Is *that* what you did all weekend?"

So she *is* paying attention.

I smirk. "I've been practicing."

"You are weird," she says. She gives me a look like she knows I'm up to something. I shrug, and she goes back to her conversation with Morgan.

"I have no idea what that song means, either, Dutch," Wes says, "but I like that line. I like it a lot. Speaks volumes."

"Mmm."

"Can you meet me by the locker rooms in five minutes?" he asks quietly.

"Why?"

"Do I really need to elaborate?" He clears his throat. "See you all later," he says, and stands up with his now-empty tray.

I finish my taco. I drain my water bottle. I bounce my leg up and down. Finally, I use Rieland as an excuse to leave early again and find Wes in the empty hallway near the gyms.

"Hey," he says and tugs me around a corner. This is the very definition of sneaking around. "I probably shouldn't say this, but I really want to kiss you right now. I've been thinking about it all day."

I bite my bottom lip. He wants to kiss me right now. I want to kiss *him*.

He leans his head back and huffs out a frustrated sigh. "Don't do that, or I won't be able to stop myself."

"Why do you want to stop yourself?" I tease.

"Because if I start kissing you, I won't be able to stop, and we have about two minutes left before lunch is over."

"Two minutes is a long time."

"Maybe in the penalty box," he says. He cups my cheek with his hand. "But it's never enough with you. Can I give you a ride home tonight after the game? I want to spend some time with you. Alone." His thumb lightly grazes my cheek, back and forth, back and forth.

"I'm supposed to catch a ride home with Carter."

"I'll talk to him."

"Carter told you he'd kill you if you so much as touch me," I remind him.

"He didn't say that, not those exact words. I'm touching you right now. I'm going to keep touching you. That OK?"

My body hums. "Mm-hmm," I say. "I'm good with that."

Wes laughs. "Carter's going to find out sooner or later. If he doesn't figure it out tonight, it'll be pretty clear when I show up to take you out to dinner."

I can't argue with that. Even if we hide our new and improved relationship from the rest of the team, Carter and Jesse and my parents will know something's going on.

"We can't keep it a secret forever," he says.

"At least until after the HockeyFest game, though?"

"OK," he agrees as the bell rings. "Play your heart out tonight. And then I'll get you alone in my truck."

Rieland pulls me aside during class to talk about the article I emailed her last night.

"Give it to me straight," I say. "I can take it."

She laughs. A good sign, I hope. "There's nothing technically wrong with the article. You have a solid opening and you hit on all the facts. You wrote the framework with the intention to plug in details of the event itself. But there's no emotion, Holland. No pull. That's the goal of good writing, to evoke emotion, to inspire action. You want your readers to become so immersed in your writing, in your story, that they say to themselves, *I want to be a part of that.*"

"How do I do that? I tried to write from the heart, like you told me. Apparently, I failed. And this edition won't come out until after the event. So they can't be a part of it, right?"

She smiles. "That makes it even more challenging. But you won't get anywhere near success if you don't fail once or twice. Maybe in this case, it's not enough to tell *a* story from the heart. Maybe you need to tell *your* story."

I nod and blow out a breath.

"There's a reason they're called growing pains, Holland. Like doing drills. Some days you leave all your blood, sweat, and tears on the ice. Some days you leave them on paper. I'll give you a pass to the library and you can work there without any distractions, OK?"

I stand. "OK, I get it. *Whatever it takes.* Thanks, Rieland."

❄ ❄ ❄

We win with our eyes closed, seven–one. I get assists on three of those seven goals.

Carter's in such a good mood, we're able to send him home without me, with little explanation on our part.

"I'm not stupid," Carter says to Wes as the three of us walk across the parking lot. "I'm on to you two. But I'll figure out something to tell Mom and Dad."

Wes unlocks his truck with his fob and opens the passenger door for me. Irritating and endearing. He lets the truck warm up for a couple of minutes, then reaches across to grab my hand as he pulls out of the arena parking lot. "Where to?" he asks, and I laugh, because his question is ridiculous for a Tuesday night with homework and still less-than-ideal road conditions.

"Wherever you'd like to take me." I play along, squeezing his hand.

Wes puts on the Barn Burner Mix as we drive through town and out on 27 toward my house—heavy, thumping beats and guitar riffs. My heartbeat seems even louder. He detours onto Satellite Lake Road, though, and pulls into the deserted, tree-lined parking lot of the Hidden Marsh Golf Club.

"In the mood for some late-night golf?" I ask.

"More like I'm in the mood for some late-night Dutch," he says, and as corny as it sounds, his words and the glint in his dark eyes as he turns to look at me send a little thrill through me.

"How did we get here, Wes?" I ask, almost shyly.

"It's a better place, isn't it?"

I love that he gets me. I love spending time with him, even if it's only fifteen minutes of make-out time in an empty parking lot, the truck running, on our way home after the game on a school night.

I hope we get at least fifteen minutes before my mom starts texting me, wondering where I am, why I didn't come home with Carter, and if I have any homework. My moment in the spotlight hasn't changed that.

Wes leans in for a kiss as I unbuckle my seat belt. His lips brush mine and then he says, "Good idea." He clicks his seat belt off. "I've got a better one. Back seat?"

I've never been so glad for a dark cab and dim streetlamps as my face heats up.

"As you wish," I murmur, and he laughs, his head thrown back.

I could fall in love with this boy, I think to myself as I open the door to move to the back and then hope to God that I didn't say *that* out loud. He doesn't laugh or say anything, so maybe I'm safe. When we meet in the back seat, I've barely gotten the door closed before he's tugging me close, and his lips meet mine with such intensity and longing, a little squeak of surprise escapes me.

I can feel him smiling and then—I'm all in. All in. Whatever it takes.

Wes deepens his kiss, his tongue exploring my mouth,

tangling with mine, I bite his bottom lip and there's that smile again before he nips mine, he covers me with his strong, muscular, hockey player body, and I try to push my own strong hockey player body closer, but we're already so close, his letter jacket is in the way, I slip my hands up underneath it, then tug at his T-shirt—a vintage look Monsters of Rock baseball T-shirt—and place one hand on his hot, bare skin, and he groans, then he moves his mouth from mine to my neck.

"You know," I say, breathless, "for someone I can't stand, I really like you."

"Ditto," he murmurs against my skin, his breath hot.

His lips meet mine again, and somehow, he flips us so that I'm straddling his lap, leaning into him, and then his hands struggle under my hockey jacket, the liner, a sweatshirt, a tank top. "Shit," he says, "layer much?"

Finally, he connects with the skin of my lower back, my side, his hands hot and smooth, electrifying me, drenching me in sensation, and he moves one hand up, over my bra, to the back of my neck, and he cups his hand around me, a movement so gentle, with so much tenderness, my heart aches.

This is so, so good.

There's a buzzing under my butt, my phone somehow wedged between me and his thigh.

Another buzz.

"Oh, shit," I murmur and pull away from Wes's delicious lips. "My mom."

Wes looks at me in a daze. "What?"

The phone vibrates again, and I pull it out from under me.

Top Shelf Hockey Mom: If you're not home in fifteen minutes, there's a good chance you won't be playing in that game next Saturday. Or any game.

Top Shelf Hockey Mom: Carter told me you were with Wes and I'd really like to know why.

Top Shelf Hockey Mom: We'll discuss this when you get home.

I hold out the phone to Wes.

He kisses my forehead. "Don't worry. Your parents love me. I got this."

Chapter Thirty-Two

WES CHARMS THE HELL OUT OF MY PARENTS.

We're sitting around the kitchen table, a plate of Mom's maple bacon blondies in the center.

"I know that I haven't lived in town very long," Wes says, "and you don't know much about me or my family, but I want you to know how much I enjoy spending time with Holland. The more time we spend together, the more we learn how much we have in common." He grins at me. "And I also want you to know that my intentions with your daughter are honorable."

I almost laugh. Is he serious? His intentions? What *intentions* could he possibly have? Personally, I *intend* to suck on his bottom lip the next time I get him alone, which I hope will be shortly after this uncomfortable conversation, when I walk him out to his truck.

"Huh," Dad says, reaching for a bar and biting off half of it. He chews and looks from Wes to me. "I thought you couldn't stand the guy."

I shrug. "Most days he drives me completely batty. But he's growing on me."

"Very funny," Wes says. "Anyway, Dutch—er, Holland—and I have discussed the, ah, ramifications of dating publicly, and we think it might be best to keep this to ourselves and our families for the time being. For the sake of the team."

"What exactly do you mean by that?" Mom asks.

"Everyone's already under a lot of pressure with Hockey-Fest coming up," Wes explains. "We don't want to create another, uh, unusual dynamic."

Wow, Wes's extended vocabulary is quite appealing.

"That's—that's very mature of you, Wes," Dad says.

This whole exchange is so awkward.

"I wanted to discuss that idea with Dutch tonight, so I suggested that I give her a ride home."

I run my thumb across my lips, still swollen from our heated "discussion" in the back seat of Wes's truck. He sees this and one eyebrow lifts in surprise.

"In any case, Holland," Mom says, sliding the plate of bars toward Wes, "you should have let us know that you were getting a ride home from Wes instead of letting Carter do your dirty work."

"Sorry," I murmur. "Are we done? I've got to work on my article."

Dad chuckles but Mom sighs. "Maybe you should have thought of that and come straight home," she says.

"Sorry."

"I may have overreacted slightly with my text messages," she says somewhat sheepishly. "Thank you for bringing her home safely, Wes."

Wes takes a bite of a blondie and wipes crumbs from the corner of his mouth. I'd like to help him out with that. "Wow.

Those are amazing. Holland tells me that you're catering the Hotdish Feed for the sponsors next Friday night. Do you need more servers? I'd love to help."

"That would be fantastic, Wes, thank you."

I roll my eyes.

"I really need to get to my homework," I say and tug Wes toward the front door. "I'll walk you out."

"Good night, Wes," Mom says.

The door has barely closed behind us before Wes backs me up against one of the stone columns on the front porch and his hot mouth is on mine. I make good on my *intentions* and suck on his bottom lip, still tasting of sweet maple-bacon blondie. I'm rewarded with a low growl.

"That was close," he says when we come up for air.

"They like you. Mom offered you treats."

"Still," he says, and his lips land on my neck. I shiver at the touch.

"I really have to work on my article."

"Mm-hmm, me too."

"You don't write for the paper," I say and gasp when his teeth nip my neck. "No hickeys. We're keeping this under wraps, remember?"

His lips land on mine again and I'm pulled out of this bitter cold night and into the warmth of his arms and his kiss.

Until I hear a rap on the window. I startle, pull my lips from his, and give him a little shove.

"Time's up, Holland," Mom calls from inside.

"Good night, Wes," I whisper.

"Good night, Dutch."

I watch as he walks backward down the sidewalk. I watch as he gets into his pickup, as he maneuvers a turnaround in the driveway. I watch until his taillights fade.

I putz around with my article, wash my face, change into an oversize Foo Fighters T-shirt, and crawl into bed, clutching my phone to my chest, waiting for a text.

He doesn't disappoint.

Wes: I miss you already.

I click on the link he sends next, a smile playing on my lips. Poison, "Talk Dirty to Me." I laugh.

Me: This coming from the polite young man who sat at the kitchen table with my parents tonight? Puh-lease.
Wes: Whatever it takes.
Wes: Sweet dreams.
Me: ♥

Chapter Thirty-Three

MONDAY. DATE NIGHT. WITH PRACTICES AND GAMES AND homework, tonight is our first chance to drive down to the Chinese Lantern.

I have to say I'm more than a little excited. And nervous. But mostly excited.

As promised, Wes picks me up. He comes to the door to say hi to my parents, and luckily, he's dropped the polite courting act. He's back to the Hot Sauce that my parents know and, let's face it, love. Because who, besides me, could ever really dislike that kid? He's every parent's hockey-playing, medal-winning dream.

Turns out he's mine, too. Guess the old saying is right: You're never safe from surprise until you're dead.

He holds my hand the entire drive to Brainerd, his thumb constantly moving, caressing, sending the most pleasant shivers of electricity through my every cell. We talk about Thursday night's game against Saint Christopher Lake (the conference goons, tough guys with more penalty minutes every year than the rest of us combined), Mom's Hotdish Feed (can't wait to see that boy in a catering apron), and HockeyFest.

The restaurant is just as I remembered: dim lighting, red walls, gold accents everywhere. Wes rests his hand lightly on my lower back as we stand in the lobby waiting for our table and looking at the photos of the owner with all the celebrities who have passed through town.

"Here's my boy, Zach," I say, and laugh.

"Oh, that's right. The big Parise fan. I forgot how much you love that guy. Don't you have his Team USA jersey from the last Olympics or something?"

I turn toward him and grin. "You remember that? I can't even remember the last time I wore it."

"I can," he says. "Dude, here's one with Chris Hudson from Dig Me Under."

"They played Lakes Jam a couple of years ago," I tell him. "It was awesome." Dig Me Under is one of those Seattle grunge bands from the '90s that made a big comeback. Chris Hudson, the lead singer, is from Minnesota.

"You went?"

"Yeah, with Hunter."

He slides his hand from my back around to my side, his fingers pressing into my waist. "Just one more thing to add to the list."

"What list?" I look up at him and his cute, dimply grin.

"The list of all the awesome things about you. I might even forgive you for that Parise business."

The hostess calls Wes's name and we follow her to a corner booth not far from the front door. "Enjoy," she says.

"I'm so hungry," Wes says.

I watch as he flips through the menu. I start to think of my own list. Awesome Things About Wes Millard. I'd probably start with his hair and his eyes and his hands and get the superficial stuff out of the way. He's funny. He likes good music. He fully understands my need for daily Foo Fighters. He motivates the hell out of me on the ice, even if he does it in a rude, profane manner. And not to sound crass or porny, but that boy can handle his stick. I like him.

"Dutch? Hello?"

"Mmm, what?"

"What's going on in that head of yours?"

I feel mildly concussed, fuzzy, looking at him across the table from me, those dreamy brown eyes locked on mine.

"I was thinking about your stick," I say.

His eyes go wide, and he lifts his water glass, gulping down several swallows.

I laugh. "Just kidding. I was thinking that when I break a rule, I smash the hell out of it."

"You're killing me. You know that, right?"

I laugh again.

"Do you know what you're going to have?"

"Oh, yeah."

"Let me guess. You always get the same thing."

I laugh. "Yep. Sub gum wonton."

"I have no idea what that is."

When the server comes to take our order, Wes has a lengthy conversation with him about heat levels and noodles versus rice. It's ducking adorable. He settles on Hunan spicy beef, extra spicy.

I'm tearing apart the last cream cheese wonton from our

appetizer to split with Wes when I look up and see Lumberjack Lewis at the counter, paying for a large to-go order.

Shit. What is he doing here? What are the chances that one of our teammates will walk into this restaurant, miles from home, on a weeknight? What are the chances that it's Lumberjack, the guy I turned down and told I didn't date hockey players? And here I am, on a date with a hockey player. With the captain, no less. We are so screwed.

"Shit." I slide over and tuck myself as far into the corner of the booth as I can.

"What's wrong?" Wes asks, popping the wonton into his mouth.

"Uh, nothing?"

"That's convincing. What?"

"OK, whatever you do, don't turn around. And scoot in."

Instead of scooting in, he twists outward to look across the restaurant.

"Wes! Scoot in!"

He turns back to face me, his jaw tight. "No. I am not going to scoot in."

"He'll *see* you!"

He shrugs. "He's going to find out sooner or later, Dutch. Everyone is. To be honest, I can't believe that Jesse hasn't let it slip."

"Let what slip?" Lumberjack now stands at the end of our table, his giant to-go bag in his hand.

"Oh, hey, Jack," I say weakly. "What—what are you doing here?"

He lifts one eyebrow, looks from Wes to me and back to Wes again.

"It's Moo Shu Monday," he says. "My folks and my little sister and I take dinner to my grandma at the senior living place. She likes the moo shu pork."

I swallow down my nerves. "Oh, that's nice."

He tilts his head. "What are you and Millard doing here?"

"We're on a date," Wes says.

"You're fucking kidding me, right?"

"Jack!" I hiss. "There are kids around. Like, right there!"

"What the fu— What's the deal? You two are a thing? A couple?"

"We're—we're just having dinner!" I say. I bite my bottom lip and dare a glance at Wes across the booth. His glare at me could melt the porcelain appetizer plate. His jaw tightens.

"So you're not *dating*?" Lumberjack says. "Five minutes ago, when I saw you holding hands across the table? Were you dating then?"

He saw us holding hands!

"Jack—" I start, but he cuts me off.

"What about that load of bullsh— b.s. you gave me about not dating teammates? Were you banging Millard all along?"

"Hey," Wes says. "That's uncalled for, Jack."

I throw Wes a look. "I'll fight my own battles, thank you."

"Oh, so this is *your* battle?" he tosses back. "Not *ours*? Last I checked, we're here *together*."

"Well, well," Lumberjack says. "Trouble in paradise already?"

"No!" I cry. "I mean—this isn't what it looks like, Jack."

Jack leans in. "I think it's exactly what it looks like, *Dutch*. Looks like the two of you are fooling around behind everyone's backs. I wonder what the rest of the team will think about this. Does Coach know?"

"This—this really isn't a thing, OK?" I say, a shaky plea. "I'd never do anything to jeopardize the team. You won't tell anyone, will you?" I look across the table at Wes for help, my eyes widening, but he says nothing.

Jack shrugs. "You two enjoy yourselves."

That's not an answer. I scoot back across the booth. "Wait, Jack!" I call after him, but he's weaving his way through the busy restaurant and doesn't turn back.

I drop my head into my hands. "I am so screwed."

Wes says nothing, not for a long time. When I look up, he's not looking at me. He's looking at some point off in the distance.

"Really?" he says. He turns back to face me. "'This isn't a thing?'"

"Wes, come on, I didn't know what to do!"

"Because it's kind of a *thing* for me, Dutch. I like you. I like being with you. You're smart and funny and gorgeous and you kick ass on the ice. I don't want to keep my feelings for you a secret. I want to shout them from the fucking rooftops."

"But—but you agreed that we shouldn't tell anyone until after HockeyFest. For the team."

"For the team, my ass. You didn't ask me to do that for the

team. You're so worried that someone will think less of you if you're dating the captain. Like that has anything to do with your talent and hard work. But I kept your secret. I haven't even told Jilly because she loves you so much, I knew she'd brag to all her friends that her brother's dating her idol."

"Way to make me feel worse, Wes!" I cry.

"Why is this suddenly my fault?"

I turn away. I can't look at him right now. I watch the cashier ring up another takeout customer. "I knew this was a bad idea. I never should have broken my rule!"

Long seconds pass and Wes says nothing. When I turn back, his eyes narrow.

"Really?" he says in a low, ominous voice. "You truly believe that? I don't. I believe that you're bigger than your stupid rule. Better than some arbitrary edict that you put in place for no reason."

Arbitrary edict? "Oh, it's a stupid rule, is it? No reason? I've got plenty of reasons. Drama like this, for instance."

"How would you even know, Dutch? What experience did you base this decision on? One date with Sweaty Chevy?"

"What—how—" I sputter.

"Showbiz, that's how."

"How dare you!"

"How dare I what? I didn't even have to ask. He offered it up after I told him you turned Lumberjack down."

"*What?* Why were you even talking to him about that?"

"Because I like you, Dutch. A lot. I thought we already

established that. I agreed to keep this under wraps, but we weren't going to be able to keep it a secret forever. You had to know that."

"Oh my God. He's going to tell everyone."

"So what if he does? I think you're worth it."

"I can't afford to lose my place on the team!"

"Why do you think you would ever lose your place on the team? Dutch, you've got more talent and drive on your worst day than half of those guys. Why can't you see that?"

"You don't know what it's like to worry about this every single day."

"I'm telling you, you don't have to worry!"

I can't believe we're sitting in the middle of the Chinese Lantern, arguing like this. "I should have known we'd never be able to make this work," I say again.

There's a pause before Wes says, "You want to know what else Showbiz said the day he told me about Sweaty Chevy? He said that he wished you'd find a decent guy, because he wanted to see you as happy as he and Morgan are." He lowers his voice. "I thought I could be that guy for you. But I guess you must not feel the same way."

My stomach flips and flips again. He's looking at me with those gorgeous eyes, those eyes so full of disappointment. He looks away when the server comes with our food.

"Can we get that to go, please?" he asks. "Sorry for the inconvenience."

❄ ❄ ❄

The ride back to Halcyon Lake may be the most uncomfortable twenty minutes of my life. My phone buzzes with text messages from my group chat with Cora and Morgan, but I ignore them.

And then: Twitter and Instagram. Notification after notification. Even something from Facebook.

What the hell? I open Twitter.

Five minutes ago, when I saw you holding hands across the table? Were you dating then?

Jack took a fucking picture. It's from a distance, so it's grainy, but anyone with eyes can tell that it's me and Wes, our hands meeting across the table next to the plate of cream cheese wontons. The bright smile on my face could guide ships at sea.

@LumberjackLewis: What do we have here? HL Hawks captain giving one of his players some special 1-on-1 training? @Hot_Sauce_17 @HDelviss

Oh no. That son of a bitch.

I close the app without looking at the dozens of replies, and I don't bother to mention it to Wes. He'll find out soon enough when he checks his own phone.

My phone buzzes—a video call from Cora. I decline and shove the phone into my coat pocket. I can't deal with this right now.

Wes and I don't speak, not one word. What would I say to him? I thought he understood why I needed to keep this close, at least for now. I thought he understood *me*.

Now I'm not even sure that *I* understand me if I was so wrong about Wes.

He pulls into my driveway, puts the truck in park. I can't get out fast enough. I unbuckle my seat belt and reach for the door handle, but he takes hold of my other wrist before I can get out. That familiar electricity *zings* through me and something like a sob fills the small space. My sob.

"Your food?"

"Give it to Jilly. Tell her I said I think she'll love it."

There's a beat before he lets go. "I don't think we should see each other anymore, Dutch," he says, his eyes boring into mine.

"As you wish," I whisper. I open the door and hold my head high as I walk away.

Chapter Thirty-Four

I CRAWL INTO BED WITHOUT BOTHERING TO TAKE OFF MY CLOTHES and read through the text messages from Morgan and Cora—basically Cora alternating between angry rants about being left in the dark and smugly stating that she knew I had the hots for Hot Sauce all along, and Morgan saying she's so sorry that Lumberjack outed us on social media.

She's not even mad that I kept this from her.

Me: I'm a horrible friend and I'm sorry I didn't tell you about my date with Wes. There's more to the story. Can you give me a ride to school tomorrow, Morgan, and I'll tell you everything? Morgan: Of course.
Cora: Yeah, and pick me up first so I can hear the WHOLE STORY. At that point, I'll decide if I forgive you.

She must have already forgiven me, though, because when they arrive the next morning, Cora hands me a travel mug of Peruvian coffee and a paper bag of homemade, deep-fried sweet potato *picarones*.

We eat the donut-shaped pastries while I relay the events of the last few weeks.

"The truth is," I say from the back seat as I watch the cold, dead winter landscape pass by, "I think I fucked up."

"You really like him," Morgan says softly.

"Yeah."

"Well," Cora says, "then we gotta find a way to fix it."

"Yeah," I murmur again, but in my heart, I know it's too late.

I don't get much opportunity to worry about how to fix things with Wes, because most of my day is spent deflecting shots about the photo that's gone as viral as you can get in Halcyon Lake. Like, one hundred and seventy-six likes and forty-two retweets by eight A.M. And a couple hundred likes on Instagram. I don't bother to read the comments. I've got Cora for that, anyway. She's in her element with all this.

Too bad it's me and not some dipshit like Dylan Rogers.

A sampling of remarks from my classmates:

Matt Sullivan: Well, well, well. You and Hot Sauce. I gotta tell you, I didn't see it coming.

Beck Bailey: So, Millard's lighting your lamp? (I reply with a whack on the arm and, "You are such a basketball player. Is that the best you can do?")

T.J. MacMillan: Didn't realize that Hot Sauce was doing a little cherry picking off the ice, too. (Said in front of Carter, who slams him into the locker bank and tells him to fuck off while I roll my eyes.)

Livvie MacMillan: I could have given you some pointers

on keeping a relationship under wraps, Holland. What, you lasted a week without someone finding out? (She has a point.)

Miracle Baxter: You and Wes are the cutest. (I hug her.)

Justin: What the actual fuck, Holland. I tell you *everything*. You're banging Hot Tamale and you don't tell me?

Me: Oh my God, Slacks, I am *not* banging Wes.

Justin: You're calling him Wes now? You traitor.

Me: Justin.

Justin: You hurt my fucking feelings, Princess, and now you're calling him Wes? And did you just call me Justin?

Me: Justin. Come on. We didn't tell *anyone*!

Justin: Carter knew. Jesse knew.

Me: He came to my house to pick me up for dinner! How could they *not* know?

Justin: Still.

Me: Stop being such a drama queen about this.

Justin: Hey! I resemble that remark!

Me: Look, I'm sorry I hurt your feelings. What can I do to make it up to you?

Justin: Oh my God, talk about drama queen. I'm just yanking your chain, Princess. I retweeted that little photo of Lumberjack's and I got about seven hundred new followers, thank you very much.

Me: *Seven hundred?*

Justin: OK, maybe seventeen.

I find Jack in the cafeteria and yank him out of the lunch line. I drag him by his sleeve out of the caf and into the hallway by the gym.

"Take the photo down."

"No fucking way."

"Take it down!"

"No!"

"It's sexual harassment."

He laughs. "Whatever. It's not."

"One-on-one training, Jack? Take it down."

"Is that supposed to scare me? I'm not taking it down." He laughs and walks back into the caf.

Later, I hear from Miracle that an hour-long conversation with his parents, Ziegler, Handshaw, and Giles and a day of in-school suspension convince him.

No matter what anyone says, no matter what those haters on social media posted before Jack took the photo down, only one person's opinion matters.

And he's not talking to me.

My only consolation is that he looks like shit, like maybe he lost as much sleep as I did. His hair looks like it's been through the ice resurfacer a time or two, and his beautiful brown eyes are shadowed and dull.

My consolation and my regret.

Wasting Light: A Blog About Music, Hockey, and Life
February 7 10:14 p.m.
By HardRock_Hockey
Even Peruvian Carbs Can't Help Me Now
Now Spinning: Chris Cornell, *Higher Truth*
(because if I'm going to be miserable,
I might as well be extra fucking miserable.)

Hello, Hard Rockers.

Remember that post a couple of weeks ago where I said I'd never felt heartbreak? Well, I'm feeling it, and it's my own damn fault. I'll just set this here for your enjoyment or your misery or whatever.

HARDROCK_HOCKEY TOP 10: HEARTBREAK

10. "A Heartbreak"—Angus and Julia Stone

9. "It Must Have Been Love"—Roxette (I can't help it.
I love *Pretty Woman*.)

8. "Nothing Compares 2 U"—Sinead O'Connor. And Prince.
And Chris Cornell. My heart breaks even more when
I hear that voice, I miss him in this world so much.

7. "Black"—Pearl Jam

6. "Careless Whisper"—Wham!

5. "November Rain"—GNR

4. "Wicked Game"—Chris Isaak

3. "Fade to Black"—Metallica

2. "I Remember You"—Skid Row

1. "Every Rose Has Its Thorn"—Poison

"Every Rose Has Its Thorn." That's where it began.
And that's where it ends.
\m/
19

Comments turned off for this post.

Hunter: If you won't let me comment on your blog, I'll text you. Take your hits and listen to your sad shit but then get up off your ass and take another fucking shot, Holland. Also. Fucking Roxette?

Chapter Thirty-Five

BREATHE IN.

Breathe out.

Breathe in.

One more game until HockeyFest.

Wes has not spoken to me since he dropped me off Monday night. Not at our game Tuesday night or yesterday's practice. Not one word. Not even to yell at me when I missed a gimme shot on Nik.

He moved to a different table at lunch.

Coach talks to me before the game on Tuesday night.

"Look, I don't need to know any of the details, and honestly? I don't really want to get involved in your personal life, Holland, but you have to understand, this is new for me. I've never really had to worry about my players—uh, getting involved with one another before. We talked about this at the start of the season, and I trust you to make the right decisions. I need to know that, uh, your, um, relationship with Wes isn't going to affect your level of play."

I gritted my teeth. "No worries there, Coach, because Wes and I don't have a relationship. He's my captain. That's all. We're not even friends."

He let out a long exhale. "OK, OK. That's good to hear. I mean, I'm sorry you're not friends. Anymore."

He pulled Wes aside for a private conversation not long after.

Now, I'm on the bench after the national anthem, my knee bouncing up and down. I grab one of the water bottles and shoot water into my mouth.

"You OK?" Carter says on his way out to take the opening face-off. "I mean, I know you're not OK, but are you at least OK enough to play?"

"I'm fine," I murmur. I don't know that it's true. We're in St. Christopher Lake, enemy territory. There's nothing saintly about these goons, some of the scrappiest and most brutish in our conference.

My first shift out, my legs shake with nerves for about five seconds, but there's something about the feel of the ice beneath my blades, the loosening of my joints as I skate, the contentment of being in the right place. My home, even when it's not home ice.

There's something else tonight. Indignation. Determination. The need to prove that I don't need Wes Millard. I don't need him at my lunch table and I don't need him here. I don't need anyone.

I get caught up in a battle for the puck with two SCL players behind their net. One of them jabs his elbow into my side repeatedly. That seems par for the course, but then the other guy gets in my face.

"Slut," he says, and I'm not sure that I heard him right until he opens his mouth again. "Saw that picture of you and Millard. When you're done sucking all the dicks in your own locker room, why don't you come spread your legs for us, bitch? We'd all fuck you."

Holy. Shit.

I shove him as hard as I can and kick the puck out of the fray, up to Luke, who misses it, letting me down yet again. The guy who mouthed off to me takes the puck into our zone, but the dumbass is offside, so we get a whistle. Number 18. Coach motions for a line change, and I get over to the bench as quickly as I can.

"You OK?" Wes asks as he hops over the wall onto the ice.

Fuck. He's ignored me all week, but *now* he decides to talk to me again?

I nod, and he skates off.

"Delviss!" Coach waves me over. "What was that about?"

I take a deep breath and think about what I'm going to say, all the while keeping one eye on the ref, who's about to drop the puck for a face-off. It's not like I don't know that this kind of crap happens every single day to women everywhere, whether they play a sport with men or not. I'm not naive. But before now, I've *never* been spoken to like this, not on the ice, not anywhere. Sure, I'm frequently called a bitch, and there have been plenty of other stupid comments: *Nice tits. You should be a cheerleader because you're too pretty to play with this bunch of ugly losers.* I've had guys ask me for my number. But nothing, nothing like this.

I tell Coach, word for word, as quietly as I can. My voice breaks.

I won't cry.

"No." His eyes narrow and his face flushes in anger. "Not OK. I will not allow that type of behavior."

He calls for a time-out as the ref's about to drop the puck and signals for the three officials to come over. Carter and Wes skate over, too.

Coach waves his hands around and points his finger in the ref's general direction, but I can't hear what he's saying. The ref shakes his head. Coach fires back. This goes on for another minute or two. The officials skate off, and when Coach returns to the bench, he is *not happy*, his mouth pinched tight, his face even redder. He slams the door closed and hits a bottle of water off the ledge into the wall behind us.

"Goddamn it," he mutters.

Wes circles in front of me like he wants to say something, but he must change his mind, because he skates back to the face-off circle. Carter comes over to the bench, leans across the ledge, and grabs my arm. "We're going to take care of this," he says.

"I can fight my own battles," I say. "I'm not going to let some shithead keep me from playing the game that I love."

My comment feels loaded, even to myself.

"We know that you can fight your own battles, Holls," Carter says, "but you don't have to."

I glance at the scoreboard. Three minutes, eleven seconds left in the first period. No score. SCL has the puck and they're putting a lot of pressure on Nik in goal. He catches a shot in his glove and hangs on to it until Showbiz circles back around and picks it up, deftly passing it up the zone to Carter, Carter to Wes, who one-times it straight into the goal before the SCL goalie knows what's happening. The few Hawks fans in the stands cheer, but they're drowned out by booing. The guys celebrate on the ice and then skate to the bench. For scoring the only goal of the game and putting us up before the end of the period, Wes doesn't look pleased. He steps into the bench and slams his stick down.

"Un-fucking-believable," he mutters, and I can only imagine what's going through his head.

Two minutes to go in the period, so I've only got one more shift to skate, if that. I watch the play on the ice, watch for my cue, stand up for the line change. And then I'm out on the ice, and somehow, I've got the puck on a breakaway, and I can hardly breathe I'm so nervous and exhausted and oh my God, if I can score this goal, I'll show that shithead how girls play hockey, and I'm still alone when I skate closer to the net, and I lean in, give my wrist that little flick, and *fuck yes* if that puck doesn't fly right into the top shelf.

I sail past the net to regroup and celebrate with my teammates, but before I can change direction, I'm slammed hard into the boards from the side, and the butt of a stick goes into my ribs, and my breath is gone, and I fall onto the ice.

Chapter Thirty-Six

WHEN YOU'RE DONE SUCKING ALL THE DICKS IN YOUR OWN LOCKER room, why don't you come spread your legs for us, bitch? We'd all fuck you.

I lean over and throw up into a plastic trash can.

The break between periods is over. Coach and Carter have gone back to the game. I'm in the locker room with my parents and SCL's medic, a gentle old-timer who checks me out and tells me I should probably get my ribs X-rayed. At that, my mother runs a hand over her eyes.

"But she just threw up again," Mom says, like I'm not there. "Do you think she has a concussion?"

"I didn't hit my head," I say.

"You collapsed to the ice."

"I couldn't breathe. I didn't black out. I don't have a concussion."

"Carolyn," Dad says and puts a hand on Mom's arm. It's the first thing he's said. He looks shaken.

"But she threw up!"

How do you tell your mother that you're throwing up because you're so disgusted by what someone said to you? Disgusted, and sickened, and so wrecked by it.

"I knew this would happen someday," she mutters, and I glare at her.

"Mom, I'm fine," I tell her.

The old-timer opens his mouth, and I expect him to agree with her. "You're good," he says. "I've been watching you. You didn't deserve to be targeted like that. No one should have to worry about this kind of thing, I don't care who or what you are." He shines a light into my eyes.

"Maybe the coach should let your players in on that bit of common sense," I mumble.

He shakes his head. "I hate to say it, and you didn't hear it from me, but Coach Olson isn't all that well-versed in common sense or manners himself."

"What did that boy say to you, Holland?" Mom asks.

"Can we talk about it later and let—" I squint to read his badge. "Dr. Schmidt here finish up." Good, he's an actual doctor. That might alleviate my mother's worry.

"No signs of a concussion," Dr. Schmidt says. "But keep an eye on her. Ribs seemed bruised but nothing more. Take her to the doctor if the pain worsens or she has any trouble breathing."

"Can I get back out there?" I ask.

"Absolutely not." Dr. Schmidt chuckles. "You're a tough little nut, aren't you? You can watch the rest of the game with your folks and take the day off tomorrow, OK? No skating. Lots of rest. You should be fine for Saturday."

I groan. "But—"

"Don't even think about arguing with him," Mom warns.

"You've got a bright future ahead of you, Holland," Dr. Schmidt says. "But tonight, you take care of yourself so that you're able to play the HockeyFest game. I'm thinking about driving up to see it for myself."

I drop my head into my hands and wipe away the hot tears.

I get dressed, and my dad, who's waiting outside the locker room, insists on taking my gear bag out to the truck. "You're riding home with us, and it's not up for negotiation."

I shrug, too tired to argue. "OK."

"Mom's up in the visitors' section with the other parents," he says. "I'll meet you there."

That I'll negotiate.

"No, I'd rather watch down at the glass. Plus, standing is more comfortable."

"You want some company?"

I shake my head. I follow him down the hall; he keeps going into the lobby and I turn for the rink. I find an area against the plexiglass where there are only a handful of young kids, no one who's going to bother me or give me any grief.

My stomach twists with revulsion and disgust every time I think of what number 18 said to me, and that's worse than the pain in my ribs. I try to follow the puck, but every time he's out on the ice, I zero in on number 18 instead. He's chippy and aggressive. He pulls a couple of penalties, but mostly, the refs don't call him on his dirty play.

I follow Wes when he's on the ice, too. Always Wes. There's a scuffle in my corner of the rink and when the ref blows his whistle, Wes notices me on the other side of the glass. He stares for a long second, his face stony, unfeeling.

Shit.

I miss him.

He looks away first, skates over to the bench.

The second period ends. I could use some coffee.

I'm surprised when Rieland walks up to me at the concessions counter as I'm pouring sugar and cream into my cup. The only straws they have are the little black ones for stirring, so this should be interesting.

"I've been looking for you," she says.

"What are you doing here? I don't think I've ever seen you at an away game before."

"I live here," she says.

"You live in Saint Christopher Lake?"

"I have to live somewhere, don't I?"

"I guess."

"Are you OK? That was a nasty hit."

I shrug. "I guess."

"Come on," she says, "I don't want to miss the third."

I follow her up to an empty corner of the visitors' section. We watch the play on the ice for a few minutes before she says anything else.

"That guy targeted you, didn't he?"

No sense in denying it. "Yep."

"Was he hassling you before the hit?"

"Yeah. He said some things."

"Is verbal harassment pretty common?"

"I guess. I mean, guys say stuff to anybody, right? But I know that players have said things to me because I'm a girl. I get called a bitch a lot. Tonight was the worst, though."

"What did he say?"

I chew on my bottom lip, debating whether I should tell.

"Holland?"

"He told me that when I was finished sucking my teammates' dicks, I should come over and spread my legs for his team."

If Rieland is surprised or shocked by this, she doesn't show it. "How do you feel about that?"

"I feel like I'm going to throw up again."

She sighs. "Holland, I'm sorry. You told Coach Giles?"

"He called a time-out and told the refs, but they didn't do anything."

"Has anyone ever said anything like that to you before?"

"Not that bad. Unless you count the shit my own teammate pulled."

"You mean the picture of you and Wes? The tweet?"

"Yeah." I swallow the heavy lump in my throat.

"I didn't see the photo before it was deleted, but . . . staff members were made aware of a cyberbullying issue."

Well, that's fantastic.

"I'll bet when you decided to be an English teacher, you

never imagined you'd be having this kind of conversation with a student, huh, Rieland?" I try to laugh, but it's hollow.

"More than anything, I wish we lived in a world where this kind of conversation wasn't necessary."

"Well, it's a man's world, isn't it?"

Rieland nods. "Can't disagree there. Holland, about the photo . . . Are you involved with Wes?"

My cheeks heat; I feel pools of saliva gathering in the back corners of my mouth. I take a few deep breaths. I am *not* going to puke.

"Not anymore," I finally whisper. "Does it matter?" I know exactly where she's going with this, but I don't want to hear it.

"It might, especially after Jack posted that photo. Coach Giles needs to take this to Mr. Handshaw so that the school can file a formal complaint against the player who harassed you tonight. I'll help however I can. This isn't OK. Not the hit, not the comments, none of it. I don't buy for one minute that boys will be boys. We can't let this kind of behavior continue. Don't let that guy get away with this."

I nod and try to swallow down the panicky feeling. "You don't believe what he said, do you? That I'm—uh, sleeping my way through the locker room?"

"No, I don't believe that. But you should be prepared to be asked that question. Especially after the photo."

"This is such bullshit!" I mumble.

"Yeah, it's bullshit," she agrees. "But it happened."

I drop my head into my hands. Damn damn damn for breaking my own rule.

But then again, fuck that. I didn't have sex with Wes or anyone else for that matter, and even if I had, that guy had no right to say those things to me. What I do with my body and who I choose to do it with, teammate or not, is no one's business but my own.

"Do you feel safe?" Rieland asks after a moment.

I lift my head and look at her. Her eyes are gentle. "What do you mean?"

"Do you feel like someone might hurt you again, on or off the ice?"

I don't know what I feel besides numb, discouraged, disappointed in the world. I feel the weight of self-doubt again.

"That's a chance I take every time I step out onto the ice. Hockey's a contact sport. You know that. Half the time the only way these guys even know they're playing against a girl is my ponytail. But if you're asking me if I think that the guy who mouthed off to me is going to sexually assault me, no. Or any opponent. Or any teammate, for that matter."

"Promise me, though, that if you feel like you're in a situation that's gotten too intense, you'll get yourself out of it. Ask for help if you need it."

I nod.

"And Holland?"

"Yeah?"

"You will get through this."

I nod again. The only way out is through.

Chapter Thirty-Seven

DAD FINDS ME WITH A MINUTE LEFT ON THE CLOCK.

"Come on," he says. "I let Coach Giles know you're coming home with us."

After a long, mostly silent drive back to Halcyon Lake, Mom does what she does best. She brings me a plate of cookies and a cup of her organic healing tea, a blend of lemon and ginger that she swears can cure any ailment. She makes up my bed with lots of extra pillows and the faux fur "comfort" throw with lavender sewn into the binding that she gave me for Christmas.

"What else can I bring you?" she asks. "Another ibuprofen?"

I shake my head. "Mom, I'm not in that much pain."

She hands me my phone. "Text me if you need anything else."

I nod and set the phone on the bedside table. I've reassured Morgan and Cora that I'm fine, called Hunter. There's no one else I need to talk to tonight.

My ribs and my head ache, but number 18's words, the snarl, the nastiness of them, bring tears to my eyes, and once the tears start, I'm too tired to fight them. I cry for long minutes, and after a while, Mom comes into my room, sits down next to me on the bed, pulls me close. I cry into her lap. I can't remember the last time I let myself cry like this.

"Oh, sweetheart," she says in that soothing way of hers, stroking my hair. "Is it the pain?"

I shake my head.

"I'm sorry this has gotten so hard for you," she says. "You are such a strong girl, Holland, and I'm so proud of you. You've always been brave and stood up to anyone who said you weren't good enough to play with the boys. Suddenly, you're getting all this attention because you're *better* than a lot of those boys, and it's got to hurt."

"That's just it!" I wail. "Why do I have to be *good enough* to play with the boys? Why can't I just be *good*? I'm a great hockey player. It shouldn't matter if my teammates are male or female or whatever. I play hockey, and I'm good at it. That should be enough."

She sighs, and it's a deep, deeply felt exhale. "You're right, that should be enough. But it's not, and you know it, and it's going to be a long time before it is enough. And until then, you'll have to put up with people saying that the school district and Coach Giles made a mistake letting you play on the boys' team. We heard it tonight in the stands after that hit. That it's too dangerous for a girl to play with boys."

"But anybody could have taken that exact hit and ended up with the exact injury! Male or female!" I cry.

"True. Not everyone sees it that way, though. You know, Dad and I are so proud of you and the boys. You're excellent hockey players, but you know what else? You're even better human beings."

I'm not feeling like such an excellent human being. I sniffle.

"Holland? Is there something else going on?"

I don't feel like telling her what happened with Wes, not with him helping out at her Hotdish Feed tomorrow night. And besides, I can't let myself cry anymore.

"I . . . I'm disappointed with a lot of things. People. That's all."

"Yes, people can be disappointing. Relationships are hard." She stands up and tucks a loose strand of my hair behind my ear. "I noticed that you didn't sit by Wes during the JV game tonight."

I shake my head. "Mom . . . can we talk about something else?"

"OK. Debbie cut my hair yesterday," she says and smiles. Wes's mom. "And?"

"She said that she enjoyed having the three of you over during the storm. She's so happy you and Wes have gotten together. And she wanted me to tell you that Tallie misses you and hopes you'll visit again soon."

My heart soars and crash-lands in the field of my shredded dignity.

"Well, Tallie is going to be very disappointed." I sniffle again.

Mom reaches out and strokes my cheek. "He can't take his eyes off you when you're on the ice." She stands and walks to the door. "Call me if you need anything."

My ribs are sore; my eyes are puffy and achy from crying. I can't find a comfortable position to sleep.

Worse than any of that is the heaviness in my heart.

I turn on the Power Loon and sigh with relief that they're

not playing "Every Rose Has Its Thorn" or "Love Song." But oh, God. It's even worse. Def Leppard, "Too Late for Love."

My phone buzzes and somehow, I know it's Wes. Is he listening, too?

Wes: I know I'm probably the last person you want to talk to but please let me know you're OK

I don't respond for a long time. Not through "The Boys of Summer" or "Roadhouse Blues" or "Rock You Like a Hurricane."

Finally, during Van Halen's "I'll Wait," I tap out: **I'm OK** and switch my phone off. "I miss you," I whisper.

I lie in bed, listening to the Power Loon and trying to sort out everything that's happened in the last few days.

Nothing makes sense.

I dig around in the drawer of my bedside table until I find a pen and the cream-colored, leather-bound journal Hunter gave me for Christmas. The cover is stamped with gold foil letters in fancy script: FULL OF IDEAS, the word "ideas" crossed out and replaced with bold black: SHIT. I open it and trace the inscription on the inside cover. *To Holland—write your heart out.*

And I start to write. I write about my first varsity game, my love for the sport, my respect for it. I write about the haters. I write about number 18 and the hit, my sore ribs, my wounded pride. I write about Big Donnie, how even though Hunter took down his letter, in my low moments, the words swirl around me like ghosts: *I, for one, will feel no sympathy for Ms. Delviss should something unfortunate occur because of her presence on the team.*

I write about my teammates, my dedication to the team, our faith in one another.

I write about my captain: *Somewhere in all of this, I fell in love with Wes Millard.*

Chapter Thirty-Eight

I AM NOT A BYSTANDER. I DON'T LIKE TO SIT BY AND WATCH WHILE my teammates run drills and scrimmages. I'm itching to get out on the ice, but instead, I'm stuck in the stands, my eyes constantly drifting back to Wes. Damn damn damn.

"Hey, Holly Hotpants," Justin calls up to me. "You a puck bunny now?"

I *hate* being called Holly Hotpants, hockey slang for a cute girl in the stands. Someday when I have a free second, I'm going to embroider "These are not your hotpants" on the back pocket of my favorite jeans.

I give Justin the finger.

After a while, the irritation gets to be too much, so I pull out my FULL OF SHIT notebook and continue writing what I started last night. I may not be able to "evoke emotion" for the *Jack Pine*, but I sure as shit can for *Wasting Light*.

I don't look up again until I hear Carter calling for me.

"Hey, Holls, come down on the ice. Coach wants to talk about tomorrow."

I grab my backpack and make my way down to the ice, shuffling in my winter boots to the bench. Justin skates over, I put my hands on either side of his waist, and he tows me the rest of the way.

"Even though we won, I don't have to tell you that last night's game was a tough one," Coach says. "Especially for Holland. Hopefully, with a day off today, she'll be rested and ready to go tomorrow afternoon. Sounds like quite a few of you are volunteering at the sponsor dinner tonight, so I'll see you there. Remember, everyone needs to be at the B tent in the Hole parking lot at one o'clock tomorrow, no later. Don't forget your gear. That's all I got."

The guys skate off, and the managers gather up the water bottles. Wes is the first to leave the ice, pulling off his gloves as he skates toward the door.

"Don't look so glum, Princess," Justin says as he taxis me across the ice. "Hot and Spicy will come around."

He deposits me at the door and walks off toward the locker room.

I move out to the lobby to wait for Carter. I pace. Back and forth. Breathe in. Breathe out. I stop in front of the picture of the 1993 State Championship team, my dad front and center, a huge grin on his face, his hair floppy and long. He loves this game, this hockey life. He must have been thrilled when all his kids fell in love with the game, too, and turned out to be pretty damn good.

I love it. I love playing, and it kills me that there are people who wanted to take that away from me. When it's time for me to leave the game, I'll leave on my own terms, in my own time.

"Holls."

I turn to see Carter, his gear bag slung over his shoulder. He's the first one out of the locker room. "You ready?"

He moves toward the door, but I hesitate. He turns around when he realizes I'm not following him.

"What?" he asks.

I look at the door that leads into the arena. I want to see Wes so much it's physical.

"What's wrong? Mom's waiting for us at City Hall."

I shake my head. "Nothing. I'm coming."

Carter throws his gear into the back of the Suburban and fires up the old workhorse. They're a lot alike, this boy and his truck. That thought leads to thoughts of another boy and another truck, and I think about Wes, and the silence on our ride home from the Chinese Lantern, the feel of his fingers around my wrist, the echo of his words.

I don't think we should see each other anymore.

Chapter Thirty-Nine

MOM PREPPED FOR THE HOTDISH FEED ALL WEEK AND SPENT MOST of today in the commercial kitchen at City Hall. She's got a lot of mouths to feed tonight: fifty-three sponsors and guests, eight committee members, and fourteen volunteer servers, all hockey players, including me, Carter, Jesse, Wes, Showbiz, even Livvie. We're dressed in black pants, white button-down shirts, and black vests Mom rented from Uniforms & More. And aprons. Black aprons tied around our waists.

We're adorable.

Ducking adorable.

Maybe a little too adorable, I think, when I find Carter and Livvie making out in the hallway behind the kitchen. I clear my throat to get their attention and they jump apart. Livvie smooths her hair and Carter adjusts his vest.

Liv smiles at me (a first), kisses Carter on the cheek, and says, "Don't tell your mom you busted us, Holland. She'll put us to work doing dishes. I need to go redo my lipstick."

"Don't worry," I say. "I'm the last person who'll rat you out."

She slips off toward the restrooms.

"Hey." I grab Carter's sleeve as he starts to walk back into

the kitchen. "Why didn't you and Liv tell anyone you were seeing each other? Were you afraid of backlash?"

"What backlash? I wanted to keep her to myself for a little
while," Carter says. "Simple as that."

I should be so lucky, for a little simplicity.

Mom gathers us in the kitchen for assignments before the
guests arrive.

"For the most part, you'll either help serve at the buffet
line or the dessert table, refill waters, clear plates. I'll need
one or two back in the kitchen with me to switch out pans on
the buffet. They'll be heavy. Holland, you're at the check-in
table, and I'll need one more volunteer to help her out up
there. Once everyone's checked in, you'll be selling tickets to
the upcoming Rotary pancake breakfast."

"What? You're not going to make me sit at a table all
night, are you?"

"Doctor's orders. You should be at home resting, not bus-
sing dishes."

"Mom."

She ignores me. "Pair up, kids, and find a workstation.
Our guests will be arriving soon."

I stomp up to the registration table and slump down in
one of the chairs. Doing nothing is exhausting. I'm used to
one or two practices a day, and most days, my own drills out
on the ice or in the basement. Today I've *sat*. The most action
I saw was when Justin towed me across the ice.

Only one thing . . . er . . . person could make this situation worse, and he sits down next to me as the first guests come in.

"Hey, Coach. Mrs. Giles," Wes says.

"Hey, Wes," Mrs. Giles says. "Holland, how are you feeling today?"

"Fine, thanks."

"Will you be ready to play tomorrow?"

"Absolutely," I say. "Won't let a stick to the ribs stop me."

"Can't keep our Holland down," Coach agrees.

Wes takes their tickets and hands them to me as they walk away. "Carolyn says to check off names on this spreadsheet as guests arrive. Here, see?"

"I'm not blind," I snap. "Why are you here? Doesn't Mom need some brawny guys in the kitchen to help with the roasters?"

"I volunteered to sit with your crabby ass. Nobody else would do it."

"How gallant of you."

Guests start to stream in. Wes takes tickets and I check off names. The enticing aroma of seven kinds of hotdish wafts around me and my stomach growls.

"Didn't you eat?" Wes asks between tickets.

"I ate." I haven't, really, since those cream cheese wontons on Monday night at the Lantern before Lumberjack showed up. Despite my body's obvious need for fuel, even the thought of my mom's chicken and wild rice hotdish turns my stomach.

Once all the sponsors and committee members have

arrived and I've checked off the last name on the spreadsheet, there's nothing to do but wait and see if anyone wants to buy a ticket to the pancake breakfast. It's going to be a long night.

"Why don't you go see if they need any help in the kitchen?" I say after a few endless, empty minutes.

"No."

"It's pointless for us both to sit here and do nothing."

"I said no."

"I'd do it if I could," I say. "Help in the kitchen, I mean. Or at the very least help clear tables. I can't stand this. I can't stand not moving."

"Stop complaining."

As crappy as this conversation makes me feel, I'll take fighting with Wes over nothing with Wes.

"Why are you being so rude?"

He turns to stare me down. "Because being around you is hard, Dutch, and so maybe I've built up a way to defend myself."

"Like a porcupine with thirty thousand quills?" I ask. "Or maybe a skunk?"

"You're impossible."

"Like looking in a mirror." My voice cracks.

I pull out my phone and pretend to be very interested in my Instagram feed.

"Dutch," he says quietly, "I saw your blog post, the, uh, shit, the heartbreak one? Everything that's happened . . . it's not just your fault, Dutch."

I refuse to look at him.

He goes on. "I didn't want to keep things between us a secret, but I know that none of this has been easy for you. And I'm sorry that things have been so hard. And, uh, I'm sorry that I made things worse."

My heart cracks again, and horrible, hot, stinging drops of water pour out of my eyes. I swipe at them and sniffle.

"Hey," he says as he reaches across the space between us and touches my arm with one finger. One finger and I'm through the roof with sensation. "Are you crying?"

I stand so quickly, I knock the chair over. "No, absolutely not."

The long, spacious ladies' room at City Hall features one entire wall of full-length mirrors and a couple of padded benches. Pretty high-class for a small-town municipal building in the Lakes Country, but they host a lot of wedding receptions for the folks who can't afford one of the big resorts.

The only place I don't see my puffy, ragged reflection is when I'm in a stall, but I can't stay in here forever. When I finally come out, Livvie's sitting on one of the benches.

"Uh, hi?" I wash my hands and toss the paper towel into the bin near the door. Nothin' but net.

"Hi," she says. "You OK?"

"Are you waiting for me?"

"Yes."

"Why?"

"Because I'm worried about you. Wes told Carter that you started crying. Are your ribs bothering you? Your head?"

"I didn't hit my head!"

"Geez, sorry."

"Did my mother send you in?"

"No."

"Did Carter?"

"No, Holland. I thought up the idea all by myself. Why is that so hard to believe?"

I sigh and sit down next to her.

"Sometimes I get the vibe that you're not my biggest fan."

She nudges me with her shoulder. "You set the bar pretty high, Holland."

"*I* set the bar, Ms. Captain-slash-Salutatorian-slash-Editor?"

"*Co*-editor," she says.

"Still."

I watch her reflection shrug in the mirror across from us. "Those things were next steps in the natural progression of things, I guess. I haven't had to work very hard."

"Salutatorian? What?"

"I've always had good grades. One day my counselor called me into his office and told me where I stood. That's all."

I laugh. "That's all, huh? So why not shoot for number one?"

"A question my parents ask every day."

"You'd think they'd be grateful, what with T.J.'s stellar academic record."

"Yeah," she agrees. "He's lucky to make eligibility after that whole chemistry fiasco."

"I don't want to know," I say, and laugh.

"Seriously, Holland, you OK?"

I shrug. "I guess."

"You're under a lot of pressure right now. You must be so nervous for tomorrow."

"Aren't you? I mean, you've got the morning game, right?"

"Who's going to come to a game at eight A.M. to watch a girls' high school hockey team with a record like ours, besides Carter because I told him he has to?"

"What are you talking about? This is HockeyFest. The whole town is going to be there!" Note to self: Get up early to go to the game with Carter.

"Tomorrow's your day to shine, Holland. You've earned it. You've worked hard for your success."

I don't feel very successful right now. Sure, maybe I'm creeping up on the team's points leaders, and yeah, I've got ten-year-old girls dyeing stripes into their hair, but I cried. In front of Wes. And now Livvie.

Like Livvie can read my mind, she says, "It's OK to show your feelings, Holland. You can do Coach's deep breathing exercise all day long, but sometimes, you just have to cry."

"Oh, really? When's the last time you cried?"

She laughs. "Oh, I don't know, every time we go to print? Or the time Jo posted that ridiculous editorial about too much snow in the parking lot? Rieland reamed me out for letting that one through."

"That post got incredible engagement."

She laughs again. "Well, what do you know. You do see the glass half full."

"Hey, I wouldn't go that far."

We sit in silence for a minute. This isn't bad. I've always been intimidated by Liv, but tonight, she seems almost human.

"So, you and Wes, huh?" she asks.

I shake my head and another fat teardrop lands on my apron. "I fucked that up, too. You said so yourself: I should have come to you for advice."

"Can I give you some now?"

"Be my guest."

"Don't give up on this. All your life, you've had to fight for what you want. Don't stop now."

I let that one sink in. She's got a point.

"Hey, Liv?"

"Yeah?"

"Thanks."

"Any time. Just so you know, I'm going to be around a lot. I kinda like your brother."

"I kinda got that impression a couple of hours ago."

"One more thing, for what it's worth." She pauses. "Anybody who thinks you aren't good enough to play on the boys' team is a complete idiot. You deserve that spot, and don't let anyone tell you differently."

With that, Livvie stands up and leaves me and my puffy reflection in the ladies' room.

I take a deep breath. I'm going to fight for what I want.

I want Wes.

When I return to the registration table, Wes and the cash-box are gone and Mom's collecting the paperwork. Only a few guests remain. My teammates are clearing tables and folding up chairs.

"Dad's taking you home, Holland," Mom says while she clips the papers together. "The boys and I will be along soon, but you need your rest."

"I'm fine," I tell her. I glance around the room.

Mom puts her hand on my arm. "Wes had to go, honey."

I shake my head.

I'm too late.

Wasting Light: A Blog About Music, Hockey, and Life

February 9 11:33 p.m.

By HardRock_Hockey

Refuse to Lose. Whatever it Takes.

Now spinning: Three Days Grace, *Outsider*

Hello, Hard Rockers.

Refuse to lose. Whatever it takes.

That's my team's motto. We're a hardworking, competitive, driven team from the middle of nowhere. We don't come from a big school with lots of money. We've worked hard—as a team—to get to where we are. Tomorrow, our game will be televised in Minnesota and across much of the upper Midwest. For the first time in our town—I mean, probably ever—college and NHL scouts will sit in the stands, watching me and my teammates.

I work my ass off for this team, for this town.

So it pisses me off when someone tells me that, because I'm female, I'm creating a distraction for the boys.

Or that I'm taking the rightful place of a male player.

Or that I could get hurt.

Or any of the other reasons that people have come up with.

I did some stupid things because I didn't want to give anyone another reason to say I shouldn't be on the team.

I hurt friends who've supported me and loved me and for that, I'm sorry.

The things I worried about happening happened. I got

hurt—physically and emotionally. But I survived the shit that came down. In the grand scheme of things, that shit doesn't matter so much. You know what matters? The people you love and who love you back and make every day better and send you videos that make you laugh. I've missed those videos, 17. I miss you.

I'm going to make this better. Somehow. I'm not giving up on you. I'm not giving up on us.

\m/

19

Comments

12:02 a.m.

You are such a sap. I've known it all along. He's a good one. #riskittogetthebiscuit

Hunter_Not_The_Hunted

1:13 a.m.

Go for it! I hope I'm lucky enough to get a girl like you someday. What channel will your game be on? Can I get it in SoCal?

MetalManiac (Jim)

1:59 a.m.

This is exactly what I needed to hear. I play hockey on a boys' team in British Columbia and I've been taking a lot of heat lately. Can I email you?

Reese Camden

Chapter Forty

I DON'T SLEEP MUCH, TOO KEYED UP, TOO ANTSY. SO I TAKE IT ALL
to the ice. I flip the barn lights on and head down the hill. It's
a few minutes after five A.M. I don't set up the pylons or even
drag the net out from the shore. I've got my stick and a battered puck and the ice. It's all I need.

The rink is fairly clear of snow, so I don't bother to shovel
or sweep. My muscles ache at first as I skate, but soon, a rush
of warmth and energy fuels me, propels me, loosens me.
Unties the knots of fear and uncertainty that have hardened
in me. The mess I made with Wes. The anger at Lumberjack
and number 18.

I'm bruised, but I'm not broken.

They might knock me down, but they will not, cannot,
knock me out.

I'm still in this game. All in.

Refuse to lose. Whatever it takes.

My breath freezes into a wispy fog and my ribs ache with
the cold and the movement. I can't remember the last time
I missed a practice, the last day I didn't do something to
improve my game. Even in summer, I'm shooting pucks nearly
every day, in the basement or at the dryland facility in town.

This feels right. The cold air on my cheeks, my blades

solid beneath me, the ice a bit rough in spots. This feels like those early days. I remember the first time that Dad slipped a pair of Carter's old skates onto my feet and held my hand as I tottered from the bench to the frozen lake, right before my fourth birthday. I'd wanted this so badly. I'd wanted to fly across the ice like my big brother Hunter, who had a couple of years on me and could already control the puck better than kids twice his age.

Hunter's the magic. Carter, the powerhouse. Jesse, the diva.

I've always been *the girl*.

Anger wells up inside me again, so I skate hard, back and forth across the rink. I peel the ice with my stops, sending big sprays of ice up, then turn around and do it again.

I am more than *the girl*.

I am the blade and the ice.

I am the puck and the net.

I am the forward motion and the stop.

I am energy. I am intensity.

I am determination and I am promise.

I am nothing you can take.

I am everything.

Everything.

All this time, I've skated for someone else. I've worked hard for someone else, to prove that I'm good enough, that I won't let anyone down. Every time I've stepped out on the ice, I've busted my ass to prove that putting me on that team wasn't a mistake. I've worked so hard to not disappoint my teammates, my coaches, my parents, even grumpy old-timers like Pete and George, but in the end, I've ended up disappointing myself.

No more.

Today, I'm playing for myself.

Today, I trust myself.

Today, I know I'm enough.

When my legs are shaking with exertion and exhaustion, I stop, skate to the goal where I've left a water bottle, and drink, my eyes closed against the early-morning light.

When I open them again, Wes is here. Standing on the snowy shoreline in jeans and his team jacket, a pair of skates over his shoulder, holding a battered stick.

I blink. My blood sugar must be low. I'm seeing things. I blink again. He's still there.

"Mind if I join you?" Without waiting for an answer, he sits down on the bench at the edge of the lake, kicks off his boots, and laces up his skates.

"I don't mind."

No, I don't mind. I don't know why Wes Millard is in my backyard at six o'clock on a Saturday morning, but I'm willing to see how this plays out.

We don't talk at first. We both sort of lazily skate around, pass the puck back and forth. After a while, he says, "You OK? Ribs?"

"Ribs are good."

"Good. How's your head?"

"My head's fine. My head wasn't ever not fine."

Well, that's debatable, I guess. I haven't exactly made the best decisions lately.

And please don't ask about my heart.

"Wes?" I stop skating.

"Yeah?" He stops, too, facing me, inches from me. I can feel his breath on my cold cheeks. Cinnamon. He's eating Fireballs at this hour?

"Wes," I start, then pause and suck in a breath. "Look, I owe you an apology."

"No." He holds up his hand to stop me from continuing. "I'm the one who should apologize. And now you're hurt. Shit."

"No, no, no. That's not your fault. Don't apologize for something that was out of your control. But hear me out, OK? Wes, I'm sorry. You've been so supportive, and I don't know what I would do without your encouragement and belief in me. You make me want to do better. For myself, for the team. For you. I can't thank you enough for that. I've been—I've been a little insecure lately, OK, maybe for, like, the last two years, and I thought I was doing the right thing by not letting anyone in. But the truth is, I want to let you in. And I want people to know that I want to let you in."

The corners of his mouth turn up and I can tell he's fighting it. He moves a millimeter closer to me. "That's a mouthful. Last night at the Hotdish Feed—I didn't mean to make you cry. Are you really OK?"

I take a deep breath, happy that the pain in my ribs has lessened to a dull ache. "I'm so much better now that I'm with you."

"Are you with me, Dutch?" he asks. Closer. Closer.

"If that's OK with you, then yeah, I'm with you."

"That is more than OK."

I grin. God, it feels like the first time I've smiled in days. "I'm glad we cleared that up. Now what?"

"I'm not giving up on us, either," he says. "So now we kiss and make up if that's OK with you."

"More than OK." I slip my arms around his waist. "Wait. You read my blog post? Is that why you're here?"

He leans down and smiles. Uh, he's so close! Why aren't we kissing right now?

"You smell like a Fireball," I whisper.

He pulls me in close. "Wanna see if I taste like one, too?" he asks, and *hell, yes*, I do, and he kisses me. And it's sweet (and spicy) and gentle and electrifying and *everything*.

"I've really missed you and your glam metal text messages," I murmur, and he kisses me harder.

He pulls away abruptly and looks at me with a gleam in his eye. "You're my favorite, Dutch," he says, and I've never been happier to hear my name.

"Never stop calling me that."

"You know I love you, right?"

Whoawhoawhoawhoa.

He loves me. My heart bursts.

"You do?"

"Yeah. I love you, Dutch. I have to admit, love was the last thing I expected to find in some run-down arena in Podunk, Minnesota."

"Hey, our arena isn't run-down. 'Podunk.' How insulting. Halcyon Lake has *two* dollar stores. That's not Podunk."

Wes laughs. "You know, I was so bitter about coming here. I mean, you can put hockey in any town, but that doesn't make it a hockey town. But the first day we were here, I went to the arena, and even though it was August and ninety degrees and humid, I walked through those doors and it was like something out of a movie. I *knew*. I *felt* it. This was my new home. Archie was there, and he introduced me to T.J. and Nik, who were on the ice messing around. Having *fun*. And you know, I couldn't remember the last time hockey had felt fun for me. Two days later, I met you, and *that* sealed the deal."

I pull away and look up at him, his beautiful brown eyes sparkling. "Sealed the deal?"

"I knew I was in the right place. You know, T.J. had told me all about you."

"Oh, ha, I'm sure he was super flattering and sexist."

He shrugs. "It is T.J., after all. But he told me how good you were and how excited he was for you to try out for varsity."

"T.J. *Macks*? *Our* T.J. said all this?"

"The very one."

"Huh."

"Yeah. But he'd only told me what an amazing hockey player you were. He neglected to tell me that you're smart and funny, or how you love glam metal and grunge, or that you're gorgeous."

I look down, embarrassed, but he reaches his fingers under my chin and pulls me back up. "Don't look away, Dutch. Don't be embarrassed. It's all true. I wasn't expecting you. You walked into the ice cream shop and I gave you a hard time and you dished it right back. It didn't take long after that to realize that I would do whatever it took to win your heart."

I laugh. "Well, holy shit, you've got a funny way of trying to win a girl's heart!"

"I'm your captain, aren't I? I'm supposed to challenge you. I'm supposed to piss you off to get you to work harder to prove me wrong."

"That's your tactic, huh?"

"Yeah. Does it work?"

"God, yes." I laugh. "You piss me off every single day."

"And look how much you've improved."

"That's enough out of you," I say, and I press my mouth against his.

The problem with making out on the middle of a frozen lake is that you're making out in the middle of a frozen lake. On skates! (We're obviously very talented.) After a few minutes of increasingly intense and somewhat off-balance kissing, I pull away.

"Wes," I say as I catch my breath. "We have to stop."

"Oh, shit, is it your ribs?"

"No, it's not that. We—we have to stop."

"Oh, OK." He sounds taken aback. "I'm sorry, it seemed like you were enjoying—"

I interrupt. "Oh, trust me, I was. I am. But the girls play at eight, and we need to be there."

He leans in for one more kiss, the lightest touch. "As you wish."

Chapter Forty-One

THE HOLE HAS BEEN TRANSFORMED.

The old school parking lot has been cordoned off and is filled with food vendors, a merch tent, trucks and equipment from the TV station. Most people are parking at the Methodist Church or the hardware store downtown and taking shuttles to the Hole. Hockey fanatics from around the area have flooded the town. It feels like summer, when the place is overrun with tourists.

The girls win their game five–zip and that sets the tone for the rest of the day. The entire varsity and JV boys' teams showed up to cheer them on, thanks to a mildly threatening group text from Carter. My appetite's finally back, so I set a goal for myself to try something from every food truck before we have to meet the rest of the team. Well, every food truck except for Third Street Rental's. Holding a grudge is one of my many talents.

Wes has other ideas, though. He tugs me over to say hi to Rollie and George and, coincidentally, Pete from the hardware store, who's setting up another space heater between their food truck and the taco truck.

"No." I pout.

"Yes." He grins.

He makes small talk, but I hang back, holding his hand, until Pete notices me and offers a gruff hello.

"Hi," I say.

Pete waves his hand around. "Good job."

I tilt my head. "What do you mean?"

"Good job. On that interview."

George coughs. "Rollie and Wes came up with a new flavor this week. Sold out already but we saved you a bag."

Rollie hands me the plastic bag of popcorn, white corn with a light frosted coating. I read the label: NUMBER 19 DUTCH APPLE PIE.

I look from a smiling Rollie to George and his grimace that might be a smile to Wes, whose grin could light up this rink at night. He squeezes my hand.

"You're sneaky," I tell him.

"I had some extra time on my hands since I wasn't glam texting you."

"Thanks for sponsoring HockeyFest," I tell the old-timers. "And always being so supportive of youth hockey. You should really consider sponsoring the girls' teams, too."

Wes bursts out laughing. "Try your popcorn," he says as he tugs me back into the crowd.

We run into Rieland in front of the merch tent. She's wearing a HockeyFest Minnesota hoodie, jeans, duck boots, and a Hawks stocking cap with a pom-pom like mine.

"Hey, Wes, Holland," she says. "I was hoping to see you today. How're the ribs?"

"Much better. I'm actually excited to see you, too," I say and then clamp my mouth shut. "Oh, that came out wrong. Sorry."

She laughs.

"I think I've got a way to fix my article," I tell her in a rush. "Well, it's more of an editorial piece to go along with the article. And the best part is that I'm excited to write it."

"Good! I'm glad to hear it. But before you can tackle that challenge, you've got to go out there and show everyone what you've got." She waves her hand toward the stone wall surrounding the Hole. "Right?"

She gets me. "Right," I say.

"But we do go to print Wednesday."

Ha. "Thanks. For everything."

"Anytime, Holland. See ya, Wes. Good luck out there." She turns and goes into the merch tent.

"You and Rieland have a lot in common," I tell him. "This irritating need for perfection. Always so demanding."

"You want me to start listing off all the things that are perfect about you?" Wes says.

"Yes, please."

My stomach growls as we walk past a food truck selling deep-fried goodness: mini donuts, cheese curds, fried pickles.

Wes laughs. "That, for one. You just ate your third breakfast. How can you be hungry?"

"I'm always hungry."

"What's your pleasure?" He reaches into his back pocket for his wallet.

"Ooh, pickles," I say, and my mouth waters in anticipation.

"You sure you want to eat those before a big game?"

"Yes. Do they have spicy ones?" I squint to read the menu. "Oh, they do, Wes. Deep-fried hotties, right there."

"One order of deep-fried hotties," Wes says to the guy in the food truck, and he doesn't even seem embarrassed.

We stand off to the side to wait for our order and take in the chaos and crowds around us.

"Amazing, isn't it?" Coach Giles says as he walks up to us.

"Coach, hi!" I say, like he caught us doing something we shouldn't be doing, not standing innocently by a food truck vendor waiting for an order of deep-fried hot pickles. Coach raises his eyebrows at me.

"Hi," he says. "So, you two patched things up, then?"

My cheeks burn, and Wes gives a small nod.

"Thank you, Saint Sebastian," Coach says. "Look, I know I told you to be careful and all of that, but you two have been unbearable this week. We need to win this game, so please don't break up again before the game starts."

Wes tucks his arm around my waist. "Not gonna happen."

"You know which tent to go to?" Coach asks, and Wes nods again. "OK, see you down there in fifteen. Not one minute later, you got me?"

"Order up, hotties," the guy in the truck calls out, and Wes hands them over. They're hot and greasy and smell amazing.

"You sure about this?" Wes asks. "These might be a little on the spicy side."

"There's only one thing I've ever been more certain about in my life," I say, smiling.

"May I have one?"

"As you wish." I hand over the cardboard basket.

"I really want to kiss you right now," he says. "How can we make that happen?"

"We could probably go make out behind this food truck," I say. "We've got fifteen minutes."

Wes laughs. "Eat your pickles."

I take a bite. "Oooh, hot," I cry.

"Hot hot or spicy hot?" Wes asks.

"Both. So good."

Wes bites one, too, and his eyes light up in surprise. "Would you believe I've never had a fried pickle before? This is amazing. It doesn't even need hot sauce."

I can feel my cheeks go warm at the thought that flickers through my mind.

Wes notices. "What, Dutch? Is it the pickles or something else got you all hot and bothered?"

I swallow. "I'd like a little Hot Sauce," I say. "With everything."

Wes's eyes flame, and he glances around. "You wanna step behind this food truck with me for a sec?"

I nod, and we duck around the corner.

"Give me a kiss, pickle breath," Wes says, and I do.

❋ ❋ ❋

Our makeshift locker room is a large heated tent that reminds me of the dragon scene in *Harry Potter and the Goblet of Fire* but with rubber flooring. A few of the guys pace and jump up and down, shaking out their nerves, but for the first time in a long time, I'm calm. We got here. We earned this. Now we show the state what we can do.

Coach steps into the tent and clears his throat. "Well, kids, this is it. You've worked hard this season, and now you get to show the entire state, possibly even other parts of the country, what you can do. I'm proud of you. But you already know that. I'm going to turn this one over to your captains."

I look up in surprise as Wes and Carter step forward. Carter speaks first.

"Well, we were all pretty excited when we found out that we were in the running to be one of the HockeyFest cities this year. Shit, when was that? Pardon my language." That gets a couple of laughs from the guys. I roll my eyes. "And then we found out we got it, and this whole town kicked into high gear. We gotta put on a good show, they said. We gotta show everyone what Halcyon Lake can do. And I gotta tell you, it's looking good. The Hole looks better than it ever has. It's like Watermelon Days and Christmas and New Year's all wrapped up in one. I heard that there's a new burger at the Full Loon, the HockeyFest burger, half-pounder with all kinds of good stuff on it."

My stomach growls at that, and Wes looks at me and laughs.

"Would you shut up already?" Jesse says to Carter. He got

called up to play varsity and is basically shitting himself about being on live TV. "Let Wes talk. You sound like a moron."

The team laughs. Wes steps forward.

"I'll keep this short and sweet. We've got a saying around here, and you all know what it is. *Refuse to lose. Whatever it takes.* Today's a big day for Halcyon Lake. For the town, for the high school, for this team. There is no place that I would rather be, and I mean that one-hundred-percent. I am proud to be your captain. I am proud to take the ice at the Hole with all of you. Now let's get out there and show them what we can do."

I love him. I'm in love with Wes Millard.

My eyes prick with emotion. Damn it.

"Huddle up!" Coach calls, and we cram together around Wes and Carter. "All in!"

"On three!" Carter says.

"One, two, three!" Wes says.

"*Refuse to lose! Whatever it takes!*"

Excitement rushes through me as we step through the doorway of the heated tent, out into the cold, down the ramp to our bench in the Hole, and out onto the ice.

This is it. This is the day we've been waiting for.

Whatever it takes.

Other than the one practice, I haven't skated at the Hole this winter, and it's good to be back. It's a picturesque setting, that's for sure, like stepping back in time. The pines on the hill leading to the Hole filter the sunlight, sending trickles of it dancing on the ice. The air is crisp and clean, with the comforting smokiness of a nearby campfire.

We warm up, get the feel of the ice. The puck connects, solid, with my blade. I'm strong and in control. Confident.

Hunter, my parents, and my grandparents are in the stands, my mom wrapped up in a blue-and-gold Hawks blanket. Morgan and Cora sit in the student section, and I can hear Cora over everyone as I skate past: "Go, Dutch!"

I can't stop smiling.

The ref blows the whistle and we line up for the national anthem, sung by Showbiz's sister, Abbie, who graduated last year. Her angelic voice reverberates off the stone walls and into the trees. It's glorious; there's no other word for it. She's going places, that one. When she finishes (to wild applause), the teams retreat to our respective benches.

One last pep talk. Carter leans on his stick on the ice side of the bench, along with Nik, T.J., Showbiz, and Brooks. Nik does his usual back-and-forth nervous shuffle. But Wes comes to the bench, closes the door behind him, and stands next to Coach Giles. I don't get it. The starting line always stays on the ice.

"Listen up," Coach says. "There's been a lineup change for the opening face-off. Dutch, get out there."

Say *what*?

And he called me *Dutch*? My eyes well up a little, damn it.

"You got us here, Dutch," Coach says. "Now get out there."

I stand, my legs a little shaky, and Wes takes two steps toward me. He grabs my elbow and leans in close to my ear.

"When this is over, I'm taking you to the Full Loon for a HockeyFest burger," he says. "And some hot sauce." He pauses, his lips so close to my helmet. I shiver at the closeness, his words, the cold afternoon air, the excitement that arrives full-force just before I step out onto the ice.

"First I want a do-over at the Chinese Lantern." I pull away and grin. "I need my sub gum wonton."

He laughs. "I love you, Dutch." He says this out loud, in front of everyone.

Justin whoops. "It's about time!"

I swallow hard and nod, my words lodged in my throat. But he knows.

I skate out to center ice.

"We've had a change in the starting lineup for Halcyon Lake," the announcer says. It's Big Mick from the arena. "Millard is out. Starting at center, we've got Carter Delviss, at right wing, T.J. MacMillan, and at left wing, Holland 'Dutch' Delviss." I can hear the smile in his voice.

The crowd goes nutso. Carter nods at me, the ref signals for the crowd to settle down, and I move into position, my stick on the ice.

The puck drops.

Acknowledgments

So many people deserve my heartfelt thanks for their support and assistance in bringing this book to life.

To my agent, Steven Chudney—I don't know what I would do without you. Thanks for your insight, your guidance, your patience, your humor.

To my editor, Erica Finkel—thank you for your enthusiasm and love for this book, your careful attention and dedication. Holland's story is so much richer and more alive because of you. Thanks to everyone at Amulet who worked on this beauty of a book.

To my Beez: Rebekah Faubion, Tracey Neithercott, and Liz Parker. Friends, I don't know that I would have survived this one without you. Thanks for your unfailing belief in me and these characters and your quick responses to urgent requests over text. I love you.

Kari Marie White, thank you for your friendship, your keen understanding, and your encouragement to dig deep. Dawn Klehr, thanks for your constant support and friendship, right from the very start and through every high and low. I'm so grateful to have you both along for this wild ride.

To Andrew DeYoung, the best debut partner a writer could ask for. Let's keep writing books and hitting milestones and going for epic.

Linda Diaz, Sara Naegle, Maris Ehlers, and Kris Jar-land, words of thanks are not enough for your excitement and encouragement. Your early-morning Facebook messages, late-night texts urging me on, and tough love to get my shit done were just what I needed. Michelle Grandia and Kate Bronstad Boyle—you both came back into my life at exactly the right time. Your friendship and support mean so much. Susan Arkell, your inspirational Instagram shares are everything, especially the one about the embroidery on back pockets.

To the UMD Gang: Jacqueline Bonneville, LeeAnn Evans, Heather Green, Katie O'Dell, Jana Oman, Jody Rittmiller, and Teresa Robinson, thank you for your steadfast friendship over the years. You are the strongest, most compassionate, most caring women I know, and I'm so grateful to call you friends.

To my family, friends, and neighbors who helped with meals and carpooling and entertaining my kids when deadlines loomed—thanks for your generosity and love for us.

I'm one of those lucky writers who can work just about anywhere, anytime, including while on weekend camping trips with the Boy Scouts. To the Scouts of Troop 563—thanks for letting me hang out at the picnic table and write. Rankila and Ryan, I'm honored that you used me as a subject of your charades skit at the campfire.

Luke Scheid and Molly Scheid, thanks for answering my questions about your hockey experience, some of which probably seemed pretty weird.

Here's to the Elk River Elks boys' hockey team, 1988–1990. My days as the JV manager were some of the best of my high school years. Those guys hold a special place in my heart, especially Matt Sullivan, Ryan Bronson, Rob Hyrkas, Nathan Cairns, and Brian Jacobson. Thanks for the memories. And to the 2017–2018 St. Michael-Albertville Knights boys' hockey team—your perfectly-timed run to the state tournament inspired and motivated me. Congrats on an amazing season.

Thanks to every musician who inspired a piece of this book, especially my constant companions Dave Grohl and Chris Cornell. Chris, not one day has gone by since you left us that I haven't heard you sing.

And always, to my big, loud, amazing family. Mom, thanks for your endless support and not caring too much about all the swears in my books. Dad, I wrote a hockey book. Thanks for all those times you drove to ER to pick me up at the arena and stood at the glass to watch the game. I miss you every day.

To my most favorite people in the world—Troy, Jude, and Halen. You believe in me, you cheer me on, you inspire me every single day. I couldn't do this without you. I love you.

Finally, to all the incredible girls out there with big dreams—you got this. Keep moving forward.

SARA BIREN is the author of *The Last Thing You Said*. She earned an MFA in creative writing from Minnesota State University, Mankato, and has had several short stories published in literary journals. She lives outside of Minneapolis with her husband and two children.